CROOKED

HONEST CRIMINALITY

CROOKED

HONEST CRIMINALITY

BRONWEN JOHN

Matador
9 Priory Business Park,
Wistow Road, Kibworth Beauchamp,
Leicestershire LE8 0RX
Tel: 0116 279 2299
Email: books@troubador.co.uk
Web: www.troubador.co.uk/matador
Twitter: @matadorbooks

ISBN 978 1 83859 503 6

British Library Cataloguing in Publication Data.
A catalogue record for this book is available from the British Library.

Printed on FSC accredited paper
Printed and bound in Great Britain by 4edge Limited
Typeset in 11pt Baskerville by Troubador Publishing Ltd, Leicester, UK

Matador is an imprint of Troubador Publishing Ltd

Dedicated to:

Matthew Purdue, for helping me with the poker aspect and reminding me that writing is cathartic.

Eleanor James, for reminding me of the simple pleasure writing can bring.

My mother, Jennifer, Karen, Carol and Andrea, who kept me sane and on the straight and narrow.

Graham, Michael and David, who encouraged mischief and the art of subterfuge.

My father, Peter W. W. John, who gave me the invaluable motto: "You can do what you like with the law; bend it, twist it, hide behind it… just don't break it."

THE FIRST
ART GALLERY SCAM
in LONDON

ONE

"Hey, fancy supporting a truly great artist?"

"Get lost."

"Aw, come on, this is my summer job and I'm working on commission – what's the big deal and rush?"

"Ash, it's me, Max. Remember, Max 'Colorado' Ying? You've been pulling the long-short con all week here."

Ashia 'Ash' Cox grinned at that. She sat back down on the steps of Trafalgar Square, watching as Colorado made his way towards some tourists. He probably had a scam of his own lined up for them. It showed business was poor in London, that she hadn't recognised a fellow con artist, let alone a good friend. It made it worse that she'd probably be the butt of some teasing when she went out tonight.

Ash grunted at that thought as a buzz in her pocket alerted her to a notification. She allowed an annoyed groan to slip out at the interruption and, half-expecting it to be some sort of push alert from her social media account, pulled it out and scrutinised it. Much to her disappointment, it was a text from one of her crew, namely Dee, asking if there had been any marks so far on their first foray into the art of the long con. According to Dee, this exercise hadn't even been worth it in the long run as they'd barely broke even before their last day today.

Ash knew that Dee didn't like the scheme; she didn't have the patience for it. She preferred the short cons, like the pigeon drop or the wine drop. But now she came to think of it, there was something in the mind of her mentor, Luke Gaines, she was sure of it. The con man was up to no good, but had not revealed his cards yet.

But there again, just like the con, it all came down to patience.

"Con artistry gives a clue in the title," Luke would say, with that small, patient smile and cool look. "So many different art forms, and patience is the key to it all."

Ash had seen it often. That paternal grin. That *Trust me, I know what I'm doing* smile. Hell, she would buy into that smile just like all the other marks in this world would, and could buy his bull. The bull that he was a vicar raising cash for his church roof, or that he was an investment banker with a deal just too good to be true.

Ash sat back on her bench, trying to spot a mark that she could use. She sighed, feeling her fingers twitch as she looked at the tourists, imagining she could hear their jangling wallets as they went passing by. She'd first started picking pockets at the tender age of thirteen, after running away from another foster home. She'd been pretty good at it, too – earning nearly £500 in her first three days. She'd been heading back to her hostel, and decided to pick on a camera hugger, as she fondly termed tourists. The guy had been perfect – tall, with greying blond hair and looking lost in his own world. She'd gone to pick his wallet and she'd felt a hand grip her wrist… that's how she'd met Luke Gaines. The man had somehow conned his way into her heart and through social services and gained custody of her, taken her under his wing. He'd taught her almost everything she knew.

"You know the National Gallery is full of the bourgeois sense of class that reeks of the patriarchy, and I am afraid that the Tate is going the same way!"

That got her attention. Hipsters were a God-given gift as far as Ash was concerned. They tried so hard to be different, yet here they were wearing the same styles with phones outstretched in front of them… they all became the same. Easy. Marks.

"Need some help, Ash?"

She turned to see Colorado approaching her, and smirked. "What happened to your little con?"

"Saw one of your hipsters push a kid in the fountain when they were trying to get a shot of Nelson. No need. Plus, I get to say I run the first art gallery scam outside of Beijing… that'll impress the folks back home."

"Colorado, you were born within the sound of Bow Bells… think you can pull it off quick?"

A nod from him, and Ash noticed the police beginning to circle the neck of the woods he'd been trying to con. Obviously the kitchen had gotten a bit too hot for Colorado's liking.

"Got a slider?"

"Joe Mahoney."

Ash nodded, and immediately got to work. She played on all the innocence that her sixteen-year-old face could muster. As the hipsters passed, she waited to make her play.

"Yeah, mister, I'm telling you, it's a genuine Paul Eyrie exhibition; y'know, the artist that makes some sort of a social commentary with each piece? He's big pals with Banksy."

Max's cockney tone was immediately switched out for a more cultured one. "You mean it?"

"Yeah, I wouldn't be standing here otherwise; I'm doing some work for my art gallery…"

Ash waited impatiently. She was sure the mark had gone, but spotted Colorado making a slight gesture with his fingers, mimicking texting. They were checking online. They weren't as stupid as she'd thought, and she thanked God that there was no photograph of Paul Eyrie on his Wikipedia page, and that 'Paul Eyrie' was an assumed name.

"But it's such a small gallery."

"Yeah; said he was sick of the pretensions of modern society, or some nonsense." She sighed, as she believed every Saturday girl or underpaid intern had the right to do. "So, you interested or not?"

"Definitely."

Another hand gesture from Max, although this time his index finger was moving in a circular motion, mimicking a reel on a fishing line. One more line and they'd hook them.

"So, the gallery. New?"

"Brand new, hosts a lot of unknowns." She sighed. "Reasonable all over, except the wages; can't wait for my GCSEs to come in."

Max snorted. That was genuine. He was about to make another comment when a young man wearing a beanie shoved him out of the way.

"Move it. You have Paul Eyrie pieces?"

From the way Max tensed, Ash guessed that this was the young man who had shoved the kid into the fountains. That helped her performance more than a little. "Where'd you get off listening in, mate? I was talking to a—"

"If you don't want me to report your foul attitude to your manager, you'll tell me where the art gallery is."

Ash smirked. "You don't know where. And I don't care. You can't afford anything. Bunch of modern-day beatniks, as my grandfather would say."

"Looks can be deceptive." The young man smirked. "Now, I'm willing to pay out; even pay for me and my friends to get in. So are you in or not?"

Ash took a deep breath and looked heavenward. "Hope my good deed pays off," she said, as if to herself, then looked at the group of hipsters, who all wore looks of smug satisfaction. She dipped her head in defeat. "Fine. Follow me."

They were so smug they didn't see the smile on her face at the inevitable mathematical conclusion she had drawn in her mind.

Hook + line = sinker.

The art gallery was actually an old office building that had been leased from Cyclops, the local fixer. There were plenty of paintings on the wall, or leaning against the wall, looking to be set up.

Dee showed the group around, as Ash leant against the wall, ostensibly watching, informing them about the lesser-known artists also on display. She was, at least, not lying about that, although the names had been changed. Gaines had bought them in bulk from the local art class, for the total amount of £90. He'd promised to make a further donation if the con had gone well. After all, Vilde, the art teacher, had been more than fair in her pricing, and it was an unwritten law of 'honest' con work that you couldn't cheat an honest person. The ones who ignored that fundamental rule normally ended up inside. Let alone, it just invited bad luck.

"This piece was painted by Paul Eyrie; it sums up the chaos of the social media age," Dee was saying. How anybody could say that about a painting of a dog dancing on the spot while a kid filmed it was beyond Ash. Colorado was looking appreciative and nodding, just like the rest of them. "This is one of the artist's lesser favourite works, so we're selling it for £1,000."

Again there came the head-nodding. The young man who was standing next to Colorado and had earned his vehement dislike was smiling. No, that was the wrong description, Ash decided. It was a baring of teeth like a predator who had prey in their sights.

"I know that kid's face," whispered a voice from beside her.

Ash jumped and slapped the shoulder of the older man who'd appeared apparently from nowhere.

"Sorry, kiddo, didn't mean to startle you none... was getting some papers for you."

"Newspapers? Hell, Luke, I can read my news online," Ash scoffed. She soon felt a light bump to the head. "Hey!"

"I meant a passport, nimrod."

"Passport? What're you up to?"

"Tell you later… how's it going?"

"Got some good marks from the looks of things. Col says he'll buy a piece too… thinks his grandma might like it for Christmas." Ash smiled and returned to admiring the action. "It's been fun using the big store."

A small smile, a genuine one, crossed his features. "Yeah, kid. It sure has."

There was something about that look and the tone of his voice which made it feel like a lingering farewell. Ash was about to push further when she spotted Dee approaching.

"What's wrong?"

"The boy wants to buy one piece for each of his friends, and there are eight of them! All from Eyrie's collection. You were fantastic as the roper, Ashy." Dee was the only one permitted to call her that. "Well done."

Ash grinned, and was about to thank her when she spotted the expression on Gaines's face as he took in the scene. He was preparing to cut and run. "Oh, come on, perhaps his maiden aunt croaked."

"And perhaps he's somebody we don't want to be meeting in a dark alley, or the son of somebody… I know the face, Ash."

"Perhaps he's been on the telly? I saw that guy from *Game of Thrones* come in yesterday, but we didn't take any payment. I was glad; I felt guilty about how his character ended up," Ash said. "We can even say that Eyrie's lawyers got us closed down because of us doing this deal… please? I mean, that's a cut of £2,000 each!"

"£1,500 for me; I'm taking my cut smaller for the art class." Gaines flashed a tense smile. "Fine. Dee, sell Max his painting for £20. I'll deal with the rest personally; that way, if it goes wrong they've only got a real good description of me."

Excited nods abounded.

"Where shall we meet up afterwards?" asked Dee.

"Usual spot in the West End; classier joint, now a con's not over until it's over. I'll use this cut to cover costs… Dee."

Dee was already in the office, taking the money out of the safe and sharing it between everyone. Dee winked as she handed over the money to Ash, who leafed through it reverently. £2,000 in readies already felt good in the back pocket. She smiled to herself.

"You have any intentions with that?" teased Colorado as Ash tucked her share into her pocket. "Or is it top secret?"

"Top secret from you, Colorado," scoffed Ash, smiling at them all. "I'll see you later."

TWO

James Redford saw her coming down the estate. He chuckled, blowing out a puff of smoke. There was no mistaking that person who walked with such an air of confidence.

Ashia Cox always cut a figure walking through the Underbrush Estate, with a certain determination in her step and her dark brown curls drawn into a chignon on top of her head. He waved to her; the way she was walking meant that she had the money for some goods that she had used as collateral for the long con that her and her crew had gone in for. He didn't offer a smile, although he truly liked Ash, mainly because she was good with the kids around the estate and, from what he could see, a very honest individual.

Unusually honest, in fact, especially given that her weekend job was being a slider and sometime pupil of the notorious con artist Luke Gaines.

Ash returned the greeting and walked into the shop ahead of him, wafting the smoke from his vape away from her face. "Christ, Jamie, you smoke like a chimney – don't you know the damage they do you?"

"If I wanted a lecture, I'd go to her indoors," he replied, with a stiff frown. "What goes on?"

"I've come in to collect," she said, with an excited smile that showed her true age. "My sovereign necklace – the job went well, Mr Redford." That showed she was settling down; the use of the respectful tone. "An—"

"Your sovereign necklace is safe here," Redford said, handing the old leather box to her. "With my small amount of interest, let's see, that will be the grand total of £1,025."

Ash didn't protest as she counted out the wad of notes, a combination of tens and fifties. She was only sixteen, after all was said and done; James Redford had taken her money illegally and, despite a fairly meagre amount being given, it had paved the way for this job. "Think that's enough, Mr Redford – just make sure." She noted Redford smiling and raising his eyebrows at her. "I'm not conning you, just want to make sure my maths is correct."

The man snorted and counted out his money on the table. "All here, Ash. Don't need to worry your sweet self. Even have some change."

"Thanks." She put her necklace on, but tucked the box that had held it into her inside jacket pocket, throwing in the rest of her funds. "You're a scholar and a gentleman?" She paused as she began to count out the change, fingers stilling as she studied it. "Hey, James, not very good at counting either."

"Yeah, yeah, and you're a scholar and a lady… we're all scholars and of good breeding… so how come there are so many idiots and reprobates in the world?" he asked, chuckling to himself.

"If I had the answer to that, I'd give you a share of the millions I'd make," she said, sliding the notes over to him. "But seeing as you're a bit flush right now, I'll leave the overcharged change behind! See you, Jamie Redford."

Redford watched with a small smile as she walked off down the street. She was something, that Ash. She needed a guiding hand in the line of grifting or she was sure to run into a whole lot of trouble later on in life. Or she'd have a very short life.

He was glad that Ash hadn't noticed his little con. It was an old trick, but nonetheless a good one – to overpay an odd bit of change. Not very much for any respectable con artist, whether they be rookie or otherwise, to notice, but it was just enough for him to sense out a liar and a cheat.

He'd tried the same sort of trick with Colorado the previous week. The little git had walked out with an excess of £30 – which he'd rather rapidly given back when chased down. The boy hadn't even had the guile to lie about it, and instead suggested that James was at fault.

James would have to make a call to Luke Gaines with this bit of information, to advise that he'd done well by at least teaching her honesty amongst thieves in this all-too-dishonest line of work.

But for the moment, he was going to enjoy his small slice of the profit as he prepared to enjoy his vape outside.

Henry Martin Holmes stood looking at the artwork that leaned against the wall, tears running down his cheeks. He'd been so cocky, handing over cash in hand to the art dealer; so happy that he thought he'd got a good deal. He'd bought them for his friends. They had taken them home, where their parents had sung their praises… he'd saved the best for Stacey Nicholls' house. He'd always fancied her.

Plus, it might've won the approval of her art historian father, Daniel. But when he'd seen it, there had been no approval in his eyes. The man had laughed as he'd joyously pointed out the flaws and explained that Eyrie had sworn off art for at least eighteen months after a particularly bad arrest in Lyon. Apparently, he'd tried his hand at counterfeiting – and had been caught by the famous Interpol agent, Du Barry.

"No, no, darling," Henry's mother assured him. "You weren't a fool."

"But, Mum, Mr Nicholls – he… he laughed in my face!" He hitched a sob. "He said it really showed how uneducated I am if I can fall for a simple con! I want it sorted, Mum!"

"Don't worry, my darling," cooed his mother. He was an only child and had been particularly ill as a newborn, something she reminded herself of daily. An art aficionado herself, she knew her darling boy had only been seeking to emulate her. "Daddy will sort it. Just you wait. Now, why don't you go have a shower and calm yourself right down?"

"Thanks, Mum."

As soon as he'd wandered up the stairs, rubbing his eyes, his mother snapped her head to the large man who was standing to her left.

"Get my husband, tell him the situation and tell him to sort it. Now."

Harry Holmes was not in his London office when the phone call was made. He was playing baccarat in Les Ambassadeurs in London, where he would probably stay until the early hours of the morning. There were no mobiles allowed at the table, to avoid distracting the professional and amateur gamblers.

Instead, the manager's telephone buzzed discreetly and, rather than bothering Holmes at his table, they called over his assistant, Leonard Hughes. Hughes was a Welshman of around forty-six, with a jowl that closely resembled that of an Old English Bulldog. He frowned as he listened, and grunted several times throughout before making a reserved announcement to the person on the other end of the line.

"I'll let you know."

Hughes hung up the phone and walked over to where Holmes was regaling several people with a tale from the underworld. He was playing casually, but his eyes flickered to the table. The others weren't paying attention as he had lulled them into a false sense of security with his tall tales of gangsters and his rough upbringing in London – he was waiting for his moment to pounce and surprise them all with his card-sharping prowess. It was the perfect way to urge them to join his celebrity cruise trip, for which he was giving a book reading and competing in the charity poker match.

"Harry, can I see you for a minute?"

Holmes looked around his rapt audience. Hangers-on, the lot of them… but they could work for him in other ways. Spread and heighten his social standing. His partner Ezra fitted in naturally with his smooth Southern charm, but he came from old money from the Southern city of Atlanta. Harry came from the worst of the worst, and even though he'd married a banker's daughter he knew he was a novelty in these settings… and novelties soon died off.

"It's important."

Holmes sighed dramatically and stood up. "Henri, I'll have to pass the shoe for a brief time." He tipped his head to everyone involved, before walking away. "What's the problem?"

"It's your son."

Holmes paused and turned back around. A tall man, he towered over his underling. He stood out among the black Armani suits in the club, his own grey suit matching his silver hair. People glanced at him. Women tittered; men glared, then shied away when he met their gaze.

"What's the little sod done?" He almost felt like a disappointment to his only son. A proper little kid, when it came down to it. He'd overindulged him as a child, he thought.

"He went and bought a fake painting – several – to show off to his friends," Hughes said quietly. "Showed one off to his crush… turns out her dad's an art expert."

"Beijing art gallery scam, read about it… so, my son's the first British victim?" Holmes chuckled. "How—"

"£10,000."

Holmes alternately froze, then felt his blood boil. His son had been made a fool of – that, in itself, was acceptable. If the kid wanted to show off and came off worst, it served him right. But to lose face *and* £10,000? A lot of honour was at stake, and if word got around that Harry Holmes's progeny had been caught out by a simple short con masquerading as a long con, he'd never hear the end of it.

"Any idea who?"

"Been asking around; seems to think it's a con man known by the name of Luke Gaines… helped train Esther Crook."

That brought a feral smile to Holmes's face.

"Sir?"

"She wouldn't have anything to do with it, would she?"

"No. At least, we don't think so. As far as we're aware, Crook is still out of the country."

Harry nodded.

"Your son described Luke Gaines, and his protégée Dee Lawrence. There was another young man being conned… and a Saturday girl."

"Sort it, make it look plain and simple. No over-complications. Get rid of Gaines and the two girls…" Holmes paused. "Girls… could always use them; make a bit of profit out of it. But nothing comes back to me on them. Got it?"

"Even if the kid had nothing to do with it?" Hughes clarified, getting his mobile phone out of his pocket.

"*Especially* if she's had nothing to do with it. Need to make examples of these people, regardless of whether they turn out to be innocent or not. It will send a message to Miss Crook that we've got another of her friends and it's cost an innocent person their life."

The Speakeasy was a small restaurant and bar in the basement of a bookshop called Ness – an additional feature to the original business. You had to give a password to enter the nether regions of the building, where there lay an old spiv palace from the '40s. The downstairs had been converted and soundproofed so as not to disturb the book thieves upstairs.

The silence in the bookshop rivalled the racket downstairs. Snappy tunes played; a combination of acid jazz and old-fashioned blues ballads. Some people were dancing on the small dance floor towards the back; others were at the bar. Ash spotted Colorado and Luke towards the middle – one eyeing the front and the second the back. You always had to have a good exit stratagem.

"You got them back?!" teased Luke, as she approached.

Ash smirked and collected a latte from the bar, then walked over to where Luke was looking at her now casually over his shoulder.

"You all right?"

"Yeah, just getting what's mine back… I thought Mr Redford might pass it on, if you get my meaning."

"You stupid little sod," snapped Luke. "Redford took—"

"I'm just joshing you. God, this gig is getting to you, isn't it?" Ash teased. "It was a good con."

"Thought up by you," said Colorado, shooting a fond smile his friend's way. "Luke was telling me about how you came up with it."

"Didn't. I'll openly admit it." Ash beamed. She was still proud of her success in helping the scheme and persuading Luke to attempt it. "I read about it, and thought, *We can adapt that.*"

"You did well," Luke said, before sighing heavily. "I want you two away for a few weeks."

"I'd like to know how you sold that to my mother," joked Colorado, sipping his coffee. "She's already freaking out about my GCSEs."

"Sold it to her as an educational trip… and it will be, for you both," Luke said as he leaned back in his seat. "I'm getting ready to retire… and I've taught you all I know. You know it's time to quit when your kids are teaching you, an old dog, new tricks."

"You can't!" Ash protested. "Christ, I've learned it all from you."

"Exactly – you're going after the big sharks in my minnow pond," Luke said quietly. "Both of you deserve better. I've booked you both on flights. Separate times, three days apart. Different destinations." He pulled their passports out of his pocket and slid them over to them.

Ash stared at the table, dumbfounded.

"You're going to Norway, Ash."

"Norway? What the hell is in Norway that we haven't got here?" snapped Ash. "And what the hell is education—"

"Esther T. Crook is out there. I've managed to persuade her to give you lessons."

The two shared a look.

Esther Crook. The name was the stuff of tall tales around the London underworld. Not many people had seen her. It was rumoured that she was straight, but in equal measure had a criminal mind that rivalled that of any wrongdoer in fiction, and she had yet to even be picked up for a crime.

"You know her?" Colorado said incredulously. "They say Holmes put a price on her head."

"That he did," said Luke with a small, sad nod. "When she came back to London, she decided to brush up on all her short cons and asked me to help out." He smirked. "She owed me a favour. So I offered you two as willing students. She'd only take one, though; seems she's rather busy. She suggested Rodney Buchannan for you, Colorado; best short-con man other than Hellion. I've arranged travel."

"What about Dee, though?! She was here before me," Ash pleaded quietly.

"You'll see me after the summer holidays," Luke assured her. "To get those results and everything… and Dee was the one who said she had her limitations."

"But, God… you do know what a big step this is?!" Ash said, looking surprised.

"Hey, I'm not going to stop being your foster dad, now, am I? Just means you've got to teach the old dog new tricks when you return, my darling, to persuade me out of retirement," he said, winking as he reached into his jacket's inside pocket and withdrew two crisp pieces of paper. "This is her address."

Ash swallowed a lump in her throat. For some reason, a trickle of ice went down her back. It felt so final. She knew she'd be back, but there was something clenching at her gut.

"I... I—"

"Look, you go get your head around it." He glanced at Colorado. "I'm going to go to the art class and drop off their slice. I'll meet you at Tottenham Court. Me and Dee will show you a few pictures of Esther so you know who's training you. Colorado, see you at the house."

THREE

Where the hell is she?

Dee Lawrence sighed as she looked out of the window at the busy street below. The poor kid was probably beating herself up, thinking that she was disappointed, when all she wanted really was for her to get home so she could congratulate her and watch some reruns of old TV series.

She smiled to herself and pulled her arms around her middle, thinking of what the reactions of her young friends would be when they met Esther. She'd been surprised by Esther's exuberance at learning the short con; as if every little detail was a piece of art. Dee saw it as a day's work and nothing more, but she respected her friend enough to know it was an art form in her opinion.

She was so caught up in the implications of the con world that she didn't pay much mind as a car drew up outside. However, she did pay attention when she saw one of the men inside fiddling with what looked like a hypodermic needle. Nicholas 'Crusher' Joseph. She'd been in school with him. A doctor of some renown in criminal circles, but he was a lackey of Harry Holmes. God, the kid… the kid… Harry had the same smile. Christ!

"Hey, Dee!" she heard from the back door.

"Colorado!" Dee fled down the townhouse stairs, rushing to the cabinet and yanking free the envelope of plane tickets and flight times.

Colorado was in the back kitchen, making himself comfortable on a chair with a glass of milk. He offered a smile.

"Where's Luke? Ash?" she demanded, looking towards the front door.

"Ash went for a walk to clear her head. Luke's meeting her in Tottenham Court; he's going to drop off the money at the art club. We're meeting up here to get…" He sat up. "Dee, what's going on?"

"Get out of here – run! We've been made by Harry Holmes's mob. Harry's son was the mark." She pressed the passports into his hands. "Run. Don't look back."

"What about you?"

"They need someone. Get my little sister, and just run."

He opened his mouth.

"Take care, Colorado. Get to Esther. She'll protect you. Now go!"

Colorado piled out the back door just as the front door was opened. Dee took a deep breath and locked it behind him. She'd seen what happened to people who crossed Harry Holmes. She'd heard whispers of what had happened to the girls who'd gone to one of his clubs looking for work… they'd not come home. No missing persons report, either. They just vanished off the face of the earth, girls in clubs with eyes too wide or tied to beds. Girls who were taken and no one knew where.

Such a fate, she knew, awaited her.

Dee closed her eyes and allowed her feelings to sweep through her. At least they had Colorado to save Ash. She didn't much like the Asian, mostly for his inability to stay on plan, but at least she knew he was loyal.

At least, she hoped so.

It was cold as Ash made her way to Tottenham Court Tube Station. The street lamps lit the street well, but their false light provided no comfort to Ash's dark thoughts. She was still stunned at the suggestion she could work the big con. That in itself was an honour, let alone being trained by the notorious Esther Crook.

The young con artist – or old, depending on who was telling the story – had been at the centre of most of the rumours about long cons from London in the last eighteen months. Kelsey Jamieson selling the Loen Skylift to eight investors who had fiddled the London Stock Exchange and made fools of themselves on an international level. Playing the old-fashioned 'Wire con on gangster Miklos Stavros, Mathias LeRoy had earned the applause of the London underworld. But nobody had seen Esther, and it was rumoured that she did not get actively involved, for reasons known only to her.

Ash turned up the collar of her jacket and hunched her shoulders against the chill.

He saved me from the streets or worse, and now he's giving me the golden goose of opportunities and I'm moping, she thought to herself.

She'd never been much of a great con woman, she thought. She wasn't much good at reading or writing, come to think of it. The only people who had faith in her were Luke Gaines and Colorado. She felt like she was betraying Dee, though. It had been all but implied that Luke felt that Dee wasn't smart enough to deal with this Esther Crook.

"Ash!"

Ash paused in her thoughts and turned around to see Colorado running towards her at full speed. She chuckled for a moment, before she saw the fear on his face.

"Col… Max, what's going on?!"

He coughed and spat out some phlegm as he stopped in front of her. "The… the guy we… we marked today, the one that bought the paintings…"

"Yeah, smart-ass hips?"

"Harry Holmes's boy," he gasped.

That froze her. "H-Harry Holmes?"

She'd seen Harry Holmes on the news not too long ago; in the USA, he'd beaten the rap for the murder of several Interpol agents and had declared outside court that it was a day for justice. His newest partner in crime, a rumoured gunrunner in the US by the name of Ezra Innocent (an unfortunate name for his job if ever Ash heard one), was in the background with a set of heavies, although his face was blacked out.

"He's got Dee… I've texted Luke to move," Colorado gasped, holding his sides. "We've got to get out of here!"

"He'll kill her!" she snapped. "We have to help!"

"We're sixteen – what chance do we have, and what the hell do you think is going to happen?! We have to leave."

"Not without Luke!"

Ash raced into the Tube station, fighting through the last of the commuters, not caring for their dirty looks or their shocked expressions. She'd lost one person in her life; she'd been in foster care. Luke had saved her from the streets. He'd fostered her, made sure in some parts of her life that she'd stayed on the straight and narrow. He'd also fostered her God-given talents, as he was fond of saying.

It was time for her to return the favour.

"Ashia!" Colorado called from behind her, and when she threw a quick glance back she could see he had been waylaid by the British Transport Police for his Oyster card. She raced blindly onto the platform and looked around.

The smell of stagnant heat and BO filled her nose. She scanned the crowd desperately. Perhaps he'd gotten to the flat – but that would be just as bad. The only reason she didn't think he'd gone there was his superstitions.

She looked around again, praying he was within her sight.

She soon saw him; spotted his dusky blond hair if nothing else. She began to walk over just to warn him. He spotted her through the chaos of the tube platform and she saw him narrow his eyes, trying to ascertain what was wrong. Then she saw a large man appear from behind him.

Leonard Hughes. Holmes's Welsh bulldog. He was just the man for this sort of job.

There was the familiar rattle of a train in the distance, and Ash looked to that, then the man behind who was also eyeing her now, as if recognising what was going on. All of a sudden, she saw Luke look down at his phone, the signal finally kicking in for a brief moment. His eyes widened and then flicked in her direction, and he jerked his head slightly towards the big man, who was beginning to approach her. She knew she wasn't maintaining the poker face that he'd taught her. She was frightened. She was terrified, in fact.

His blue eyes flickered in sudden defeat, and he mouthed, *Run.* He then took several steps towards the platform, and raised his voice. "It's just too much! Harry Holmes has done for me, Luke Gaines!"

Sensing what was about to happen, Ash turned and ran. She heard the screams of the commuters, only now stimulated into action by the screech of the Tube train. She screamed too as she ran up the stairs, colliding with Colorado.

"What the hell is going on?" he demanded.

"Luke... Luke's dead..."

"Holmes's men?"

"Sacrificed himself for me, just like Dee did... we have to get out of here."

"Where to?! He'll find us!"

"We've never been arrested; there are no photos." She shoved him up the stairs and they ran, dodging past the Transport Police who were all too focused on a suicide than on two teenagers, and into the night air. "They don't know us. They just have descriptions, and what good is 'a black kid and an Asian kid'?!"

"You still haven't answered me..."

"Where else?! To Esther's!"

"She'll kick you out! And what clothes do you have? Can't exactly go back to the house; he'll be waiting."

"Don't have anything in your life that you can't walk away from in a second," she said. "Everything I have is gone, and the safest place I can be right now is in Norway with her."

Colorado pulled her into a small side street as blue lights flashed by.

"You follow me?"

"Fine. I'll put the word out."

And with that, the two separated, disappearing into the immersive blue lights and London mist; neither seeing the other's reaction as they realised how badly the con had gone astray… all from the wrong mark.

PUTTING HER
ON THE SEND

OR

HOW TO BOW OUT
WITH A PLAN

F O U R

The plane was cold.

The lights were down.

To all other intents and purposes, it was the perfect time to hide and rest.

Yet to Ash's overactive mind, it seemed like she was the only person in existence; even with the pilot up front. She wrapped herself in the tiny, ineffectual airline blanket, uttering the softest of curses.

She didn't know how she'd got here. She couldn't remember much, just fear and blindly following instructions from people she didn't know but Luke did. People who had hidden her away and managed to get her onto the flight, and had told her that they'd arrange things with Crook and the British social system before they vanished into thin air.

This plane was actually going to land, and they were going to make her get out in this foreign country with only the clothes on her back and Esther Crook's address stashed in the back left pocket of her jeans, and her passport in the right.

None of those helpers had offered comfort, although then again, Ash thought she'd probably have spat in their faces if they'd suggested they could make things better.

Even now, wrapped in rational rage, Ashia Cox had made a decision.

She was going to kill or con Harry Holmes if it was the last thing she did.

The Loen Skylift had a stunning view of all the fjords and lakes, let alone the Briksdal Glacier. Ash thought of this as she journeyed up it, looking darkly onwards. The messenger who'd met her off the flight had informed her brusquely that Esther Crook was at the top of the Skylift, eating dinner and recovering from a busy night of work. Ash had felt her stomach sink. A con artist who did honest labour didn't seem much like an honest person to her. It felt like a trick of the light. She groaned at the thought as the Skylift ended its long journey. Sticking her hands into her pockets, she walked out and up to the small cafe.

There was a waitress serving and three couples sitting. Ash read them quickly. Two honeymooning couples – at least, that's what she assumed from the way they couldn't keep their hands off each other – and a tourist. An older woman was looking out of the window; next to her, a younger woman with dark rings under her eyes was tucking into a meal and ignoring the room.

"Pardon," Ash said, stopping the waitress. "Have you seen Miss Crook?"

The waitress nodded and pointed towards the window. "She's there."

Ash followed her gaze to where the two women were sitting. There was a table between them. Ash thanked the waitress and sat down, ignoring the young woman and looking at the older one. The woman eyed her and returned to her book, apparently snubbing her company.

Ash coughed into her hand. "Well, this is a nice time to prove myself to you, Mrs Crook. I've been doing some cold reading. The two couples over there are from the cruise ship; the younger couples who can't keep their hands off each other are newly-weds, possibly on honeymoon. The older couple has probably been contentedly married for many years, judging by the design of their wedding rings. On the cruise for an anniversary." She smiled and looked at the old woman, who was looking at her with… disdain? She knew she'd have to brush up her technique after all. "Shall I do you, Mrs – oh, congratulations; I didn't know you were married – Crook?"

The older woman merely shook her head at the apparently unwanted and unwarranted conversation, before standing up quickly and rushing out, muttering as she went. Ash watched her go, surprised by her agility. Perhaps she wasn't supposed to approach her? She'd explain that she'd never got the instructions.

"Well, you need to improve your cold reading," said the young woman who had been sitting next to her. She had a lilt of an accent which bordered between French and English.

"You what?"

"The correct term is 'pardon'," corrected the woman, smirking as she continued to cut her meat before shoving a liberally sized piece into her mouth. She chewed and swallowed, picking up her water and taking a sip before continuing. "And you heard. You're not good at cold reading."

"I don't know what you're talking about." Ash stood as the girl stopped drinking and returned to her meal. She'd barely gotten into the country and she'd already been made.

There was a gentle clatter of knife and fork as the girl looked up at Ash through hooded green eyes and flashed a smirk. "You were right about one of the young couples. The others were all wrong. The couple you asked about, Mr and Mrs Nielsen, are having a baby and that's why they can't keep their hands off each other. They're making up for *future* lost time. The cruising couple are having an affair, but their partners are on board and this is the first time they've had the opportunity to be truly alone. I would bet my poker winnings that the one man has vertigo and the other lady a bad head… possibly both sides are playing each other and having affairs, thinking the other party doesn't know. Mrs Hansen, who you scared off, is very hard of hearing and struggles most ferociously with it. She thought you were going to jump her and rob her."

Ash stared at her as the 'cruise couple' began to pass.

"How's your husband's vertigo?" the young woman said to the woman she'd just accused of having an affair in a friendly tone of voice.

"Doing very well, thank you, Miss…?"

"Esther Crook."

It took all Ash's strength not to collapse into the seat in shock at her youth.

"We met at the captain's party. Remember? Your dear wife had a headache?"

There were a few more nods of acknowledgement, and Esther summarised a fictionalised version of events aboard the cruise before they took their leave. She then turned to Ash.

"Esther Crook. People will believe anything if you say it with confidence. Now, unless I'm mistaken, you're Ashia, right?"

A nod.

"Thought so."

"You?"

"Why, certainly I'm me," Esther mocked.

Ash continued to stare at her. She couldn't be older than thirty. She certainly didn't look like the mastermind everybody made her out to be. It made her angry that she'd already been conned. That this mere girl, who looked barely older than her, had conned her! Had a reputation that was envied…

"Would you like a bite of what I'm eating?" Esther said, sipping from her glass of water and returning to her food. She gestured for Ash to sit down, which she did. "It's veal schnitzel, potato salad, home-made ketchup and lemon. It's delicious, really." She sighed. "Would you like something *else* to eat, then? I'd advise either the waffles or the strudel."

"I've seen people eat; I'm here to work," muttered Ash, throwing an accusatory look at Esther, who didn't seem concerned and continued with her meal. "Get me?"

"I get you; I just don't need to follow you." Esther's green eyes flicked to her, and she smirked. "Listen, you may have eaten on that airplane into Stryn, let alone between whichever godforsaken London airport and Oslo, but I've not eaten since an all-night poker game. I am allowed to rest."

"You win." A curt nod. "How much?"

"None of your concern," Esther responded sharply. "And it was illegal, so you can keep that question to yourself, too. God knows I won't be prosecuted for grifting, but illegal poker…"

"Why do you bother with con work, then? You could stick to an honest day's work," Ash sneered, folding her arms across her chest petulantly.

Esther looked up properly then, and emerald-green eyes collided with dark brown. The eyes were the windows to the soul, according to Gaines, even those of a con artist; but one look at Esther's told Ash nothing beyond that they were green. Even that might have been a lie. It was no wonder that she was an excellent poker player.

"A good con artist doesn't get caught. The mark thinks his plan, which he fell into via greed, has fallen through and they're out by a few monetary assets. If they have worked it out, they've got to admit to criminal activity." Esther downed the last of her water. "I've advised on most of the big jobs… if it wasn't for my damned promise I'd be out there now. And before you ask, no, I'm not discussing the promise. So here I am, a year off – a gap year, you Brits say, right? Right – and stuck here when I could be with Mariana Lei out in Hong Kong, running that long con on the Hong Kong Stocks. By the way, if you have shares, sell them next week."Ash narrowed her eyes at the sarcastic tone as Esther pushed the plate away from her. "And anyhow, it's all to do with confidence… thanks for putting me off my grub, by the way."

"What do you mean, confidence?"

"Before 'con' became taboo for those honest citizens, it was just an abbreviation of 'confidence' – that damned thing I've had endless lectures about."

Esther stood and tossed money onto the table, throwing a "Thank you" to the waitress before gesturing for Ash to follow her. When Ash didn't move quickly enough, she began to walk off, and cut off the protest as Ash quickened her pace.

"You didn't want food – instead you put me off mine – so we leave at my pace. My home is a mile from here; we can walk."

"So all con artists are saints?" mocked Ash, as the two exited the building and began a long walk down an embankment which led to some woods.

"Any industry has rogues," replied Esther insincerely, kicking a rock with particular vitriol. "We certainly do, or Luke wouldn't have been murdered. Someone must've been on the inside."

Ash looked at Esther, ready to snap at her, but instead she found herself trying to read her. Esther's expression was glacial to say the least, but there was a slight squint to her eyes which revealed that she was trying to be sympathetic. Ash changed her mind about her being 'too honest'; human emotion seemed a foreign affair.

"Good news travels quickly… I am sorry."

"I want to get even with the guy that did it."

"There's enough time for that. For now, though, we get our heads in the game," responded Esther, as they came to a small wooden cottage. "My home."

"You bought this?"

A nod.

"They said on the flight how much these cost…"

"Ill-gotten gains pay well." Esther walked to the door and opened it. "Get in."

Ash sighed and stepped indoors, smiling as she looked around. The cabin was attractive in a rustic kind of way, although it was dark, even in the afternoon sun. Esther smirked softly before turning on the lights and closing the curtains, then heading outside and beginning to close the shutters.

"Don't believe in natural light?" Ash asked, attempting to sound cavalier, although she caught a glint in the window before Esther closed the shutter. She did it for protection.

An equally cavalier answer came. "I play late-night poker with the local police. We play in the dark, so I have little use for daylight." She freed her long, dark hair from its ponytail. "You're as anxious as a cat on a hot tin roof. The best spare room is downstairs."

"I don't want sleep. Slept plenty on the plane. And I don't have anything any more, bar the clothes on my back. He's helped kill Luke… he killed himself to save me. He's done God knows what to Dee… I want to beat him. I want to—"

"Hold on! Hold on," Esther interrupted, raising her hand and managing to stop Ash's tirade. "I know you want to get even, but I can't in good conscience train you without knowing the full facts."

Ash paused. Her rage and guilt at what had happened overwhelmed her, and then came the realisation that Esther had so little information to guide her in what needed to happen. She wet her lips and sank down onto the sofa like a rag doll.

"Well? I'd like an answer. *Parlez-vous Anglais?!*"

"His name is Harry Holmes. London—"

"Gangster?! Are you freaking nuts?!" Esther's eyes widened in shock, and she prowled towards her. "You don't even know the basics and you're thinking of trying to sell me the idea of going after the nastiest son-of-a… that's an insult to dogs. You don't know anything about him?!"

"I know he killed Luke." Ash didn't even have fight in her voice any more.

"He's pissed on other people's parades too… but most of them have the good sense that they are born with to stay well enough away from him."

"You're afraid of him too?"

"If you're in your right mind, you're scared of him," Esther stated emphatically. "I'm not frightened of any bogeyman, if that's what you mean."

"Then what're you thinking?"

"I'm thinking of how many ways the man can kill me on any given day!" she snapped, running her hands through her hair. "He has agents in all the three-letter majors. Christ, you are green," she snarled, realising that Ash didn't know what she meant. She held up five fingers. "FBI. CIA. MI6. MI5. ATF." Esther put a finger down each time she spoke with concentrated emphasis. Once all the fingers were down, she waved her hand exasperatedly in the air. "And that's not even counting Interpol or any other interested law enforcement agency in the world. All those have figures in that would willingly give over info to him. He's friends with the former Mayor of London. He's got the backing of three newspapers. He's smart. He's hard to con. His damned wife puts Nazi-stolen artworks on display. She's proud of it, and he's got so many people in his back pockets that every raid has failed. Damn it all!"

Ash listened, her eyes widening slightly. "You've been thinking to mark him?"

Esther smirked, then shook her head. "I've been waiting to." She sat down on the edge of the sofa. "The problem is, he's a legal eagle, totally. He's a mark that's difficult at the best of times. He's got the interest of honest men at the aforementioned agencies, and believe me, they have some interest in me."

"But you've got an interest?" Ash interrupted.

"And a promise to consider." Esther threw back her head and gave a short bark of laughter. "Yes. It'd be the con of my short career."

"Promise?"

"The Interpol agent that was murdered, shot dead in a steakhouse… four years ago? Tied to the crime was Mr Holmes, who wasn't such a big name as he is now in gun-running. Heading the investigation was a young woman. Remember?"

Ash closed her eyes and pictured the photograph in the

newspapers. It had been international news as it had been so blatant and brutal. The woman had been shot dead in a diner, and it had all the hallmarks of a mob hit from the '20s – several bystanders had also been killed. "A woman, Anne…"

"Anne Crook. She was the one murdered, and I feel it only fair to share that she was my mother," Esther said quietly. Ash watched the pain briefly swathe her neutral expression before the mask returned. "Well, my father was part of the investigation with her. By the way, he's a federal agent in the States."

"You're joking? He could run us in?"

Esther shook her head. "Got to prove it, and I don't have a paper trail, as the now-obsolete expression goes. Not that I'm supposed to know he's my dad… very overprotective parents." She walked to the kitchen, and Ash could hear water running. "Want a glass?"

"Please."

Esther returned, holding one glass out to her, filled with water.

Ash took it numbly and took a long sip, coughing lightly at the coldness. "Sorry… what do you mean?"

"I con him into thinking I don't know he's my pop and he lets me think he believes it; we're both fantastic con artists and it works better that way." Esther looked around the room. "Anyway, when my mother died, he made me promise not to go after Holmes until I had a rainmaker, and it seems you walked right through my door like a proverbial black cloud… and by that, my dear girl, I mean you were as thundery as hell. Nothing to do with your skin colour, I can assure you of that." She shook her head. "But… I need to work out if I can do this."

"But why? Why would he warn you?"

Esther smirked. "That's another tale for another night. Now, if you'll excuse me, I have some ruminating, meditating and sleep to catch up on. As I said, best bedroom is by there. Good morning, goodnight."

And with that she exited, leaving more questions than answers in her wake.

FIVE

Ash saw very little of Esther Crook over the following two days, during which she seemed deep in contemplation, playing hands of solitaire. She'd then disappear out onto the fjord, walking with her hands in her pockets and looking thoughtfully into the distance. She'd been put onto learning her cold reading in the restaurant, both to prove Esther wrong and to improve her own skills. Ash also continued to hone her own skills in the art of pick pocketing.

Esther arrived back on the second day to find a decent haul on her kitchen table, at which she flashed one of her characteristic smirks. "An excellent haul," she noted, sitting down. "Been thinking it over, your proposition…"

"You mean the con? I mean, you told me you had an idea?"

"More than an idea; a perfect one… But there's one problem," she said, pointing at Ash. "And that's you."

"Me?!"

"And Colorado. I don't feel safe enough, little rainmaker, because of who Holmes is."

"What sort of excuse is that?! I'm telling you I want to do it, and you're saying—"

"You know so little about him." Esther sighed and patted the seat next to her. Ash joined her. "The man won't kill you. He'll probably sell you to the highest bidder or stick you in a brothel. He has five in London alone, which, as of yet, have galled the international agencies for being near impossible to break."

"I'm willing to take the hit," Ash offered.

"I have no doubt. The graveyards in the Old West are full of young men and women who were willing to take a hit for the glory and old frontier justice." Esther patted her hand. "Plus, I have to deal with the fact that you're a foster kid. They're probably searching for you after the death of Luke. They'll want to know what he was up to. How'd he die? Bad news travels fast, but detail, not so much."

"Threw himself in front of a Tube train to stop them getting to me; cause chaos."

"Left hand doesn't know what the right hand is expecting... he was a con man right up until the end," Esther said quietly. She leaned back in her seat and considered. "He planned for you to be away?"

"From the night I left, yes... I just left without my clothes."

"That at least is believable," Esther sighed, and twisted her dark hair over her shoulder. "This will have to go. Cut it shorter – do me a favour, kid, and look me up some actresses with boy cuts."

Ash went to her phone and began pulling up images of actresses. "You do know you're... what? Twenty-five?"

"Au contraire; I'm as old as my teeth and as young as my head – all of twenty," Esther said thoughtfully. "I'm in."

"Wait, you're kidding?" Ash asked, spinning to face her. "You're in?! After two days of doing nothing?"

"Different time zones, friend," Esther said, with a small smile as Ash handed her the phone. "One thing about the long con is that you have to have patience and a good crew... and I must say, the students of the long con, you and Colorado, will be most fortunate."

"Patience? I think I'm going into the wrong line of work," Ash hissed.

"Relax, friend." Esther huffed as she stood up, and fiddled with her long, dark hair again. "Things are going to come together, and after tomorrow you'll be learning more about the long con than you ever wanted to know."

"How long before we get to him? Get to the bare bones of it?" Ash asked, scowling.

"You really hate him, don't you?" Esther smirked. "I've got somebody new for your pal Colorado to meet tomorrow."

A confused look.

"I do remember my promise to take him on… but then my own plans changed so I sent him to Rodney. Now they've changed yet again, I asked Rodney to release him. I'm putting him with a very old friend of mine by the name of Gregory Mathias LeRoy, affectionately known as Mattie to myself, and by various other names." She rubbed the back of her neck before walking to the cabinet by the fireplace and withdrawing a silver card holder from within. "Now, please do remember that the doors and windows remain locked whilst I am not here. If anyone should ring, they will use the name Annie. Not that I expect anyone. And if you'll excuse me, I have an appointment with the tourist board and the local police. Don't expect me come morning."

Harry Holmes straightened his tie as he exited the interview room. He smirked at the frustrated look on the face of DCI Rebecca Banks. She'd been chasing his tail for years, especially in the light of the murder of that persistent agent from Interpol.

"You do realise that the ravings of a lunatic have no bearing on a suicidal moment?" snapped his latest associate, Ezra Innocent, as he stood by the doorway, watching the proceedings with one overlarge bodyguard who didn't interrupt the American with the smooth Southern accent. "Heaving him in here when clearly the man had suicidal tendencies?"

"It's all right, Ez."

Ezra glared, and Holmes winced. Ezra Innocent despised any abbreviation of his name, and had once punched one of his underlings for committing this offence. Holmes had watched the man go down like a lump of gold, as a glimpse of a smile ghosted across Ezra's face and, with an apology, he returned to his poker game like nothing had happened.

"Ezra, I should say. DCI Banks is only doing her job. After all, that poor man killed himself so dramatically, and calling out my name. I do hope you find those dear girls too."

He grinned to himself. Ezra had taken one the previous day, apparently for some 'friends' to have fun with. His men had already done some beatings but not too much – after all, people paid less for damaged goods.

"That is my intent," DCI Banks said darkly. She looked at Ezra with barely contained contempt. "And you should find better friends, Mr—"

"Innocent, my dear lady," he said politely. He opened his mouth to say more, but was interrupted by the beep of his phone. He shook his head. "My apologies. I have been awaiting this for days." He walked out of the police station, flanked by his bodyguards.

Holmes watched him go, before smirking at Banks. "Banks. I hope we don't meet again too soon."

She offered a glare, and he chuckled as he walked out down the corridor, snapping his fingers at Hughes.

"What happened to the black kid? Any news on her?"

A quick, sharp shake of the head from Hughes, as he followed his boss with staccato steps, reaching into his pocket. "No. Kid's vanished. No trace. Hunted, although I do believe Gaines was in contact with Crook."

That stopped him. "Think he's sent her to Crook?"

Hughes shook his head. "Not sure. The Lawrence kid didn't talk. I'll take care of this one personally."

"You could include that Crook girl."

"I won't chase her, sir. Ezra's boy is on her; best they have." He sighed. "When's Mr Innocent taking you to his guns?"

"When he's ready. He wants to make sure of us."

"He's been doing that for near enough five years," Hughes said, pausing to catch his breath as they spied Innocent pacing outside.

"I'm of the same mind as him: keep your friends closer than your enemies." Holmes smirked nastily, before walking outside to join his associate. He was glaring at his phone. "Problems?"

"Daughter in the States," Ezra offered. "The darling girl seems to be under the mighty suspect conclusion that I do not wish for her to have any fun."

"You never mentioned you had a daughter," Holmes said, surprised.

It was true. Ezra had been a guest at many meals and events hosted by Holmes and his family. Holmes had put emphasis on his family and their importance.

"I don't mix my business with… family matters," Ezra said quietly. "I think it'd be easier if we moved things forward slightly. We do, after all, have that poker tournament. High-stakes poker games are always relaxing."

"Whoa, Ezra, my friend," Holmes said, raising his hand as Ezra began to pace towards his car. "We must make arrangements to meet your darling daughter. You wore the gold band for show."

"My wife's dead. So yes, Harry it is just for 'show'. My daughter and I share an intermittent relationship due to this." Ezra took a deep breath. "I may as well have buried my daughter with her mother. It was shortly before I met you. Now, if you'll both excuse me, I have more immediate concerns right now."

"How did she… er… die?" Hughes asked, too late for Holmes to stop him.

Once more Ezra paused and then quirked his head back to Holmes's lieutenant, disdain filtering through his green eyes. "Not that it matters to a second-rate nimrod like you, Mr Hughes, but my wife died in a shooting thanks to my business… associations, as I would like to say." He climbed into his car. "The Delaney Hotel, thank you."

"One more question, Mr Innocent… what's the interest in Esther Crook?"

"The shoot-out my wife got caught up in was the result of Esther Crook's mother, Anne Crook's, activities. Her father has Esther well hidden, but when I get to her, your foreplay last night will seem like a day in paradise. Au revoir, gentleman and understudy."

"Rise and shine, my little lotus blossom."

The next morning, the shutters of Ash's room were torn open and the bright early morning sun burst through. She sat up sharply and rubbed her eyes.

"What the—"

"It's all come together, kid. Need to catch the early flight into Oslo for some decent clothes for you two, but we'll get it without a hitch."

"Wait, you gussying me up?" Ash asked, rubbing her eyes and finding an amused glint in Esther's green ones. "Hold on."

"You know, in *The Sting*? There is this fantastic fruity named Rag in the background, where you see all the con artists coming together? Imagine that music because this is it. Now get your ass up before you really piss me off and I go after him alone."

"Wait, what?" Ash called, jumping out of bed and running behind Esther. "You've been away two days and you expect me to be up and at 'em?"

"Precisely; Luke said you weren't thick. Now move your ass."

Esther explained, as she laid out her playing cards that she seemed to have eternally stashed in her pocket, that there would be four others joining her to train Ash and Colorado in the scam, as well as helping her organise it. Wyatt Trammel, Christopher Adams, Buck Singleton and Eleanor Hyde – the truth be told, the names meant very little to con-artistry aficionado Ash. But then, the best con artists in the modern world were the ones you heard whispers about, and the masters were the ones you hadn't heard of.

After a three-hour drive to the regional airport and an hour's flight to the capital of Oslo, Ash felt ready to throttle someone. But Esther was nothing if not an excellent poker player, happily engaging in a friendly game with Ash, although Ash sensed that she was just being played, especially when she won more than a few of the games that Esther had set out.

When they arrived in the city, Esther had called a taxi and immediately headed to a large building where she made herself comfortable and began to reign supreme. They were now in a narrow dressmakers and tailor's shop staffed by two individuals: Johan, who was fitting Ash now, and Bill, whom Esther had embraced tightly and who was making her a cup of tea.

"Make sure she has at least nine evening gowns, and I *mean* at least," Esther said as she sat in the dressing room, reading a newspaper, while Ash was fitted. "And make sure that they walk the line between simple and eye-catching. Think you can hook it up in one night?"

"Hey, if I can get Jo Osborne his kit done for Franco's gig, you know I'll do it." The younger man handed Esther her cup of tea. "How should I take payment? Favour owed, dinner in a nice restaurant, percentage…?"

"Flat rate, Bill."

The words hung in the air, and Ash paused in pulling her boobs into a more flattering position as a sudden realisation washed over her.

Esther Crook wasn't expecting to walk out of this con alive.

S I X

Any thought of returning to London was ruined when Esther had gone out of the room, phone in hand and speaking in clear, short sentences –some littered with French and others in plain English. The tinkle of the shop bell indicated that she had left.

"How long you known her?" Ash asked Bill when she stepped back out of the changing room, dressed again in her casual jeans and T-shirt.

"Since we were sixteen," Bill replied, with a fond grin and taking the chosen items of clothing to one side.

"Is she as good as they say?"

Bill threw a glance at Ash. "Better. She's something like royalty in our line of work."

Ash offered a grin. "Have any tells?"

"Yeah. When she's telling the truth she's lying to you"

Ash shot him a confused look as Esther returned indoors.

"Ash was just asking if you have any tells."

"Yeah, bull ones. Come on. My associates have arrived." Esther pulled at her shirt. "Do you still have my measurements?"

"No need to measure you again, Es," the man assured her in his calming tone of voice.

His colleague, however, was not so calm. "Es, I expect to see you here to pay me."

"Now, now, Johan, no need for dramatics. You know me." She offered a smirk that only seemed to make him hug her. "I promise when this is over, I'll visit."

"Don't make a con promise."

"Can't con an honest man," she said softly. "You can only con with conviction." The two shared a soft, if sad, laugh before a steely resolve came over them. "I'll send each of them to collect it."

"And yourself?"

"Eleanor will come in with the details," she said quietly. "We've got the gist of the plan, but this involves fancy footwork to say the least."

"Just need to explain and get everyone on board?"

A tight nod in return. "Brother, you don't know how right you are." She tipped her head to him raising her fingers to an imaginary hat in a salute, before she and Ash exited the shop and strode towards a taxi.

"The Magnificent Hotel, please. Honestly, people have no taste. Chaos. Good name for a hotel. Or Hudra – like the siren of the Norwegian shores."

"Perhaps it'll live up to its expectations?" Ash said.

Esther smirked.

The Magnificent lived up to its appellation, standing as a huge red-brick building in the centre of Oslo, with a smart drive scattered with selected big-name cars. Esther merely rolled her eyes at Ash's surprised look.

"How can we afford this?" Ash asked quietly.

"We can't," Esther said, walking confidently up to the receptionist. She waited for the woman to raise her head before speaking again. "Hello, I'm Esther Lambert, Interpol." She flashed a badge with a smirk.

The young woman nodded.

"Me and my associates have booked a room; I believe Mr Adams is arranging it?"

Another tense nod, a quick gesture to the computer screen, a surreptitious putting of card keys into an outstretched hand, and Esther thanked her, jerking her head for Ash to follow her to the stairs.

"At the risk of sounding like an idiot, did you just pretend that you're an Interpol agent? You know, the International Police?"

"Nervous, already?" Esther smirked.

"Yeah... well, we're kind of international criminals now. And we're winding them up?" Ash stopped on the stairs.

"As good as any Swiss clock," Esther stated, fixing her with a green-eyed glare. "You ever been fingerprinted, bar entering or exiting a country?"

"No."

A flash of that annoying ingratiating smirk again before Esther returned to her walk and her gaze back up the stairs. "Then don't concern yourself."

"You genuinely enjoy this, don't you?"

Esther's green-eyed gaze didn't waver a jot from her focus up the stairs. "Our world isn't theirs. They are grey and we are Technicolor in their eyes, until we wash it away. It's a behind-the-scenes, wink-and-you'll-miss-it world. It's not built on the humdrum; it's built on adrenaline and the knowledge that, if everything is done right, we get away. If we don't, then it means we are not very good con artists. We border with the good, the bad and the goddamn ugly. Now move it. I know of one very annoyed gentleman who'll be yelling if I make him miss his lunch."

"Esther, get your ass up here before the pizza goes cold," boomed a deep voice from a floor above. Esther broke into a grin and hurried up the last few steps so she could see the tall man holding the door open for the two on the correct floor.

"There he is... still treated as a kid, Buck?" she returned, smirking. "Am I that blatantly obvious?"

"You're a whole mess of tells to those of us that know," the man replied, heading back indoors. "Pizza is free game now, Esther."

Esther shook her head, shoulders shaking in silent laughter as they headed upstairs, falling into an easy step together. They soon came to the allocated floor, silent and slipping down the corridor as light as feathers. Esther walked up to the door and knocked three times. It opened immediately to reveal the twinkling brown eyes and smiling face of a tall, moustached man. Without more ado, he offered Esther a hug.

"It's good to see you, Miss Crook," he greeted her.

Ash gave a small smile as she saw the poker face drop for half a moment when Esther embraced him back, and a glimmer of a childlike smile on her face as she relaxed. "Esther, are you going to introduce me?"

"Buck, Ash. Ash, this is Buckley, or rather Buck, a very good friend and an outrageous flirt."

"I can't help my natural magnetism." He winked at Ash, who stepped slightly behind Esther.

"I was just teasing, you don't need to worry," Esther said, voice suddenly concerned. "Man is all muscle and no brain."

Ash merely nodded; she already knew that she was safe with Esther, and that they needed each other right now. As the other two caught up briefly, she looked around the room.

The hotel room overlooked Oslo in all its grandeur and finery. There was a large table in the centre of the room where a young man – from the look of him, not much older than Esther – was sitting typing frantically into a netbook while simultaneously checking a tablet to his left. Another man left the bathroom; an older man who merely kissed the crown of Esther's head as she passed – a definite change from the young woman who came from a bedroom and squealed loudly when she saw Esther, and the two shared a tight hug.

"Christopher Adams," said the older man of the three. There

was more than a hint of danger in his voice. "Me and Buck are your outsiders."

Ash couldn't imagine the two as con men – their appearance screamed 'police', from their stance to their shoulder holsters that she had felt during the brief hug Buck had just given her.

"These two have successfully run several stings, all from the outside," Esther said, sitting down opposite the younger man. "Wyatt here is the computer whizz." She began laying down cards next to the other young woman. "Eleanor here is a very old friend."

"Despite being the same age as my colleague," said the other woman, before tapping the card at the top. "Low or high?"

"Unless you have the power of clairvoyance, you know my answer will be in the negative for your bet," Esther sighed. "Eleanor is also one of the best ropers in the business."

"Says the master," Eleanor said, smirking as she lifted the card. It was a tarot card. "You have got to teach me that little trick."

"Little tricks are what save people's lives in the con world; you ought to know that by know," teased Esther. She glanced at Ash. "And that is a precious gift that all grifters learn."

"Along with the greatest lie," said Eleanor with a small smile. "Three valuable little words for peace and quiet: 'I am fine.' Works every time."

"Very true. Now, we can either discuss the weather or we can get back to the con at hand."

Suddenly, Esther leaned forward and began drawing on a napkin. It wasn't beyond Ash's notice that even Christopher Adams had begun to watch with muted interest as the young con artist scribbled.

"This little drawing represents the art of the con." Esther threw her pen aside dramatically. "And doesn't it do well?"

Slightly unsurely, Ash took the napkin and brought it forward slightly so that she could see the image clearly. It was a circle with three arms coming off it. Inside the centre of the circle were the words *The Con*. The three arms had different words on; the first arm being *Motivation*, the second arm was *Opening*, and the final one *Good Reason*. Beneath *Good Reason*, Esther had scribbled Luke Gaines's name.

"This little thing represents everything we need to know?" she asked, getting a terse nod in reply. "Doesn't seem like much."

"It isn't. But we work with what we know."

Esther leaned back in her chair. "The first thing we need is motivation; we need to know our mark's reputation and what'll guide him into a con. Mr Adams?"

Chris nodded and pulled out a folder from his inside jacket pocket, put it down on the glass coffee table and removed several photos. "This is Harry Holmes; he's a gangster. Being chased by the ATF and the rest of the three-letter agencies, but so far has been successful in dodging them. Always looking for higher things to raise his profile and social ranking... that's why he married a banker's daughter. Their son was born six months later."

"More like a shotgun marriage," muttered Eleanor. "The old boy is a Roman Catholic who's being watched for inside trading by the City."

"How'd you know that?" asked Chris, looking at the young woman with surprise.

"My – honest, may I put in – father has an interest; works the corporate banks as a stockbroker. And the business dealings are all at Companies House, for anyone who cares to do any proper digging," Eleanor said, picking at her nails. "Holmes's daughter is desperate for some recognition of her own. Seems she wants to be known as something more than a gangster's moll. She gives regularly to charity and is an all-round lady behind closed doors."

"Behind closed doors, she's a megalomaniac," Esther broke in, as she threw out the cards that she'd just withdrawn.

"Her institutes despise her and she keeps one set of artwork under lock and key, although she's never revealed to the outside world why that is. Every six months it undergoes a switch between LA and London," Buck agreed. "Right now, everything is in LA.

Seems that there was a raid arranged a month ago and everything had up and left."

"Strange for an evaluator, let alone if she's chasing the glories," Eleanor said, leaning forward. "Seems like she only went with him to wind up Daddy Dearest?"

"Exactly. They only holiday together once a year to the Seychelles, and she hasn't been seen attending any of his PR events for at least eighteen months... but he still offered to buy a ruby for her."

"So he probably thinks of that old saying, 'Lucky at cards, unlucky in love.' Could be the reason he's joined this tournament?" Esther said quietly.

Christopher Adams gave a deep chuckle. "It could very well be. By all accounts, he is a fair gambler." His green eyes flashed at Esther, who was leaning even further back on her chair if that was possible, and looking into the distance. "He has been involved in the murder of several Interpol agents, but he beat the rap." His deep, gravelly voice was harsh with anguish. "From what the leaked psych reports have said, he is always looking to look like a hero but is disliked even by criminals as a snake."

Esther nodded. "From what I know, he's jealous of con artists, but equally admires them as they are the genteel of the con-artist world."

"Genteel?" Ash said, startled. "Joe Public seems to think we're the worst criminals of the lot."

Esther chuckled at Ash's incredulous tone. "There's criminality even in criminal circles... people who give us a bad name."

"I suppose that's a good thing," Eleanor said, with an amused smile. "Otherwise everyone would try what we're doing. Holmes is trying to con the public into believing he's a good man."

"He's a backwater gangster from the wrong side of the tracks and is terrible at trying to look good." Esther flicked a card onto the table. "Honest con artists tend to get away with being respectable citizens. And there is an art to it."

Ash leaned forward and nodded. "Just like that man who sold the Eifel Tower, what was it, four times?"

"Ah, yes, our beloved Reverend Victor Lustig, right up there behind the villainous Lou Blonger and the Old West brother Soapy Smith… there you have it. Our names go down in legend; gangsters' lives are forever tarnished. Now we come to our opportunity, or, rather, our opening," Esther said, with a small smirk. She pointed at Eleanor. "What did you find out, El?"

"I'm your best friend, Es, and I don't like it. He's a celebrity guest on a cruise. The cruise is notorious for its select guest and its games of Texas Hold 'Em poker."

Esther flashed a smile of triumph.

"Don't smile yet. If he feels he's losing, he cheats. He has also been known to beat the living daylights out of people he loses to."

"Ah, perfect. You can't con an honest man," Esther said proudly.

"And he wants *you*? I know you have a history with him due to her mother, but he *really* wants you. Doesn't care about *anyone* else but you, and possibly your old man – your family has a way of winding him up? I would like to meet your old man."

"Ah, my old man, the maestro of irritation." Esther smirked. "I promise to introduce you formally when this is all finished with, El."

"I'll believe it. It's the perfect time to reel Holmes in… the cruise at the very least." Eleanor smiled at her friend. "Get him angry and get him in."

"Depends on what route," Wyatt said, speaking for the first time. "You are going to be doing the long con?"

"This game has been in play a long time, Wyatt. No need to stretch it out any longer than it needs to be. I've already got people sorting out the big store in London. Just hope he takes the bait quickly for us. Eleanor, I need you in London."

Eleanor looked up sharply.

"You'll still need the clothes, so call in and see Bill. They should be done by the time you leave here."

"Where do you want it?" Eleanor asked, already getting to her feet.

"Speak to Mattie. He owes me a favour; he'll know the best place. Tell him to have a word with Nancy, too." She sighed. "But it needs to be ready double quick." A sudden flight of concern crossed her face, and she looked at Buck, who was grinning as if reading her mind. "Is Ezra Innocent going to be with him?"

"Might be, we don't know." Chris chuckled at her discomfort.

"I've heard of him, he's nice," said Ash. "You know, a good villain, if you get my meaning?"

"Naivety is not an asset I need... Innocent has been after me for years. We have a long, nasty history and I have no time... but all the time in the world," Esther said, frowning as Eleanor threw her a concerned look. "El, make sure if you run across him, you go the other direction."

"Wish you'd let me know; heard rumours of people asking about you, Es," said Eleanor, putting on her coat. "You sure you don't want me on the cruise with you?"

"Most certainly not. And people can ask. If Wyatt's done his job correctly I'll have a new passport and ID shortly."

The young man smirked. "Don't know what you'd do without me, Est. New passport, new ID and tickets booked for the cruise tomorrow night."

Esther smirked and stood up, crossing to the window and looking across the bay.

"So you're just reeling him in on the boat? Then big store in London and Denver?"

Esther nodded.

Ash gave an enthusiastic smile. "That sounds great, Esther. Full stop."

"Always makes me nervous, full stop," Esther said, barely loud enough to be heard. She looked down at the phone she'd so surreptitiously pulled from her pocket and shook her head at whatever was on the screen. "Full stops, I mean. Just like their American counterpart, period. Strange things in both the grammatical and other usage; they make everything sound final and ominous. Full stop."

SEVEN

"It's huge."

"Makes you wonder how they stay afloat," agreed Ash, as the two boarded the cruise liner. "Have you not seen them?"

"Usually when they come into bay in Norway I'm in bed," Esther said, smiling sadly as the officer took their tickets.

He regarded Esther's passport with a frown, then a steady smile. "What an unusual name. Darnell Voleur?"

"Rather thought 'Darnell' was pretty," Esther muttered, then, looking at the man before he opened his mouth any further, "'*Voleur*' is French for 'thief'... smart-ass."

Ash snorted as the man sniffed, though realised that the insult had been a joke on the parts of Chris and Wyatt. She handed her own passport over and waited for her key card to be printed.

"Miss Voleur and Miss Azeri, you've been assigned to State Room Number Four."

"Fresh flowers daily, if that could be arranged?"

Ash nearly dropped through the floor into the water in shock.

"There seems to be heightened security here?" Esther continued quietly.

"Shouldn't cause you any problem, Miss Voleur," said the security guard. "There is a famous jewel being exhibited."

Esther quirked an eyebrow in obvious confusion.

"Only here for the gambling?"

"*Oui,*" Esther said allowing a bit more of a French accent to slip through.

"The Star of Burma is here, along with a study of other jewels on loan to Cross-De Braun Casinos Ltd."

"Richard Burton failed to purchase it for Liz Taylor, you know; one of his only failures on the gemstone side of things," Esther said to Ash, who was still gaping. "Thank you. I must see it – not right now, though. Anyway, have my bags been taken to my room?"

A quick nod.

"Thank you. We don't need an escort."

Ash jogged lightly behind her friend as they walked through the cruise ship. A small gesture from Esther's hands indicated that she should not speak until they were in the room.

This was exactly when Ash flipped. "You seriously booked a state room?!" She was debating whether she admired Esther's ingenious spirit of commerce, or whether throttling her was a viable option. For all her precautions, it seemed to her that Esther was flaunting the fact that she was on board for all to see.

Esther threw down the file and nodded, taking off her hat. "It draws attention to the fact that a big player's come into town," she said, smirking. "Or, in this case, pleasure boat."

"I still don't get why it has to be on this thing?" Ash asked.

Esther offered a small smile as she put her suitcase on the bed and began to unpack. "Here begins the lesson: you don't want to be a mark, so stop thinking like one. Now, tell me: what does the ocean have that no law-abiding country has… and I just gave you a clue?" She sat on the edge of the bed and waited patiently as she pulled out some evening attire as well as the files that Adams had given her.

Ash opened her mouth.

"And don't say, 'Fish.'"

"Wasn't going to… wait – you said, 'Law'."

Esther looked up and nodded.

"There are different laws in international waters… this is a gambling ship?!"

"Perfectly legal. All monies go to the charities of the winners' choice." Esther smiled as Ash looked at her in surprise. "But Harry has got a false charity in his name."

"This is why you've been building up a reputation?"

Esther nodded again.

"You wanted in?"

"I've been invited twice, but as I told you, I needed a rainmaker," she said, leaning over to pick up a particular file. "So, we rob him of his charity money… I think Samaritans, because when I win the trophy I might just mention Luke's name."

"You're a real piece of work, you know that?" Ash said, smiling as she slung her things onto the bed. "Guess it'll suck to be playing when I'll be mixing with everyone."

Esther looked at her with an idle grin. "Like hell. I need a spy in the camp. Plus, you need to practise cold reading. There's no better place to learn a person's tells. Apart from church."

"You know, Gaines would've said that he didn't know if you were kidding or not," Ash said, pausing in her unpacking. She looked at Esther, who was wearing a small, sad smile. "You're after Holmes, like me."

"How come you ended up in foster care?" Esther asked.

"Never knew my dad; Mum died of breast cancer when I was six, so I ended up being kicked from pillar to post," Ash sighed as she remembered. "Well, I ended up turning away from my foster home and bumping straight into Luke. You?"

"My mother was great. Brought me and my twin brother up practically solo." She offered a slight grin at Ash as she unfolded a T-shirt. "Yes, there are two of us in this world; no, we don't feel each other's pain; and no, he's not a con artist… well, he is a fixer.

My mother was a teen mother like yours, but worked her way up in the respectable world... got too close to Holmes, though. My dad and her caught Holmes, so he thinks, and they get married. Holmes gunned her down." Esther sighed, and looked at the dresses in the case. "And the day I bring that bastard down will be the happiest of my life."

"But you never said how you got into the con-artistry line?"

Esther chuckled. "Don't like mystery, do you?"

The two began unpacking to the best of their abilities, while flirting with this new line called honesty.

"If you must know, my surname has travelled down the line for several generations, possibly back to the time of Queen Anne of England, and I do believe my father's side of the family is a host of reprobates too." She considered. "Might even run into my grandmother as well... hence why I need eyes."

Ash beamed. It was a high honour for any con artist to be asked to be eyes for the main man. Dee had always been the slider for the team back home. It was a good role, but one that you only trusted your closest allies with. "Mean it?"

"You are the left hand of God, consider that," Esther said, smirking. "And your first act can be to get your ass out there and see if we can find out about Harry."

"But we know Harry; that's what the files are about?"

Esther chuckled. "My dear child, I like to play God in my small universe and listen to the inner workings of the organisation. Now, if you'll excuse me, I have a tournament to win."

"Ever think you should quit while you're ahead?" Ash asked, looking at her. "You know, you could come up against somebody as good as or even better than you."

"Unless my father is on board, that is highly unlikely, and, as he always told me, 'Faint heart never won a flush.' Come on, let's go."

"You know, the problem with most business ventures,

especially growing up on the estate I did: you were judged by your class."

The tour had been a terrible idea, especially aboard this cruise ship, considered Harry Holmes as he looked around the stage. Ezra had long since given up paying his business partner any mind. In fact, he was shuffling a set of cards and talking quietly to his bodyguards who flanked him. He had yet to participate in any part of the tournament, preferring to stay on the outside. The scanty crowd just seemed to feed his general annoyance, and every now and then Ezra's green eyes would flicker in Harry's direction, then to the crowd; then he'd sigh as he returned to his game.

"What a fascinating beginning to your promotional tour."

The host was a young man who seemed fascinated by all aspects of Harry's life, even the boring front that he'd had set up. Initially, he'd feared that the host would have to be replaced; his incessant questioning had made Harry fearful of Interpol. When he'd suggested this to Ezra, the latter had pointed out that paranoia was unnecessary, especially given that his precious book containing all his business dealings was safe in LA.

"Now, please remember, ladies and gentlemen, that Mr Holmes will be available to watch play in the poker tournament tonight."

Harry raised his hand, to muted applause from around the room. He glanced to his right, and smirked. Hughes had had to stay behind in London to keep an eye on his business interests, and to keep his other eye out for that black kid who'd conned Harry. He'd been forced to bring along his left hand, Andreas Paulsen.

Paulsen was waiting to the side of the stage. The tall, usually calm Swede was twitchy with anticipation.

"What's wrong?"

"There's a rumour that Esther Crook is on board."

Neither noticed another man pause in taking a sip from his whisky chaser.

"Got a young girl asking about her."

"Show me."

The two men headed to where the tournaments were taking place, although they stood at the balcony overlooking the games. There were three circular poker tables, with several young ladies and young men playing. But while two games looked as if they were being prepared to be settled, at the third table there looked to be an epic match taking place between an older man, two younger men and one young woman. The woman was focused on the game and had no inch of concern on her face.

"There's the girl who's been asking questions," said Paulsen, pointing out a young black girl calmly watching the affair. "Been asking about Esther Crook."

"Find out anything?"

"She's with a woman called Darnell Voleur. Only know that she's a decent player."

"She'd cheat at yoga." Holmes saw the girl smile at the calm poker face of the young woman, who merely sighed and raked in her winnings from this hand. "Is that the woman she's with?"

"Yes, that's Voleur."

Green eyes flickered in the light, and a predator-like smile crossed Holmes's face. "Keep Innocent from the tables. I want to see Miss Crook play."

Ash watched as Esther stood to stretch her legs and walked over to where she was standing, flicking her nose, mimicking the similar gesture from *The Sting*. Her skill had blown everyone away from the table, and most now kept a discreet distance. Ash turned to face Esther, as enthralled as the rest of the spectators by the three professionals as they practised their craft.

So far her questions about Esther Crook had revealed a begrudging admiration for the young con artist, much distanced from the revulsion she felt for Harry Holmes. She'd delighted herself with her cold reading, making several new friendships along the way that could prove to be handy in the future. She'd learned that

Harry considered himself a novelty, and that the cruise was evidence of this. He wanted to be reputable, but the people he yearned to join regarded him with the same contempt as they did hardened criminals. His seminars had been half-booked and it was rumoured that he had paid big to get in and forced several 'decent' players out.

"Anything new learned?" Esther asked quietly, joining her.

"You've made an impression. You have just been invited to dinner with an Australian geologist and her grad student," Ash snorted, though she saw Esther smirk. "What?"

"Catch the name?

"Dr Victoria Jones, and the boy with her is a Russian; Anton Something-or-Other. Why?"

"You never know when it might prove handy to be friends with a graduate geology student," Esther said, picking up a glass of water and taking a liberal sip. "Such a nice game."

Ash grinned. "So, easy pickings?"

"Wouldn't stoop so low," Esther said, smirking. "Come on, I'll get you a diet drink of something."

"I thought you were on the bourbon?" Ash paused thoughtfully. "Shouldn't I drink so as not to look out of place?"

Esther chuckled. "A teenager would definitely look out of place drinking in this kind of place. And I'm not in the habit of breaking the law."

Ash nearly choked. "Not in the habit of breaking the law?" she laughed. "You're a living legend! All those jobs that you've helped plan out…"

"You *know* I have never been formally charged with any crime?"

Ash scoffed. "Never?"

"Not even questioned. My reputation is built on being invisible. Living legends can't be charged." Esther offered a smirk. "Now, stop thinking like a mark, and I'm going to teach you a very precious motto."

"That being?"

"'You can do what you like with the law; bend it, twist it, hide behind it... just don't break it.'"

"Now, where's there fun in that?"

Esther chuckled. "There's none whatsoever. Just to point something else out whilst you're brushing up on your observational skills, I've had one – singular – bourbon. Not multiples. One. Now, it's on to the soft drink. Got to have an active mind." A mist came over her eyes as she looked at the table. "I will love and leave you. I believe my allotted time is over."

A crowd gathered around to watch the final two competitors for the quarter-finals play. The man Esther was playing with was Brett Higgins, a young American. The other player had dropped out due to the two's professionalism and quickness in hand. He now stood to the side of the game, watching just as eagerly as the others.

Ash watched as Esther fastidiously played the cards, and then Brett Higgins began to deal out the cards for their fifth hand. Unlike the other competitors, who had made small mistakes that turned into large ones, so that Ash could root out their small tells, she could see none.

"Raise."

"Okay, call."

There was a sharp intake of breath around the table as the tall American put out his cards.

"Two pair."

Esther let out a small sigh, then threw down her own two cards. Around the room, there was a delighted, astonished laugh as she pulled in the money with a small smile.

"Three of a kind," the croupier said with a nod. "I'd like to advise an end to the evening's events. Games will start at three o'clock tomorrow."

"Thank you for the game, Mr Higgins," Esther said, standing and shaking his hand. "It's rare I get as good a game as that. My compliments."

"Pleasure, Miss…?"

"Voleur. I hope to play you again soon," she said softly.

"If you are so inclined, we could meet again tomorrow for a friendly hand?"

A tilt of Esther's head.

"Winner buys a coffee?"

"Thank you. Will ten o'clock be agreeable?"

"Most."

"See you then… again, a true pleasure." She glanced at her winnings and handed approximately £2,000 to the croupier. "Thank you, sir."

She walked away, thanking people as they offered her their hearty congratulations. Ash smiled as she stood next to her. Esther raised her finger to indicate silence as she downed a glass of water.

"Let's get out of here," Esther said.

The two began to walk back to their cabin.

"You know you're better than most of them?" Ash asked, walking alongside her mentor.

Esther gave a nod.

"Then what's the issue?" she continued flatly.

"Someone might be a ringer and surprise me," Esther said, with a shrug. She flexed her fingers and gave a satisfied sigh. "Come on, I need to rest before tomorrow's games. I'm going to be early. I've offered to be the croupier for the children's illegal chemin de fer match. Bless their little black hearts."

"No more games? How about blackjack?"

"No, and before you ask, I don't count cards… just enjoy the game." Esther smirked as they headed to the lift.

"Not exactly illegal to do so," Ash said, as they stepped into the lift and headed towards the state rooms.

Esther chuckled as the express elevator headed up. "Just frowned upon." She reached into her bag and pulled out the key card for their room. "Besides, I tend to lose at blackjack. You know, my father, for his sins, has tried to teach me that damned game. He swears he's going to kill me some day because of my lack of prowess."

"You lose?"

"You don't tell Eleanor; that jerk will want to play it all the time." Esther swung open the door and entered into the dark, stepping into the bathroom immediately and closing the door behind her. "Get some shut-eye; we have a good few hours. There'll probably be a huge announcement."

Ash nodded and looked at the beds that had already been made up. She sighed and turned on the lights, then began to pace to her bed, only to be caught around the mouth and jerked back into a hard, male frame.

"Who the hell are you?!"

She let out a scream against his hand, and attempted to bite, only to receive a shake.

"Who are you? Prowling around, asking questions!"

"Vin, drop her!" Esther's voice was icy.

The man didn't release his hold over Ash's mouth.

"Now. She's a friend of mine."

The man looked down at Ash, then grunted and released his grip, throwing her to Esther, who caught her with ease as she stumbled. The man sat in the chair on the balcony, pulling out a bar of chocolate from his pocket and taking a bite. Esther regarded him coldly.

"Changed your hair."

"You've not. What're you doing here?"

"Had a tip-off and been looking for you for Innocent. He's set his hound toward this kid here. Sorry, darling; joy of my job." He directed his blue eyes at Ash, and she continued to keep her distance. "Seems like she's afraid of me, Est."

"Who in their right mind wouldn't be?"

"If we were in our right minds, we wouldn't be in this job, would we? Full stop?"

Esther flinched at the terminology before guiding Ash to the bed. "Devin is a bounty hunter, Ash." She sat Ash down on the edge of her bed, but remained standing herself, to eye their guest. "And definitely a full stop I concern myself with."

EIGHT

"You know this... this... renegade?!"

"Renegade... Good word. And yes. Vin here is an old friend. Bounty hunter for Ezra Innocent, who normally keeps me informed of his movements." Esther raised her eyebrows.

"You play both sides?" Ash asked, looking at the man in disgust.

"He is also a good friend of my father and has an excellent misdirection in place; for example, if I am in Lyon, he says I'm in Monte Carlo. I am due a trip down the Riviera... perhaps when this con is over."

"Damn it, Esther! You brought a kid here? And as if I haven't been trying to direct you away from here?!"

"Ah, I was wondering why you were here," Esther confessed. "I take it that you are not here on a pleasure cruise?."

"Watched you play, Est. He'll know who you are and he's sent his hound dog after this one." He waved his hand at Ash, who was glaring at him.

"Couldn't you persuade Holmes to let Innocent take us both?" Esther asked.

A tense shake of the head.

"No?"

"No. Innocent is only interested in you." Vin stood up and prowled slowly towards her and put both hands on her shoulders. "Get out of here."

"I'm on an ocean liner in the middle of international waters... how am I supposed to?" she asked, shaking her head.

"Find a way to hide amongst the crew..." He paused and squinted. "You're running a damned con?"

"What do you expect me to do? I kept my promise to the letter, until the rainmaker came."

"And what about Ezra Innocent? You do know they are partners?"

Esther continued to look defiantly at him.

"You know, don't you? You're up to no good, you conniving, sly little brat of a fox!"

Esther smirked. "In the words of my dear father, 'A fox isn't sly, just can't think any slower'."

"Yeah, yeah." He cuffed her head playfully. "I'll settle myself in the bathroom in case Holmes's goons try anything." He pointed at the safe. "Your derringer is in there. I managed to get it through security."

"Probably as wait staff," scoffed Ash.

Vin paused a moment before pacing onwards to the bathroom, grabbing sheets along the way.

"Waiters and waitresses I hold in higher regard," said Esther, patting Ash's shoulder. "Don't worry. Devin there is reliable; I'd place my life in his hands. Anyhow, he was curious more than anything... you and old Vin should get along. He had a rough upbringing."

"Esther, shut up. I can still hear you."

"Yeah, you old sod," Esther riposted with a gleeful grin. "Thought she might like to know you're just overprotective."

"Damned right. Get some rest; I have money riding with your old man on you losing to that American, Brett Higgins, tomorrow. You do know he's beaten near enough everyone here?"

"And such a young face… ah, well…" Esther suddenly paused. "The old man knows I'm aboard?"

"Mm-hm, and told me to tell you," Vin stuck his lathered head around the door, "that if he has to come rescue you from some stupid con he will not be best pleased."

"He can be what he likes," Esther said, frowning. "I intend to enjoy this tournament, like it or not. I'm intending to enjoy my five-card game of stud… hell, might even let the kid think he's going to win."

"Esther, you're going to lose to that kid on purpose," Vin said in a knowing tone of voice.

Esther waved him off and he chuckled, winking at Ash, who smiled despite herself.

"I guess you're the only person in the world who'd get insulted if someone called her what she is. A good soul."

"Not insulted… embarrassed." Esther turned to Ash. "Now go to sleep. It won't be easy, but we have a good watchdog out there."

Ash shot Vin another look over her shoulder.

"Nothing will happen while he's here. Promise… just don't drink his coffee."

"Don't see what problem you have with my coffee, Est," Vin called out.

"None; makes a fine paint stripper," Esther retaliated. "But if you should ever meet Ezra Innocent and he offers you an out, I make it clear to you here and now, you take it. Regardless."

"I thought you didn't trust him?" Ash asked quietly.

"He's a man of his word. Been promising to throttle me for donkey's years." Esther smirked. "Always one step ahead. Don't trust him, but if he offers his word you take it… it's about self-preservation. I've told Vin the same. Thank God he's not aboard."

The card games were simmering down for the evening, apart from a few friendly hands being played. Old-fashioned five-card stud, well after the croupiers had finished. Ezra Innocent was smiling in the low light as he sat, legs outstretched and overlooking the sea with a measured eye, a bottle of bourbon resting to his left with a half-full glass dangling from his loose fingertips. His two bodyguards sat silently to the side, quietly resembling two sheepdogs waiting for their master's orders.

He looked at peace with the world. It almost felt a shame to disturb him, Harry thought to himself. Then he thought of Esther Crook, who'd escaped his grasp once, and if he had this man's backing then he'd get her back into his hold.

"Ezra," he said softly.

Innocent glanced up at the intruder.

"I have news for you about Esther Crook."

"Not one to beat around the bush, Harry," said the gentleman, returning to gazing at the sea. "Last I heard, she was hiding out in Norway."

"She's on board, travelling under an assumed name," said a man appearing from behind.

Holmes spun around to see the man who had come in silently, unseen, to break into their conversation.

"Just left her now."

"Why, Devin, I thought you were protecting your asset. Harry, this is an old friend of mine, and my watchdog, as it was, Devin."

"Some watchdog."

A raise of the eyebrows from Ezra.

"I mean, I found her before him."

"Devin has been running with the foxes and the hounds, under my instruction," Ezra said. He tilted his head curiously as the other man plucked the untouched whisky glass up. "Please, have a glass, Vin. Do you know what her scheme is?"

"The stuff you drink is too fancy for my taste, Ez." A shake of the head while Ezra grumbled at the name. "She's enjoying the poker, more than anything. Looks like she's retired."

"People like her don't retire," said Holmes, deciding that he didn't like this man one bit. If the kid had retired, it meant they wouldn't have the opportunity to try to con her… or for her to be in his debt. "They find cons."

"They also have a strange moral code," Ezra said, smirking into the drink that he'd lifted to his lips with apparent casualness. "I happen to want to let her know I'm aboard." He chuckled at the disbelieving expression on Holmes's face. "As my *own* moral code still tells me that, as a Southern gentleman, I am obliged to meet her and attempt to find out her scheme." He looked across at Devin. "Go back before you're missed."

"You trust him?" Harry asked as Vin nodded, giving Ezra a small almost-salute before walking off back indoors. "He did protect her first."

"'Trust is another con', in the words of my darling mother," Ezra said, sipping the last of the bourbon. "I just want to ruin her. Like you, I suspect that she's up to no good… but I have a plan for that."

Morning was ushered in by several knocks on the suite door by their steward delivering a late breakfast in bed. When Ash had awoken and dressed, she'd found Vin sitting drinking coffee and eating a Danish pastry, his long brown hair tied into a ponytail, and looking more comfortable now.

"Mornin', Ash," he greeted her.

She grunted.

"Est went out in the early hours, no doubt to help the kids out."

"Figure she'll be banned from the blackjack tables?"

"Nah, she wins too much on them," the man stated with a chuckle. "Lets people think she's terrible… Eleanor's been trying to draw her in for about four years."

"She told me she couldn't play," Ash said, sitting down opposite him and pouring herself a coffee.

"Ambrosia," Vin said, his voice suddenly a touch sad. He shook himself. "She tells people that. Every con artist needs to be poor at one aspect… and she'd not be a croupier for the kids' game if she were. Why anyone would bring a kid on board a ship while they gamble is beyond me."

"Honing their senses?" Ash joked lightly.

"Possibly." He looked thoughtful.

Ash shook her head.

"At least they're with them… some would dump them or use them for a con."

"Is that what got her into the game?" Ash asked quietly.

Vin shook his head.

"Her mother?"

"Her mother… I knew both parties… when Holmes killed her it turned the kid remorseless." He bit his lip. "Determined to see him through, but she didn't know enough to kill him. Nearly got herself sold into the trade for that."

Ash looked up sharply.

"She broke into the mansion he had in Hollywood – let's just say, as the kid's proud of saying, she ain't no thief. Proved it when she got caught breaking in… but he figured he would make a profit on her. Kid was pretty and a virgin. Worth every penny of hard-earned money, and she'd be a prize. Barely saved her from that one. You know how Holmes has a chipped tooth?"

Ash nodded.

"That was Chris getting her out… broke his jaw in three places too. So her old father decides to make her promise to wait for a rainmaker."

"That'd be me."

Vin nodded. "I guessed… has she told you what the con is?"

Ash was about to say when she caught a glimpse of something in Vin's eye. She didn't know what, but it wasn't good. She thought of Luke Gaines in the darkness of the dramatic end of his life, and yet his words of wisdom: *Scratch the lie – kick the truth in the teeth and go with your gut.* "No. Well, not much. She's enjoying the poker right now; been playing illegal matches in Norway."

Vin clicked his tongue, obviously unsatisfied with her response. "Well, she's just like her dear father, paranoid bastard."

Who trusts you with his daughter? Ash felt herself tense before saying casually, "Probably waiting for an idea."

"More likely." He sipped his coffee. "Innocent's aboard."

"You what?!" Ash snapped.

"Innocent is aboard." Vin sipped his coffee again as Ash jumped to her feet. "And where are you going?"

"I got to warn her – if she knows Innocent's aboard she might pull the con!" Even to her own ears, Ash knew she sounded like a whining sixteen-year-old. Selfishly whining.

"So you're thinking of yourself, not the kid?" Vin snorted. "And she trusted you to be her slider?"

"She told you?"

"Guessed." He stood. "What else can she be planning solo?"

Ash felt like snapping that she had a team, but bit her lip. She didn't trust Vin. She didn't trust herself, either. Esther had warned her that two people seeking revenge was a recipe for disaster. "Where are you going?" she asked quietly.

"It's near enough time for the poker match; figure I can be a friend and warn her." He threw a look back at her. "I reckon it's the least I can do."

The ship was large enough to lose yourself and your soul on, with various games played in different areas. There was also a cinema and a swimming pool. Vin had investigated the pool area while Ash had gone to the cinema – and, nearly two hours later, Vin with suspiciously wet hair and Ash wearing glasses that looked like 3D glasses, the two agreed she was in neither spot.

"She must've gone to the coffee shop," Vin said quietly as he glanced at his watch. "Would've heard if she'd been caught dealing that kids' match she was on about."

"Is that Esther Crook you're discussing?" came a scratchy voice from the left.

Both spun around to see a young man studying a rather large emerald necklace on the display stand of a nearby shop. His green eyes flicked up at them, before he returned to making a note in a notepad. He offered a curved, innocent smile.

"How'd you know?" Ash asked curiously.

"I met her this morning with my geology professor after breakfast. I'm Anton Pavlov." The young man offered a slight quirk of the lip and a hand outstretched. Ash shook it quickly, as did Vin. "We're going to be meeting later for dinner."

"Know where she's gotten to?" Vin asked quickly.

"Look where the crowd is." Pavlov gestured abstractedly and returned to his examination of a new ruby and emerald that shared a display case. "They've been going half an hour, and it's been an even keel."

Ash and Vin moved to the atrium staircase. Looking down, they could see a throng of admirers surrounding a small coffee table, and Ash spotted Esther's scarlet leather jacket and what she took to be Brett Higgins's shoulders.

"Thank you," Vin said to Pavlov, heading downstairs immediately. He glanced at Ash as she paused, continuing to admire the scene from above. "Ash, I'll meet you down the front?"

"Of course." She paused to look back at the student, who pushed his glasses up his nose. "Thank you for your advice, Mr Pavlov."

"If I may, I'd like to request that dinner between myself and Miss Voleur solo? She seemed to be very interested in the Burmese ruby," he said, not looking up from his study.

Ash was about to give a pointed response, but then she turned smartly on her heel and headed downstairs. She soon found Vin, who was smiling at the ongoing game and brought her forward.

"Rare you see this, iffun you ever do," he said with a certain satisfaction. "Ash, watch two masters at work."

From Ash's perspective, the poker game was going well. Both parties had decided to use circular chocolate mints wrapped in green foil from the coffee bar to symbolise coinage, although it was more a matter of enjoyment than a proper game. It was also gathering a steady stream of admirers of the fine art; even Vin's lips had twitched when Esther had dealt a particularly fine flush. It was olden-day poker in a modern-day setting, and if Ash closed her eyes she could imagine the scene playing out on the old Mississippi riverboats.

"May I join you?" It didn't sound like a request.

Ash looked at Vin, who was growling at Holmes's appearance. Harry Holmes looked out of place in his casual jeans and shirt, in comparison to Esther and Brett Higgins, who were casually dressed but somehow fitted into the entire scene. They both glanced at the interloper.

"Just don't expect conversation."

The infamous gangster's lips twitched; the twist of them was nowhere near a smile. It reminded Ash of a predator eyeing a particularly sweet morsel, and it sent an unpleasant shudder through her. The son had the same expression.

Esther merely glanced at him, as did Higgins, a look of utter contempt on both their faces. "You seem to have an interesting effect on people, Mr Holmes."

The lips twitched again, and Holmes reached for the pack of cards. Esther, however, picked them up before he touched them and began to cut them, shuffling them and dealing left-handed.

"Very impressive, Miss Voleur."

"It was a case of learn to deal left-handed or stop playing. I like my cards too much," Esther said shortly. "Anyway, I play well either way, as Mr Higgins will ascertain."

"That I will."

Despite having no play in the game, Holmes began to filter his fingers through the forfeited cards. Ash watched as both players tensed up. It was considered poor conduct, and it was evident both sides recognised the transgression.

"Sir," Higgins's soft Texan drawl held menace, "please desist from going through the discarded cards. You have no right to a game."

"Not committing a crime." Holmes smirked.

"Well, as my father always says, 'Worst crime a man can commit is interrupting a poker game', so you must be committing at least a dozen other crimes." Esther looked up into Holmes's cold eyes. "You are interrupting a private play for pleasure. Myself and Mr Higgins had a rather stimulating game yesterday. And this is proper poker... as you are no doubt aware."

"But, Miss Crook... or is it Voleur?" Harry mocked, and Ash saw Esther cock her eyebrows with open disdain. "I couldn't quite keep up."

"Crook. Voleur is a family name, but I forget you didn't know your father, isn't that right?"

Holmes glared, his ears turning a subtle shade redder. Ash hid a snort behind a cough as Esther returned to her card game with increased nonchalance.

"Please leave the table."

"No, no, would much rather watch." He pulled out a chair and sat next to Esther. She grimaced at the closeness and returned to eyeing her hand. "A dead man's hand... how appropriate."

"Sir, your manners are abysmal," Brett Higgins said quietly. "Myself and the lady were trying to enjoy a friendly card game."

Ash turned away from the game, as a man crossed the room slowly, followed by two bodyguards, but with a panther-like grace.

"Mr Ezra Innocent, on your left," Vin said quietly in her ear.

Ash trembled, though she felt Vin at her back, keeping her eyes fixed on Innocent's approach. A curt nod in his direction from Vin. Ash winced at that. But Esther had said he needed to preserve himself here. Ash was stunned by the youth of the man. He looked barely into his forties with dark hair and sharp green eyes that took everything in. A smart Armani suit which showed off his square and tight body, but then there was a glint from his mouth...

Ezra slid into the now-empty seat as Esther dealt the hand, all too focused on the 'friendly' practice. She was smiling at something Higgins had said and agreeing when she glanced in Ezra's direction. Instantly, her poker face fell. Even when there had been a flash of annoyance with Holmes, she'd maintained an ice-cold expression. There was now only true, unadulterated fear.

"Oh, Miss Crook." Holmes was grinning now at her wide-eyed stare at the man. "I believe you know this gentleman?"

"It's a pleasure again, Miss Crook."

"Innocent."

N I N E

Esther briefly tapped the top of the cards, almost in frustration, as she saw Holmes smirk and step back allowing for Innocent begin playing. She offered a small, reassuring smile to Brett Higgins, who glanced between the two with growing anxiousness.

"Mr Innocent is an old acquaintance," Esther stated to Higgins.

"Seems a surprise to see him?" asked Higgins.

"I thought you were still Stateside, Mr Innocent?" she said quietly.

"Business needs."

"I heard you were doing business with reprobates, but this? This is a new low." Her eyes flicked to Holmes. "You do realise the part he had to play in your wife's death?"

"And Mr Holmes has given me a rather compelling account of your duplicity in it… surely you realised that I would be waiting?"

Esther nodded curtly. "Mr Higgins and I enjoyed a rather excellent game last night. We're playing for who pays for the coffee."

"Fantastic odds," Innocent agreed, smirking. He stood.

"Though if you don't mind some disagreeable manners, Mr Higgins, I'd like to facilitate Miss Crook's coffee."

Esther shook her head. "If you'd like, we can play a game ourselves? If Mr Higgins has no objections?" A quick shake of the head before Esther glanced at her watch. "And then if you'd like to facilitate me, as you'd say, to go to this convention on the Star of Burma?"

Ash tensed, as did Vin's hand on her shoulder, as Innocent could be seen considering the offer.

"And your friends join me?"

"Only me and the kid aboard, Mr Innocent," Esther said quietly. She looked up. "Mr Higgins and me are just competitors."

Innocent nodded and sat down, taking off his coat in one swift movement and hooking it to the back of the seat. "Mr Holmes, I have a feeling that you should step back and watch the game and give us privacy for our conversation on this…" he pondered over the word, "…matter."

Ash watched as Esther settled into the game, playing evenly with Innocent and completing her game with Higgins. Higgins would have the honour of not buying the coffee, which she promptly gave to him and asked for him to pick her up a cup of tea and some sweet tea for Ezra Innocent. She received a slight tilt of the head as an acknowledgement of a well-played hand and game. The teas arrived shortly afterwards.

Ash felt her eyes water as small mistakes and tells became apparent through Esther's nerves, the gambling man playing opposite revealing nothing that she could see other than a small tap at the top of the cards. Esther looked to be bearing it well, though there was a slight tremor to her hand as she dealt one card. Ash couldn't see Vin, but she could hear his sharp intake of breath as Ezra Innocent laid down the last card and produced a stunning full house which reduced Esther's hand to nothing.

"I feel here is the time to complete our sojourn. Competing, or just enjoying the amateurs?" Esther asked cordially as Brett

Higgins returned to her side. "Thank you, Brett. I hope to see you later."

He looked hurt at the dismissal, until Esther pressed a light kiss onto his cheek, a chaste but polite goodbye, for now at least. "I hope to see you too... perhaps we could meet for dinner?"

"I'm afraid not; a friend has promised me the conversation of a doctor who is an expert on the Burmese ruby that's on display. But I can promise myself for afternoon tea? Shall we say three o'clock?"

"I'd say that's fine."

She smiled at his eagerness, before he headed off and she took her tea and sipped from it. Ezra Innocent waited politely, gesturing for his two goons, and Ash felt Vin tighten his hold on her before bringing her over to them.

Esther cocked her eyebrows at Vin before shaking her head. "Should've guessed you'd be helping him, Vin," she said quietly.

"Self-preservation," Vin said but Ash could feel his hand slacken on her; obviously a sign that she understood that this was necessary.

"Big word; learn it from the dictionary? Oh, I'm sorry." Esther put on a taunting air of apology. "Vin the turncoat is dyslexic, Miss Azeri. Or just plain stupid."

Despite knowing it was an act, Ash gasped at the harsh words before Esther's arm was snatched by Innocent. She winced and threw an angry look at him.

"Manners maketh the man, let alone woman, Esther Crook. Accept this and take a lesson from it, as I do detest a sore loser. Accept it as part of my education on good poker and we will alight together."

Esther kept her gaze steady before nodding.

"I'm glad we agree. Now, I believe you were wishing to see this famous gem?"

"I believe that was a condition of the win?" Esther nodded again, and Innocent's grip slackened. "I'm not bringing Holmes."

"Lady's privilege," Innocent said, smirking. "But this is not a—"

"I rather guess you're going to say this is your show? Fine, then." Esther tilted her head. "Let's go."

The group began their walk to the exhibition, Ezra and Esther talking lightly between themselves as the two bodyguards, Ash, Vin and Holmes followed in perfect silence.

"You know the exhibition is worth several million pounds?" Esther was saying conversationally, and it took a squeeze to Ash's shoulder to reveal that Esther was talking to her. "Quite a steal."

"If you can get by the security," Ash said politely.

Esther walked around the security guards, Ezra Innocent's hand at the small of her back, and if Ash hadn't known about the underlying fear that had ruined the game, she would've said they were an affectionate father and his daughter, despite the fact that Innocent looked barely old enough to have an adult daughter.

"Fascinating things, jewels," Esther said politely.

"Very. Did you know that the ruby, when worn, is considered by Hindus to protect you from the Devil?" Holmes said thoughtfully. "It's a shame about the flaw in the ruby that's the centrepiece here."

"It is; if it was an emerald, it would've been considered even more beautiful. We French, as you know, call them '*jardin*', which means 'garden', because they resemble light coming through the greenery. I must admit, I have an open admiration for an honest gardener, like I have an admiration for an honest cop," Esther said, with a fond smile directed at Innocent, who folded his arms across his chest and raised his eyebrows. "They dig around in the dirt and get very little for their reward."

"A lot of dirty history behind the Star of Burma?"

"A harbinger of death to whoever holds it; I've heard the stories," Esther said, turning her attention to the ruby.

"The unfortunate Russian royal family have held it; it was also held by… was it your grandfather?"

Esther offered a tight nod.

"One of the greatest cons against—"

"Hellion?" Ash interrupted in surprise. Both turned, and she blushed. Even *she* had heard of this con.

Hellion was a con woman notorious for her smooth style and for leaving chaos in her wake. She'd supposedly conned eight businessmen in three months, resulting in the collapse of Les Cheveliers, a French bank. It had been one of the best cons of the late '80s; a con artist known only by the unattractive moniker Potvin had managed to convince Hellion to purchase a ruby for a con of her own. The ruby had been a fake, and she had put a curse on the man, promising swift retribution.

Esther offered a small smile. "Her con name is Hellion. My paternal grandmother, as it happens. The last time I saw her was last year, when I walked away with the majority of her poker earnings… most upset, she was, too." She clicked her tongue in abject dissatisfaction. "I walked away with £400,000 in hard-earned cash and she still accused me of cheating – as if I would cheat in Monte Carlo; it's practically the Notre Dame of the gambling world."

Ash looked across at Esther, who raised her eyebrows at the sudden admiration she knew was coating her expression. "You're part of that."

"My brother and I are the last in the line of both sides of the family, may I add; an exceedingly long line of reprobates, crooks and generally disreputable people," Esther said, smirking. "And no, he falsely claimed it was the ruby in question that had been stolen. He sold it to many famous people and got jailed, because of that and because of his varying other enterprises. My mother barely escaped the man. She became an Interpol agent because of it." Her eyes hardened. "He didn't deserve to bear the name Crook."

"That I can agree on," Innocent said softly.

"Doesn't soothe the pain, though, that the man took your wife in the same moment he took my mother," Esther said softly. "You see, Ash, my grandfather, Paul Crook, was obsessed with killing my mother, and unfortunately in his triumph on achieving this, he also killed the wife of Mr Innocent, a bystander at the scene. He and Holmes share the same reprehensible nature – honour amongst gunrunners and all that. Hence, his wish to kill me… my father's favourite."

"I'd settle for knowing what he looks like," Innocent said with a smirk.

"As if I'd tell you."

He looked at her. "Two generations of family wiped out in two days, one by Potvin and Potvin by Chris Adams—"

"Potvin slipped off the side of a building making his escape. That's hardly Chris's fault."

"—it makes me wonder why you've brought in a kid to a con," Innocent said, ignoring Esther's indignant interruption.

"Who says I'm running a con?" Esther asked.

"You. I know you." He sighed. "My accursed Southern gentleman charm and manner compels me to tell you that, if you do not find a better way to spend your time, you will face a storm unlike any other."

Esther leaned forward, looking hard into the businessman's eyes. She didn't flinch. "I don't fear storms, Mr Innocent. I have no problem with you, but I assure you with my best intention that I am not pulling a con on you. In fact, my aim in this tournament is just to win." Her eyes flicked to Ash. "She's a friend, like I said. Nothing more and certainly nothing less. She has no cards to play."

The two shared a tense look before Holmes coughed subtly, Innocent breaking his gaze from the young woman, who immediately stood in front of Ash.

"Kid's not worth protecting," Holmes said dismissively. "Would be easier for you to give up the game than—"

"I'm not on any game, unless you are talking about that *Highlander* film, which I might watch tonight!" snapped Esther. "I'm here enjoying myself and, last time I checked, withdrawing from the formal contest. It'd seem someone has poured poison instead of honey into the judge's ears." She tossed her head back defiantly. "I'm no card shark, Mr Holmes."

"Most swan-like neck, Miss Crook." In one swift move, Holmes had caught the nape of her neck in his palm and forced it back, looking like he was appraising her as one would a horse.

Ash made to step forward, only for Vin to grab her hand to stop her. She threw him an angry look, but then saw that his other hand was resting by a large bowie knife tucked into the waistband of his jeans that she hadn't even noticed.

"I am inclined to remember some of my associates being most enamoured with your looks back then. And I know several young men who would pay good money for you here and now... let alone the fact that you broke a few orders when you got away last time."

"And I seem to remember that I was saved by Chris Adams," Esther murmured. Ash watched Holmes's fingers retract swiftly, Esther flashing him a true smirk when she rubbed the back of her neck. "Still getting pain in your jaw?"

"Shut your mouth."

"The girl is under his protection too, so if you want a piece of me, try it."

Holmes glared hard at Ash, and Ash felt Vin's hand on the small of her back, quick and reassuring. His own gaze was on the man, and Ash could swear she heard him growling.

"Down, Vin," Innocent ordered, in the same moment as Esther shot Vin a piercing, warning look. "We're just having a pleasant conversation."

"Nothing pleasant about it," the bounty hunter said tensely as he held Ash. "You've done what you wanted: warned her off as a Southern gentleman."

Esther smirked. "The other one is no gentleman." She turned her attention to the ruby once more. "Biggest of its kind, you know? It's colour is known as a pigeon blood red, Vin?"

"I've seen pigeons and they aien't red," Vin drawled.

"Very funny," Esther said as she bent down to examine the ruby again. "I'll take your warning under advisement, as I realise after this point I will be fair game."

"I'm glad." Innocent smirked before jerking his head again. "Gentlemen – which includes you, Mr Holmes – let's go!"

The men, with the exception of Vin, strode off and Ash shot a final glare towards Holmes, who walked away into the distance, throwing a smirk over his shoulder at them.

"What was that all about?" Ash asked, frowning as she looked at Esther, who stood and watched their retreat darkly.

"Marking of territory," Esther said quietly. "If he gives you a way out, you take it. No bull. Just take it."

"Aren't you playing?"

"Not any longer; the poker face is down. The very first thing that Holmes will do is spread a whisper that I am here. It's not worth the effort of denying that." She shook her head. "And don't change the subject. If the man offers you an out, you take it."

"You're still frightened?"

Esther nodded. "Not of him. Holmes is one loose cannon that Innocent's barely reining in. He killed your foster father; more than likely sold your foster sister into sex slavery. Yes, the son of a bitch is well suited to being my grandfather's heir."

"He's a gunrunner."

"Yeah. So?" Esther shot her a dirty look.

"So? Shouldn't you be taking him for everything he's got?"

Esther let out a sharp bark of laughter that near choked her, so Vin answered for her.

"Even Est has people she won't mess with, and he is one. As mentioned, he's hung up over his late wife."

"And factor in that I want Holmes, and it kind of messes with the best-laid plans." Esther leaned her head on the glass. "As they say, they fall apart."

Ash stared at Esther hearing the desolate tone of voice and

seeing the misery on her face. Even though the con hadn't even begun properly, she knew that her chance at Holmes had slid through her fingers like sand.

"Tonight is an evening off from the gambling dens," Vin said, rubbing his chin. "Now, are you sure you're not plotting any con?"

Ash bit her lip, waiting on Esther to explain her con to her father's friend, but was instead surprised by the sharp cough that Esther gave.

"I told you the other day, Vin, as I will tell you now: I have no interest in Holmes. I'm scoping for someone else entirely."

Ash looked at Esther, who straightened her back and kept looking at Vin without a hint of concern on her face.

Vin waved his hand exasperatedly in the air. "If you were, you wouldn't tell me, right?"

Esther nodded, giving a small smirk.

"After—"

"You – I emphasise the '*you*' here – not telling me that Innocent was aboard, hence why you were here?" Esther patted his shoulder. "Vin, I love you to pieces but I know when to cut my losses." She gestured to Ash. "Come on. Let's go to our room and figure out how we get out of this one."

Ash nodded, although she smirked when Vin went to go with them.

"You stay away from me right now." Esther planted an affectionate kiss on his cheek, and Ash chuckled at his faint blush. "Be seeing you."

The two women headed off, silent and brooding. All that careful planning was slipping through Esther's fingers like sand through a sieve. They wandered back to their room and, as Ash shut the door, she sank down onto the floor, back braced against the closed door.

Esther sat down and pulled out the omnipresent deck of cards. She raised her hand to flick them and shook her head, walking to tip water out of the vase overboard. "Just as well they hadn't gotten round to putting the flowers in here."

Ash hung a sign from the doorknob. "*Do not disturb…* I just hope everyone takes the hint."

Esther grunted her agreement and began flicking the cards into the empty vase.

Ash sighed and sat on the edge of the bed, taking off her glasses to clean them. "What do we do now?"

"This is a setback in my original plans. I'm sorry, Ash." Esther sighed heavily. "It just means I'm going to need to become a tailor."

Ash scrutinised the lenses of her glasses as she cleaned them, throwing a curious look at Esther. "What do you mean, tailor?"

"I need to make adjustments to my plans," explained Esther, sighing as a card missed the lip of the vase. "Shows I'm stressed when I start missing the targets."

Ash nodded, sitting cross-legged again. She chanced another glance at the mail. "You've had messages from both that grad student and Brett Higgins?"

"I promised dinner to one and coffee to another," Esther agreed, sighing again.

"Do you fancy either?"

Esther shook her head and chuckled at, Ash had no doubt, the innocence that lay behind the question.

"Do you fancy Vin?"

The card that she had been flicking sailed over the target as Esther snapped an indignant, "No!" This was followed by another soft chuckle. "No, no. Vin has been a pain in my ass since I first met him." Esther stood and stretched her back. "Finer cold reader I'm yet to read."

Ash snorted. "Never would say that."

"Watch out for that 'Aw, shucks, I'm just a simple Texan' routine." Esther bent down to pick up the card, admiring it briefly before flipping it around to reveal an Ace of Spades. "Good card to lose, because all he is doing is a routine song-and-dance." She glanced at her watch. "Ash, go enjoy the benefits of this boat. I've got some rearranging to do."

"Don't you want me—"

"Go on. Enjoy yourself. I'm poor company right now." Esther sighed and practically threw herself into the seat she'd occupied before. "Regardless of time, I feel I must ring my father. Hearing him tired and pissed off might just cheer me up."

Ash paused and touched her friend's shoulder. "Is there anything I can do?"

"No... I'll give you a call if I get an idea." Esther sighed.

"Well, it's not that we can escape. We're prisoners with our guards being Mafioso types," joked Ash.

Esther sat up at that.

"Est?"

"You're a genius. You're a bloody genius!" Esther sprang to her feet. "We're back in business." She gestured to the safe. "Get the iPad."

Ash burst into a grin and ran to the safe, punching in numbers swiftly. She retrieved the iPad and handed it to Esther eagerly. "What're you up to?"

"I'm calling The Nun."

Ash paused. She'd heard of the Nun. A fixer who even arranged the fixers' gear around London – not many people had seen her, though, and where her mysterious nickname came from was beyond anyone. Esther started a video call on her iPad, foot wiggling impatiently.

"Esther, why do they call her the Nun?" Ash asked innocently.

Esther snorted. "Apparently, she conned the Pope."

"What?"

A woman appeared on the screen. "Universal exports."

"Nancy, you got to stop using the James Bond stuff. One of these days you're going to get arrested by the copyright lawyers," Esther joked, ignoring Ash's confused look. "Nancy Nunn."

Ash glared at Esther, who winked.

"Now, from the first con artist to the best living one. What can I do you for?"

"I need a Spanish Prisoner."

TEN

Eleanor Hyde liked being in Nancy Nunn's neck of the woods. She was coming to see if there were any ideas here, or, rather, if Esther had given her any instructions. Waiting on Nancy gave her a chance to wander around the place.

The aircraft hangar was attached to a warehouse and had been one of her favourite places to come when she was training to be a con artist. It was usually stocked with items belonging to Nancy's father's company, A Wish; a perfectly respectable production company that provided props for television and films. An oversized fixer's office, with enough respectability that no one could guess the number of cons that had passed through here. A con on top of a con.

She had to admire the contradiction of this particular con. It was simplicity and complexity combined behind the scenes. It was fair to say that Eleanor believed that con artistry was a calling, much like the priesthood, comedy and writing. After all, as far as her parents knew she was studying for an International Relations and Creative Writing degree.

She was just celebrating this con internally when she heard the tread of someone behind her. Eleanor turned around to be met with the sight of a middle-aged man, and her eyes squinted. Leonard Hughes. She knew him. A sniffer dog and the right hand of Harry Holmes. She'd heard a whisper while setting up shop that he was supposed to be haunting London for his boss. What he was searching for was anybody's guess, although Eleanor had a funny feeling that it was something to do with Ash.

"Hey, you."

She gestured naively to him.

"Yes, you. Know who's running this joint?"

Christ, your Welsh accent ruins any chance of you sounding like a '30s Chicago gangster, Eleanor thought rudely. Instead she picked out a crate of glasses and came out with a cockney accent: "Good question, mate; been here all day on my Jack Jones."

"Christ, a cockney – well, who runs it?"

"Feller by the name of Nunn; he's off down the Beeb or summat." She knew nobody did business with any of Holmes's men, especially after the death of Gaines. "What can I do ya for? Come for a butcher's hook around the joint?"

Hughes shot her a superior look. "Don't think I don't know what you're doing."

Eleanor near enough laughed at that, behind the confused if annoyed look she offered to him. Chance would be a fine thing. "Listen here, Taff. I'm working and I'm collecting stuff for that new drama… remake of some BBC drama or something."

Hughes sniffed. "Pretending it's a respectable business."

Eleanor sighed and put both hands on her hips. "Look, mate, I'm busy right now. I've got to pull at least nine boxes from the hangar before the boss's daughter has me checking out all the cars out the back. What do you want?"

Hughes grimaced. "Wondering if the proprietor is available?"

"Mr Nunn? Nah, up in the Smoke today, and then heading to your neck of the woods down the Gower." Eleanor pretended to consider. "Think he's back on Tuesday." She heaved her crate. "Show you out. I'll take you down to the car."

Eleanor escorted him down the stairs, eyeing the man with deep suspicion, although this piece of acting barely hid the revulsion behind her eyes. She was relieved when Hughes eventually began to walk behind her.

"Miss, you might still be able to help me."

Eleanor spun around to glare at him, portraying her annoyed cockney worker with ease, she felt, although it could have had something to do with her absolute hatred of the man.

"I have a photograph of a young lady that you might've seen around the place?"

Eleanor propped the crate on her hip and snapped her fingers as he withdrew a sheet of paper. A printed photo from a Facebook page. "Haven't graduated to a smartphone yet?"

The man growled.

"What?"

"You don't like working Saturdays, do you?"

"Do you?" she said sarcastically. She looked down at the photograph and raised her eyebrows at the sight of Ash's smiling face looking back at her. "Should I know her?"

"Her father committed suicide a few weeks ago. We're concerned for her safety."

"If you're the Old Bill, I'm Tinkerbell." She handed it back to him. "What do you want her for?"

"None of your business; we're just concerned," said Hughes. He pulled out a card. "Know where she is?"

"Nah, not seen her face around here before." Eleanor took his card and in the process nearly dropped the crate, Hughes catching it before it fell. "Shit. Sorry, and thanks. Here, lemme look again."

Hughes granted her another look.

She shook her head. "Nah, but tell you what, guv – I'll be sure to call ya if ya want."

"Ta."

Eleanor waited for him to jump into his car and drive off before chuckling to herself. So arrogant and self-assured had he been, that he'd not felt her deft hands pick his pocket for his small leather wallet. She pulled out the photograph of Ash and raised her eyebrows. Seemed Hughes had been busy at the worst of times. She'd been assured by that little twit Colorado that he had deleted Ash's social media history when she'd gone to see how he was progressing with the long-con man Mattie LeRoy.

The way his training was going, Eleanor was right to not trust him as far as she could throw him. The little sod didn't like learning from people not much older than him, and had seemed jealous of where Ash had ended up. She'd have to check in with Esther about that... they definitely didn't need holes like that in the operation. LeRoy had already opined that perhaps the better option was a less respectable con artist such as Hellion, who only served their own purposes and to hell with anyone else.

"Good job," called Nancy from the office window where she was leaning out. "Very classy."

"Can't beat the classics; it's a good old distract-and-grab." Eleanor smiled wistfully. "I was shown that down Bleeding Heart Yard... that's where I met Esther first."

"Talk of the Devil and she shall appear – Esther is on the blower," Nancy called out the window.

Eleanor nodded and ran up.

Nancy was leaning on the office door jamb, frowning. "I think she's gone mad."

"The Spanish Prisoner?"

Ash listened to the discussion as she watched Eleanor chew over Esther's decision. Esther looked at ease with herself now, a maestro waiting in the wings for her orchestra to catch up with her latest alteration to a well-known composition. It was just a shame that the con was a very well-known one.

"Everybody from here to eternity knows the Spanish Prisoner," Nancy said, frowning.

"Can you arrange it or can't you?" Esther snapped.

"Of course I can," Nancy said indignantly. "Just feel it's not worth it, is all."

Ash spoke her next thoughts aloud. "He likes the classics. He knows we know that... he won't be looking for it. Make it so obvious that he wouldn't look for it."

"The art of hiding in plain sight; what we are best at," Esther said, leaning forward. "Now, can we do it?"

"Course we can, just involves rejigging the original plan," Eleanor agreed, flicking a blonde lock of hair from her eyes. "Just seems nuts to me. But then again, nuts have always worked." She paused. "I bumped into a Mr Leonard Hughes here today, in fact."

"On the prowl? Copper?" Esther asked, as Ash came forward to look at the screen. She glanced at the younger girl. "Or an old enemy?"

"Enemy," promised Ash, scowling. "I thought Colorado deleted all my history?"

"Wyatt did," finished Esther. "He must've left the final bits of that up to that little twit. Say, where is he? I haven't heard any reports."

"Gone out short-conning. Can't see what Luke saw in him." Eleanor coughed into her hand. "But we got a problem. Neither Holmes nor Innocent is going to let you go easy."

"Oh, I always have a plan; just waiting on a response," Esther noted confidently. "Look, get the little short-con artist to my dear grandmother, and can you get the ball rolling for everything? I've basically got my end done up as tight as I can."

"Thought you said it had gone to pot?" mocked Eleanor, who received a glare from her friend. "The worst-case contingency plan?"

"But of course. I'll see you in London day after tomorrow."

Ash turned at that, raising her eyebrows.

"All will be explained soon enough."

"Why do I feel like that's a lie wrapped up as a gift?" Ash mocked.

"Probably because you know damn well it is." Esther shook her head, then took a moment to glance at her watch. "Can only say I'm grateful that Brett wasn't recognised by Mr Innocent."

"Not recognised?"

"Every single madness has at least three methods," Esther said. "Now, if I'm not careful I'm going to be late for afternoon tea." She stood and stretched to her full height. "And you are not invited – go find yourself something to do."

Ash snorted. "Practice?"

"Find something. Have fun. Count this as your leisure time."

"Leisure time on a pleasure boat, indeed," snorted Ash.

"Spend it wisely. I'm going to enjoy myself." Esther patted her stomach. "And eat until I'm full as an egg, as you British say."

"And you, French?" teased Ash.

Esther smirked. "*Ventre affamé n'a point d'oreilles*. Words are wasted on a starving man." She tilted her head in a silent farewell before exiting.

Ash watched from across the crowded restaurant as Esther crossed the floor. She was dressed in a low-backed dress and wearing what looked to be a genuine smile as she was greeted by the grad student. The two shared a kiss on the cheek before they sat down, Esther thanking the server for pushing in her seat, and then slipping into the conversation with great ease. She looked a consummate professional flirt. She raised her eyebrows when Brett Higgins joined them; he didn't look unwelcome, however.

"All very polite and professional," Ash said aloud. She shook her head and went back to her meal.

She enjoyed her own company, realising that Esther had recognised her need for solitude long before she herself had. The young woman who rarely ate, and when she did seemed to breathe her food in, had seen that Ash needed some rest. Whether she had taken her own advice was a different matter. Ash wondered idly if Esther was running a con on either young man, and kind of hoped not. They seemed thoroughly decent; Brett had even held the lift door for her when she'd been running up from the pool this morning. She watched Esther finish her dessert before walking over to Ash's table and crouching by her protégée.

"I have a business meeting," she whispered. "And I need to cancel my entry in this damned tournament."

"I know you wanted to win. I'm sorry."

"Ah, don't apologise. Never, ever cry over spilled milk. It could be worse. It could've been good champagne," Esther said, with a dark chuckle to herself. "As my beloved grandmother would say. Look, go back to the room; Brett's going to show me some stuff when my meeting is done with."

"Sure you'll be fine alone?"

"Brett? He's a doll, don't worry." Esther patted her arm. "Make sure you put on a decent film, something like a cowboy or a… I don't know…"

"I'll put *The Magnificent Seven* on; I know how you like a good cowboy." Ash grinned, having once caught Esther sitting up in the middle of the night watching *Rio Bravo*. There had been a childlike innocence on her face. "Or perhaps a good horror?"

"Hammer Horrors," Esther advised, before turning to Brett, who had just joined her. "Now, if you'll excuse us, Prue and I have a few drinks and tales to share."

Ash tilted her head thoughtfully as she watched the two make their exit across the room. She felt like she had been conned somehow, but couldn't put her finger on how. After all, they were laughing together and looking comfortable; it looked and felt nice. Sometimes cons got under your skin and you began seeing shadows where there was no light to cast any. Ash shook this thought off and finished her dessert. She thanked her waiter before heading off down the corridors, smiling at the young officers as they talked to other guests. She'd forgotten how invigorating the formal evening had been, and right now she was off the clock and could enjoy her own—

Ash gasped as she suddenly felt hands grasping under her arms. She was gently lifted a few inches off the ground.

"Mr Innocent needs a word with you, miss."

She felt a butt of something press into her back.

"No funny business, now."

Ash scowled as her arm was grasped more firmly and she was manhandled down the corridors to a new state room. She paid attention to the two guards now. Both were broad and taller than her, although the one was an older man with grey hair and the other a younger black man. The black man knocked the door and waited.

"Who is it?" called a smooth Southern accent from within.

The black man gave an exasperated sigh. "You know damned well, Ezra. Brought the kid, just like you asked."

"Give me a moment." There were a few moments of perfect silence before the door opened and Ezra Innocent stood there, distractedly fixing his mother-of-pearl cufflinks while his cravat was loose. "Ah, you've brought my guest. You may leave us."

The bigger man kept his hold on her. "What if she runs?"

"Why, Jesse, the young lady has too much manners to run." Innocent looked at Ash, who gave a small nod before he returned to fiddling with his cufflinks. "See, Jesse, Nate? She knows that, no matter my manners, a man who frightens the great Esther Crook is worthy of being frightened of. And she damned well knows that I will break her back as good as look at her if she doesn't get inside this cabin."

Ash took the hint and stepped into the state room, glancing around. It seemed even more spectacular than her room, as she noted its grandness and, on a dresser, a photograph of a young woman and a young man horseback riding. She could see the man was a younger Ezra Innocent, not much younger, Ash guessed but happier at least with a smile that lit up his face. However the woman's face was more blurred and hidden.

"My late wife." Ezra's voice came from behind her. It was

friendly enough, but she felt like it was laced with arsenic. "Sorry for the rude intrusion into your evening plans that you may have had."

"I would've thought you would be playing poker, Mr Innocent," Ash said politely, before noticing the two silhouettes – one female; one male – on the balcony. She turned to face him, to see him tidying his cravat in the mirror, although his green eyes studied her astutely. "I hope my kidnapping hasn't intruded on your evening."

He glanced at her, a thin semblance of a charming grin on his face, before standing up straight-backed and nodding. "No, no. You're not intruding." Ezra brushed himself down, picking at an imaginary piece of lint on his lapel. "In fact, I have a business proposition for you." He pulled a pocket watch out of his breast pocket. "And before the evening poker matches, of course."

"Business proposition?"

"I, unlike my colleague Mr Holmes, am not blinded by ambition, greed or, frankly, baser needs." He offered a small smirk. "I know that if I am to get Esther Crook where I want her, then I must allow her to con Mr Holmes. I think the man deserves it. Dee Lawrence is safe, by the by."

Ash threw her head up in surprise.

"I sent her in the direction of Christopher Adams. You may or may not know that the gentleman is a member of the ATF. Her father's boss and a thorn in my side. I think the gentleman has put him on the case to protect her. Thinks that Vin is untrustworthy. Don't blame him. But nonetheless, your friend is safe."

"Thank you, sir… but I know there's a 'but' involved?"

Ezra chuckled. "Wise words. Yes, yes, there is a clause involved in my kindness." He walked with a panther-like gait towards her. "You know, as my dear – how shall I say this? Acquaintance, Esther would put it – that there is nothing better than money in your back pocket; than a signature on a dotted line." Innocent reached into the top breast pocket of his waistcoat and withdrew a sheet of paper. "I want you to sign this. I realise that, as a sixteen-year-old – yes, Miss Cox, I do my own research, which Mr Holmes has so far skipped over in his overzealous attempts to get Crook – you are not of age, but I have been assured by my lawyers that this is totally binding. This form will save you; Esther bargained with her own life for you." He gave a dark chuckle. "That dancing around in the exhibition was to make sure of your safety. However, I want her, and you're my in."

"You can't be serious?! Esther's my friend. And I was always told never to sign on the dotted line for anything."

A shark-like smile and a flash of the golden tooth made her unease grow. "Yes, but I know about your friend. I'd rather guess which proverb holds more water at this time."

"And why should I?"

"My dear, the object of any con artist is to be a painter and to fill the world with colour and bright lights for their con. And whilst the rest of the world is submerged in admiring the art, the con artist is holding an umbrella, feet not even wet, avoiding the Technicolor deluge they have created. Unfortunately, you find me beneath this umbrella with a healthy dose of paint stripper." He stretched his fingers. "Choice is yours."

"What's this do?" Ash asked, holding the paper.

"This, Ash, turns you state witness… or, rather, informant to the mob."

"I told you there's no con."

There was a rapid knock at the door, and Ezra jerked his head up as the second of his goons ran in. He looked flustered, and was followed shortly after by Vin.

"What's going on?"

"The Burmese ruby has been stolen."

PLAYING THE CON

ELEVEN

Basically, it was simple. It was as simple as pie, if you asked Esther Crook at the very least. It was as simple as acquiescing to the search of her room due to the theft of the ruby, and as simple as bowing her head in recognition of some guilt when it wasn't found in her cabin.

It all just came down to timing.

And her mark, Harry Holmes, was as punctual as a Swiss clock. The perfect target for Esther Crook, in all honesty. She had timed his routine to precise motions. While Holmes thought he was watching her, she'd enjoyed hiding in plain view.

Every day he took his morning constitutional around the deck. He tended to note if anyone different was on deck, so that had quickly been ruled out. He would then sit by the pool and watch her when she took her swimming lesson, occasionally joined by Innocent.

Since her calm dismissal of Vin, she had no doubt the man would be watching her from afar, so had kept to a normal routine, all the while calmly directing.

The ring would be pickpocketed by none other than Ash while Esther was practising her swimming. Ash had no doubt, based on her study of the man, that he'd notice when he was reading – he always made a habit of letting it glint in the sun.

The girl was observant, Esther thought as she smirked into her hot chocolate and looked out onto the waters. Gloriously international, where laws were so feeble, and yet minds were sharp. He'd undoubtedly accuse her and demand that her rooms be searched; Esther would play the role of the accused, delivering enough insults to infuriate and push the man over the edge into blind rage. Then Ash would approach him with the ring and pretend to double-cross her. It was a finely tuned piece of music in which the purpose was to reveal that Ash was in some sort of servitude to Esther, and to get the man to trust her.

Once that was accomplished, she could hang the man from the ceiling.

Ash's own performance would come later on in the day when the theft of Harry Holmes's wedding ring was revealed and she'd been revealed as an innocent party. Then she could deliver it to the rooms. It would be short, but the way she handled it would be key.

Ash had asked a few questions which Esther had answered before Ash had left again to enter the mind of her character, much like a method actor. Esther had been amused at that, and remained so. It was the art of the con that she'd had drilled into her own head, and she knew that a part of it was acting. When Ash had come back, Esther had tested her. Asked her about her school, her childhood, her favourite film, where she dined on board – and how poor was her poker, and how good was her blackjack? Did she listen to the news or was she strictly interested in the download chart?

Ash had been accurate and nonchalant in spinning her web of deceit – if thrown, she'd managed to improvise, and if she'd shown hesitation it had been the natural kind. Now Esther could understand why Gaines had been so admiring of her. She was good. Very much like Esther herself, if she thought back to her younger days.

She stood to rid herself of a few newly acquired kinks in her back and leaned on the railing of the balcony, staring harshly into the water. Before every con she worked out the physical angles required, but at this stage she equally convinced herself that the world would come to an end. As a poker player, she played each hand as it came and kept some close to her chest, so tight, in fact, that she threatened to paper cut herself to death with them. She knew that she had accounted for everything, even Innocent, in every sense of the word. But there were angles. So many different angles that she factored in, and yet couldn't.

"*À confesseurs, médicins, avocats, la vérité ne cèle de ton cas*," she said, lightly and thoughtfully. Ash threw her a confused look, and Esther snorted. "It's a French expression: *Conceal not the truth from thy physician and lawyer*." She sighed as Ash shook her head. "We're as ready as we're going to be."

"Can we count on everything?"

"As much as we can." Esther stood and grabbed her backpack, which contained her swimming costume and her towel. "From this point on, you are my subservient and you don't much like it."

"I can understand why." Ash scratched her nose as she stood, looking around the room. "This is the last time we'll be here, isn't it?"

"Apart from our little hook-and-line session? Yes. Make sure you take anything valuable in your backpack." Esther sighed as she packed away her cards, putting them into her leather jacket pocket. "One valuable lesson in this career, is that you should never have anything in your life that you can't walk away from in a second."

"Is that all you've got?" Ash asked, filling her own backpack with her precious goods.

Esther nodded.

"Not much."

"Everything I hold dear is right here." Esther pointed to her temple. "Memories nobody but death can cheat me of… and I've always wondered if I can con him."

"Death?"

"Or the Devil himself. You know, there's a grave in Liverpool; I forget the name of the gentleman, but in any case, his tomb is built in the shape of a pyramid. He was supposedly put in there sitting up, cards in hand. He is, according to the story, sitting at a card table and clutching a winning hand of cards… with a deck of cards opposite."

"Who's he going to play?" Ash snorted.

"The Devil. Story goes that this keen Scouse gambler had beaten the Devil once, and the Devil was so mad that he swore that when the scouse gambler died, he'd arrange another game. And in that game the Devil promised that he would win he'd claim his soul. So the old sod says that his body should never be committed to the earth as a means of cheating Satan out of claiming his immortal soul." Esther chuckled to herself. "Got to admire the con."

"Which one? The tourist crap or the story?"

"Both. I'd kind of like to go down as a dead living legend." Esther crossed her eyes comically before standing. "Let's get going. Never know; we might see Prue."

"Prue?"

Esther flashed a smirk again. "Brett. Brett Higgins. You'd do well to remember that nickname."

Ash shook her head.

"Now come on. The fish is going to need to be on the line by close of day today."

Harry Holmes was sitting, enjoying his coffee and admiring the view from the poolside. And not the natural beauty of Norway, either.

Esther Crook was diving into the water from a small platform, dressed in an all-black swimsuit. He smirked nastily into the rim of his cup as she shot an angry look his way. He'd heard she'd pulled out of the tournaments last night. Even if she had no con on, it would cause a dent in her criminal finances. It was an added bonus that she'd not be able to con anyone aboard.

A kind of childish glee filled his belly as he looked around at the surrounding scenery. She was still pretty, and whatever deal Holmes had made during their short meeting only a day ago was worthless to him. He had a score to settle with her. He could remember her first escape. She'd broken into his home in Los Angeles with the intent of killing him. Barely sixteen years old. It had only been his wife's entrance that had saved him, and only the distanced intervention of Esther's father had saved her.

A frown marred Holmes's face as he saw Brett Higgins join her with the grad student, interrupting his ornery and sadistic recollections of that fateful evening. The three shared a laugh over something before Esther pulled herself out of the water.

"Azeri, coffee, now!" she snapped in the direction of the teenager, who was sitting reading and occasionally looking out at the water. There was a frustrated sigh, and then a second call. "I don't want to listen to it; coffee, and get yourself one too."

Holmes chuckled at the glare directed at the young woman, who was now standing at the pool's edge, talking lightly to the two men. He sighed and stood with his own coffee, deciding to take the better seat of the two once the girl had moved on. He walked leisurely towards the seat, seeing like-minded people scoot away from what was already, in his head, 'his' seat. It would no doubt amuse Ezra – yes, it was a pity the man and the sunrise were not on speaking terms. They could share a laugh over this.

He was so focused on this thought that he didn't notice the approach of the teenager, who walked straight into him, tipping coffee onto him – barely missing more intimate areas, at which he howled. On the other side of the pool, Esther Crook was laughing hard at him.

"First time you've done something right today. I do like a bit of slapstick; do you do Buster Keaton stunts too?" she mocked, before throwing a look at the teenager. "I'm going to my cabin; don't disturb me." With that, she walked off.

"Oh, sir!" the girl said, obviously shocked. "I'm so sorry."

"It's all right; just stay away from me," Holmes snapped, wishing he could also snap the neck of Esther Crook for this.

The girl attempted to wipe at him, taking his book from him and resting it on the seat.

"I said it's fine."

"Well, I'm still sorry, sir." The girl rushed off, blushing faintly.

Holmes shook his head and sat back down. It took several moments for him to notice it. To notice the lightness of his finger – something so comforting and familiar had been taken from him and he didn't know how. He just knew something…

He looked down at his empty wedding finger. Rage immediately consumed him. He didn't know how, but he definitely knew who.

Esther Crook.

"This is a serious accusation, Miss Voleur."

"Just call her Crook and have done with it."

"I understand, and of course, who this Crook character is, I don't know!" Esther leaned on the doorway to the cabin. She'd been waiting patiently for the stewards to arrive. She'd heard the commotion coming down the corridor, and chuckled to herself.

"I demand my ring."

"You can demand and I'll tell you again, I don't have it." Esther sighed. "But you are welcome to search the room for it."

She stood, arms folded, as the security walked ahead of her into the state room and began the search. It was the second one since the previous evening. She had suffered this indignity along with the rest of the ship. Thanks to the robbery of the ruby, there had been a thorough search of every cabin and mouse hole aboard the ship. She walked to the champagne ice bucket.

"Am I permitted to drink?" she asked, gesturing at the bottle. "There are few things I can't stand, and one such thing is drinking a Dom Pérignon '53 above the temperature of thirty-eight degrees Fahrenheit. It's as bad as being… I don't know, I'll think of an analogy later. You can check the bucket – as you can see, nothing but ice." She received the briefest of nods from the security. "Thank you."

"It'd seem Miss Voleur's room has been searched thoroughly."

"I'm telling you, she stole it! Honestly, it's the truth!"

"Every decent con man knows that the simplest truth is more powerful than even the most elaborate lie." Esther sipped her champagne as she leaned on the doorway and looked in at the ongoing search. "It is quite possible that you took it off when you went swimming."

"I haven't been swimming," snarled Holmes.

"It's an occupational habit that one who becomes an expert at lying eventually, or should I say *conveniently*, forgets how to tell the damned truth." Esther glared at the steward. "As you can see, there is nothing here. I have been searched for both the damned ring and the damned ruby, and now, if I'm honest, I'm bored." She looked hard at the gunrunner. "If you don't want to be a victim then don't act like one. I can assure you, I've spent the morning drinking coffee downstairs with Brett Higgins. I only recently went up to the pool and just got back. Where you seem to think I've been, and in case you didn't notice, I wasn't anywhere near enough to you to filch the ring. Though why the hell I am explaining myself to you of all people, I have no flaming idea."

The steward and security conducted a few more cursory checks, although they made no eye contact with her as they searched the inside of the cabin and even the balcony. Esther sat at the desk and opened a book that she had resting on there, ignoring the constant glare that Holmes was conspicuously giving her.

"I can only apologise, Miss Voleur," said one of the security men.

Esther nodded.

"I'm certain Mr Holmes has made a mistake in identifying you."

"I'm not going to lose sleep over it," Esther said, raising an eyebrow.

"What do you mean, 'certain' – she obviously stole it! All the evidence is against her."

"What evidence?! I was in the same place as you when you sat down," Esther snapped, frustration breaking through. "If I'd wanted your damned ring, I would've used it as a bet." She glared. "Christ, you're an idiot. Just get the hell out of here, the lot of you!"

She watched them depart and waited, closing her eyes in moderate complacency and total calmness. Now it was out of her hands; she had no further cards to play in this act of the carefully rehearsed play. It was all on Ash's young shoulders. Esther could afford to rest.

As the door opened she looked up and smiled at Ash, who showed off the ring dangling from her necklace.

"Nice work, kid. He'll be nice and hot." Esther wiped her forehead and grinned, ebullient in victory. "Hot enough to blow a fuse and definitely hot enough to want to murder me at the least."

Ash grinned. "May as well wait. Haste has no blessing."

Esther shot a confused look at her protégée.

"Haste makes waste... it's Swahili."

Esther grinned. Christ, the kid was looking at her with hope. Gaines knew what he'd been doing. "I'm rather fond of an expression my mother taught me and my brother. Patience is a virtue and the best warrior of its master: time. Very poetic"

"Which are we?" Ash joked lightly.

Esther chuckled and nodded.

"Hey, you didn't say what the way out was?"

Esther shrugged. "That's my job right now, as it happens."

Ash stared at Esther as she shrugged. So blasé. So calm. Yet she saw some of the nervousness – or was Esther conning her? To be honest, she really didn't know if Esther was being serious or joking. She was impossible to read.

"Get going. Before he calms down." Esther picked up the phone from the table. "Got an unpleasant call to make."

Ash took her time to exit, and chuckled as she heard Esther's voice.

"Yeah, it's me. Listen, I got a favour to ask ya… no… no… list… will you stop yelling at me?! I haven't even asked you yet! What the hell's the matter with you?"

Ash walked calmly and slowly down the corridor, turning sharply to the left and rehearsing her acting presence to the final nuance. Her name was Ashleigh Azeri, her father had lost a bet at poker with Esther Crook, and she was the collateral. She hated the young woman for that. It made her an indentured servant, and although she liked Esther as a person, she knew better than to fake that.

She knocked on the door to the cabin. Paulsen, the goon that Holmes kept around, opened it.

"Yeah?"

"Esther Crook sent me."

There was a call of assent from within and Paulsen allowed her to slide into the room. She looked around. It was smaller than Innocent's – talk of the Devil, as he walked from the balcony, flanked by the more congenial black man, Nate.

"Yeah?" Holmes snapped.

"She's told me to give you this," Ash said, pulling her necklace off and holding it up to the light.

The platinum ring glittered, highlighting the years of imperfections and delicate scratches on the less durable metal. Ash took a breath, remembering how easy it had been to slide the ring from Holmes's finger once she'd hurt him by banging into him and spilling the coffee on his more delicate areas. Holmes's ice-blue eyes stared at the band of platinum before he sprang to his feet. Ash stood coolly, though inside she was shaking. Innocent had crossed the room in a few strides, his gentlemanly persona gone. Now there stood a dangerous man, and luckily Innocent placed himself between Ash and his business partner.

"You thieving—" Holmes began.

"Easy, Harry," Innocent cautioned. "What is the meaning of this?"

"She wants him angry to con him."

Holmes and Innocent glared.

"You ruined her poker season. There wasn't a con in existence before then. You tipped her hand."

"I could throw you overboard, you cocky little—"

"Wouldn't do you any good, anyhow," Ash said, as Innocent tensed. "She got the fundamentals of an idea for a con *without* me down. Now, I can either con you, or get even with you."

"She's been hanging around with Brett Higgins and that Russian student a lot. They got a play?" asked Nate, arms crossed against his chest. "You're not the only one that watches."

Ash shook her head. "Nah. She fancies the one. The other she amuses herself with." *Scratch the truth, then cover it with bull.* She heard the voice of Luke in her ear. *Then take the offensive.* "If you don't want my help, just say and I'll hand you back your ring and we'll meet through the con, but you'll be a hell of a lot poorer."

Holmes's breath was evening out now, the rage simmering down again and that cold, calculating smile crossing his features. "Did she tell you I was into movies? Sounds like *The Sting* to me, where they shake down—"

"Not all con artists consider *The Sting* to be the Holy Bible of con artists," Ash said, scowling. She pulled the ring off its silver chain and put it on the table between them. "It's up to you, but regardless, here is the ring back."

"Why the double-cross?" asked Holmes quietly.

"Because I am sick of her telling me what to do, how to eat, how to look, to act like the slider, act this and act that, and never letting me in. I've been doing this since I was thirteen; I know what I'm doing."

Holmes gave her a contemptuous look. Ash rolled her eyes at that; better to act like a spoiled brat who had had enough of education.

"You're a smart kid if nothing else."

"Great, glad to know. See you on the other side of the con, Mr Holmes." Ash turned sharply on her heel to exit.

"You got time later?" he asked.

She merely nodded.

"I expect to see you portside at three o'clock sharp."

"Next to the cinema. She's going swimming with Higgins." Ash coughed into her hand and then grinned, adding in what Esther had said to her earlier as part of the con. "Seems she has a pet name for him. Prue."

For some reason, Innocent's eyes widened briefly and a snarl came over his features as Holmes's dour expression lit up with an outlandish delight.

"Prue! The family name; Proulx. No wonder they were playing good poker with each other, Ezra! The twins are together."

Ash looked up sharply.

"It seems she didn't trust you all the way, and with good reason. She's been playing with her brother. Who's the older twin?"

"Never sure," Innocent hissed, his emerald eyes looking balefully into Ash's. "It would seem, Miss Azeri, that you've been with the Crook twins."

Ash felt her mouth dry up, realising she'd sunk Esther and now her brother. Whereas Holmes, at this moment, seemed untouchable, Esther now had a weak valve to test. Ash forced herself to straighten her back proudly. "Three o'clock. Portside. Cinema."

She headed out, walking the part as well as acting it. She felt her stomach lurch as she walked to the starboard side of the ship, and, once reassured that she was fully out of the way of Holmes's and Innocent's goons, she ran to her shared cabin. She found it locked and knocked on the door, only to be met with a tired-looking Brett Higgins.

"Are you Esther's twin?" she demanded immediately.

Brett merely raised his eyebrows with amusement. "So we're not dead in the water, then?"

"I don't think so," Ash admitted as the man allowed her in and ruffled his auburn hair with a fond grin. Esther was sitting cross-legged on her bed. "Why didn't you tell me—"

"That there may be other members of my crew aboard?" Esther asked calmly as she looked at some papers. "Easy. I needed Cael – oh, I do apologise; I've just realised I've not introduced you properly. This is Caelan Brett Proulx Crook. My baby brother."

"By all of two minutes." He smiled, shaking Ash's hand before joining his sister. He sat in front of the mirror and pulled out a large bag. "Do you know how long it took me to get that through customs?"

"Probably as much time as it took you to build your reputation as state champion when you were born and bred in Lyon." Esther looked at her brother, who was now dampening a rag in some sort of liquid, which he began to apply to his nose and cheeks. "Very nice touch."

"You know me, sis; I've always got a plan…" He glanced at Ash, whose gaze was flicking between them in confusion. "Sorry. Forgot that you're new to our double-talk. And, in answer to your earlier question, she needed you to slide one side and me to sit and watch the other."

"Mother never could work out how we cheated at Twister." Esther chuckled. "Did he swallow the tale?"

"Looks like it," Ash said. "Why didn't you tell me?"

"Holmes has never seen my brother," Esther said, smirking. "And I guessed that Vin would be aboard once I told my father of my idea to con him."

"Does she know about Chris being Dad's boss?"

"Vin mentioned it," Ash said, deciding to keep Innocent out of the equation for now. "Although, I startled him when I mentioned Christopher Adams was involved."

"For good reason; let's just say cat and mouse is an understatement for those two," Caelan said, pulling latex off his nose to reveal one very similar to Esther's. "He's going to kill you. I've had ten texts a day with at least three graphic descriptions of how it's going to go down and how you will go down with him."

"I'm protected by the law that he so carefully follows." Esther grinned to herself. "The joys of being an ATF agent."

"And the reason you got Christopher Adams involved?" Ash asked.

"Easy; the Nun couldn't arrange our documents in time, and let's just say I'm not above manipulation to get my own way. Wyatt did the best false documents possible, though he's no Terry Nunn." Esther smirked. "Now his use is over with, I can go on with my original plan."

"We got a way out?"

"We're Crooks," Esther said, looking offended.

"We always have a way out," clarified Caelan, with a wicked smile.

At three o'clock sharp, Ash was looking into the soulless eyes of Harry Holmes. Suspected brothel king, gunrunner, all-round bad guy. Innocent was sitting next to him, although his eyes were closed in silent contemplation, it would seem.

"What'd you tell Crook I said?" Holmes asked finally.

"Nothing of importance; creative swear words," she said, shrugging ambivalently. "Just enough so she believed me."

"Smart move." He looked out again at the sea. "What do you want, Azeri?"

"I want Crook. Not dead, mind you; just somebody to out-con her," she said, deciding more than a slice of innocence was needed. "Just want her to be taught a lesson, you know?"

Holmes nodded. "Okay, so you got my attention. Why me? Why not him?" He gestured at Innocent, who opened one eye, gave a huff of slight laughter, then closed his eye again.

"Well, if I'm honest, I didn't know about Innocent or he would've been my first port of call," Ash said, and Ezra flashed a gold-toothed grin before continuing his silent, closed-eyed meditation on God knows what evil. "But I need somebody who looks legit enough, and someone she hates enough to go chasing."

Holmes nodded. "So, a slice of revenge on two fronts?"

Ash gave an exaggeratedly tired nod. "Yeah. Listen." She fished in her pocket for the card that Caelan – had pressed into her fingers so gently earlier. "This is going to go down in this warehouse, that's all I know; so far at least. Look, I can meet you once she explains the full scheme, then I can let you know… that's what you're after."

"And you?"

"A sense of pride that I got the untouchable Esther Crook," stated Ash. She breathed out. "And, of course, the invaluable gift of the London Metropolitan Police deciding not to breathe down my neck!"

That got both Holmes's and Innocent's attention.

She suddenly felt her phone vibrate in her pocket. It was just a photo of Esther raising her glass at the poolside. "I've been missed." Ash jumped to her feet. "Look, meet me at the Liberty Clock. I can show you what I mean then. If you can make it about three-ish?"

"Fine. I figure if you're lying, I can kill you." Holmes paused and looked at her. "If I'm not there at quarter to three dead on, you're on your own, kid."

Ash nodded, before tearing off in the direction that Esther had meekly suggested, let alone a more demanding one asking for her to bring coffee.

Caelan and Esther were sitting portside, in very easy conversation, when Ash found them. All in fluent French, their mother tongue. Ash paused a moment, seeing the calmness between them. Things were beginning to make the tiniest bit of sense.

"Hey, come join the fun," Caelan said, waving her over. Ash sat on the edge of the seat, handing him his coffee. "How'd it go?"

"I think I got the hook in; just warned me he was gonna kill me."

"The hook is definitely in, then," Esther said, putting her hands behind her head, smirking at them both. "If they don't threaten to kill you, then they're not sunk." She sighed, and then winced at the reverberation of distant helicopter rotors. "Christ. She's early."

"When does she ever run to time," Caelan said with a groan.

The approaching helicopter interrupted the game of basketball that Vin was enjoying with one of Innocent's goons. It interrupted Ezra and Holmes's poker game with Paulsen. It interrupted every poker game in the place, in fact. Everyone pointed and looked out; nearly everyone saw the name on the side of the craft: *Cross Enterprises*. Whispers abounded as people walked to windows and railings to watch the helicopter land. It was no doubt the owner of the ship, Isadora Cross-De Braun.

The helicopter landed towards the back of the ship, the motors juddering to a slow and steady halt. People emerged from their rooms and their games to watch as the infamous and beautiful philanthropist and owner of several casinos disembarked.

Isadora Cross-De Braun was a rather imposing woman, and she stepped forward to meet the captain. The man tilted his head apologetically and began a spiel. Unfortunately, for him at least, she had begun her own angry diatribe.

"You have disappointed me. It took me far too long to acquire this piece and it should be on display in my casino, but I chose to hand it off for a charity event." She sighed and looked out over the crowd, before smiling at the four approaching, helmeted figures.

"I'm taking my team back. I will be leaving four behind as well as Mr Christie – my insurance investigator."

The tall man offered a hand for the captain to shake.

"Don't worry; Mr Christie has verified each of my team's identities."

The captain tipped his hat to each crew member, each one loading a few items on board. "We did our utmost for security."

"And a poor job it was." Isadora sniffed. "The money I wasted on this damnable place's security…" She threw a look around before smirking. "Plus, I hear some of my best rivals have been pushed out due to unfounded rumours about the criminal intentions of one of the finest poker players I have ever met. You can't con honest people, you know."

Harry Holmes, who'd been approaching with Ezra, promptly stopped.

"Ah, the rogue himself," Isadora remarked.

Holmes preened with intention.

"Ezra. How are you?"

Ezra ignored Holmes's stunned look at him being addressed so casually and yet insultingly. "Fine. What the hell is going on?"

"I've come to collect my supposed security team," Isadora said, scowling at the group who were now seated comfortably in the helicopter. "Leave other associates in their place?"

"Esther Crook – I take her to be one of them, M-Mrs De Braun?" Ezra stated, a strain barely noticeable in his voice.

"No; last I heard, Esther Crook was in Norway. Girl damn near cleaned out my casino last year." A feral glare came over Isadora's face. "I'll be glad to get hold of her again."

"Ah, well, Mrs De Braun," began Holmes, earning a dirty look, "I don't know if you know who I—"

"Yes, you're that idiot man who tried to buy the damned ruby from my late husband," she snapped. "Fool! And then my PR man says you'll be good for trade and your book tour is worse than being a sinner sat in a church."

Ezra coughed discreetly.

"Now, if you'll excuse me, I have to be going." She threw a look at them all again. "Men!"

With a few more indignant mutters, she gently took the arm of a young man who'd offered it and reboarded her helicopter. Soon she was giving sharp verbal reprimand (if her facial expression was anything to go by) to her pilot. The helicopter took off, people ignoring the announcement from the second in command that the ship was now back in territorial waters and gambling would need to cease for a short time.

"That, my friends, is proof that there is a God," Ezra's bodyguard Jesse said.

"Or the Devil himself exists," muttered Ezra. He turned to Vin, who was wearing an amused smile. "What's wrong?"

"Just figured out that those people who left, were they undercover?" he asked the captain, who nodded. "Any chance one of them was named Voleur? Just, she promised me a coffee earlier and it'd seem she's—"

"Yes, sir. She left just now, along with Brett Higgins and Mrs De Braun's niece. I wouldn't like to be in the penetration company's shoes. The test they did didn't work in the long run."

"Or, rather, one long con failed."

Vin chuckled to himself as Innocent and Holmes both let out a litany of curses, but frowned as Holmes snapped to Paulsen, "Get hold of our little bird and ensure they sing. Tell them I want to know where she walks and where she goes, and ask where that Crook kid would've sent the kid that conned my son back to. I haven't forgotten her."

Vin winced as the two walked away, and looked at Innocent. The dark-haired man was shaking his head with what could only be described as incredulous amusement.

"It really was a game of charades played with charlatans," said Innocent with a huff of surprised laughter.

"But I'm still worried about Holmes and Ash, Ezra," said the bounty hunter. "She is one of those famous full stops that Esther Crook concerns herself with."

"One could almost feel sorry for her… *almost*." Innocent smirked, before tidying his cuffs again. "But then again, I can't wait to hear the full story from Miss Azeri of how they made their exit."

"I don't know how you managed it, but you did," Ash said, shaking her head as she took off her helmet and looked down at the rapidly disappearing cruise ship. "Shame we didn't see the tournament through."

"The chess game that you've put yourselves into seems much more interesting; it's a shame I have to be back in San Marino by tomorrow." Isadora was powdering her nose with a compact as Esther took off her helmet and looked at her. "I was rather hoping you'd spend tonight in – no, rather, I insist you spend an evening with us."

Esther groaned. "Do whatever you think is best." She raised her eyes heavenward, though whether for a solution or absolution, Ash couldn't make out. "You normally do."

"Your father really is letting your manners slip, Esther… you've not introduced me to your new friend."

Esther raised her eyebrows.

"What?"

"Manners aren't your forte… even if you do pretend to be a lady of substance."

"Esther…"

"Ash, I'd like you to meet Isadora Cross-De Braun."

"Yes; philanthropist and owner of that yacht," Ash said, earning a scoff from the twins. "What?!"

"Oh, Esther, you know the best con artists are the ones we never hear tell of. Just whispers." Isadora laughed, pleasantly, although Ash winced, as did Esther. There was a falseness behind it. She offered her hand to Ash and fixed her with a hard gaze.

"I'm also known as Helen Bassett-Gardener, Marian Starkey… or you may know me as Hellion." She looked pointedly at Esther, who raised her eyebrows. "Now, my dear granddaughter, I'd like to know what exactly is going on."

TWELVE

Number 13 Cuckoo Lane.

It was lucky that Ash did not count herself amongst the unfortunate souls who believe in fate, fortune and all that stuff. But even she felt a trickle of concern.

Thirteen was the traditional number of steps up to the gallows. Twelve up, and then one final step; the long step down. The cuckoo, who stole the nests of other birds and pushed their eggs and chicks out – if that wasn't a damned omen, she didn't know what was. She shivered against the cold morning air of her home city and pretended it was the London chill that was disturbing. Despite her earlier buoyancy over her first official con, she had now settled into despair. Holmes hadn't given a solid answer. She was on the cusp of something big, and it all hinged on the urbane gangster wanting to get his hands dirty… and that was luck.

'There is no such thing as luck; it's an arbitrary excuse for a plan not coming together,' Esther had said with a firm finality that brooked no denial when Nancy, upon seeing her friend, had remarked on her good luck.

Esther had waved off Ash's concerns last night when they'd arrived in from Monaco, after an all-too-brief stopover for the helicopter to refuel. Hellion had been more than obliging, as Esther had recouped any losses from on board the ship on the poker table, all the while keeping a studious distance from the watchful eyes of her grandmother as she relined her coffers.

Caelan had mostly been on the phone and showing Ash how to rig cameras to their advantage. Once satisfied, the trio had made their way to London where Eleanor had been waiting, impatient but joyful when she saw them.

Caelan had retreated to bed immediately when the group arrived at a Covent Garden apartment that had a housekeeper who had balefully glared at Ash until reassured by both the money Esther had pushed into her hand and Esther's assurances that she was not an enemy. When she'd eventually retreated to slumbering safety in a large feather bed, Esther had been still awake playing solitaire at the table with a snoozing Eleanor opposite her on the couch. When Ash had awoken, Eleanor had been awake and informed her that Esther had gone for an early morning walk on her lonesome. It would seem the twin preferred her own company while in London, as judged by Caelan's own dark glare out onto Covent Garden.

Memories apparently, unwelcome, made their way into their minds.

There had been no time for breakfast as Caelan and Eleanor told her but she'd managed to dodge away to visit the old haunts from a distance.

She looked longingly at the shop opposite, memories more pleasant resurfacing. The times spent in the old "Tea Leaf" cafe, no she wasn't selling the place to marks. To her it was the good old-fashioned greasy spoon that London was infamous for – had all been good memories. Esther had warned her not to go to any old haunts, no matter the temptation, especially with Holmes's goons hanging around. She muttered a curse under her breath and returned to casting a longing look at the window, just as one of the girls put up a sign: *Fresh Apple Pie.*

That stopped her dead. She considered her options. Surely, there was no harm in just going in and grabbing her crew some pie? It might sweeten their dour moods. Ash nodded and crossed the street, opening the door. She was about to call out a greeting when the door to the men's toilets opened and Holmes's lackey, Hughes, stepped out.

Once again, Ash froze. So did Hughes. The two stood, eyes locked; hand on fly for Hughes and Ash still halfway through the door. Hughes unconsciously doing his fly up was what spurred Ash into action. Three actions to be precise. In her first movement, she spun on her heel, in the second she had torn open the door and in the third set off running. It was lucky, Ash thought to herself, that she had had that burst of adrenaline and realisation in the moment before the irate Welshman did. She heard yells behind her, but kept running. She turned sharply down another street, dodging into the early morning traffic. Why the hell wasn't it rush hour? Things were too quiet to be bobbing and weaving through these streets. She glanced behind her, cursing as she saw the Welshman gaining on her. While her adrenaline was reaching its end, his was just beginning, the shock having worn off.

It was difficult to keep track of her direction as she followed all those bends, hearing the pounding of heavy boots in the alley behind. She had to get out of here. She should've listened – *That's twice you've not listened in London, and it's going to cost you*, she cursed herself.

She skidded to a halt, gasping for breath. Hughes was still a decent distance away, but gaining fast. Ash looked around, before spotting the familiar Tube station sign. She let out a loud huff of relief before running over, dodging through the commuters and blending with the crowd.

The traffic lights that were between her and salvation turned to amber, and she threw a frantic glance as she came to a halt. Hughes would catch her if she waited. With a decisive if fearful nod, Ash began walking towards him, hands raised. Hughes's piggish face adopted a predator's snarl of a smile, and he slowed. Ash walked forward about twenty feet before she heard the traffic resume its ponderous journey.

Then she ran.

She darted across the road, throwing a cursory look to both sides, her right leg barely missed by a black cab and scarcely hearing the loud beeps of the traffic, let alone the yells of the drivers. Ash ran down the staircase into the Tube station, blending in with the commuters. Not expected, but a good escape.

Once out of sight among the crowds, she took off her jacket, threw it quickly to the side and began looking through her bag. All con artists had to be magicians, and vanishing into thin air on command and in plain sight was one of the most valuable lessons that Dee had drummed into her when one of their short cons had gone wrong in Trafalgar Square and they'd been running from several agents of the law.

With social media being a necessary element of con life in recent years, identities were hidden behind items of clothing never worn, and Ash had long developed the habit of keeping a spare jacket in her bag along with various little items to 'destroy' herself.

Her profile picture on Facebook always featured her with glasses; never her favourite wire-rimmed pair that one day would probably be slung over the nearest bridge into the Thames. She took them off, keeping an eye on the stairs as there was a lull in the human traffic, and switched them for a pair of severe horn-rimmed ones. Hughes had evidently got caught at the lights, as she had been hoping he would. She took out her hooped earrings and replaced them with a pair of studs that Dee had given her for her last birthday, before putting on her pearl necklace. She stuffed her jacket into the bottom of her bag, and then walked upstairs, joining a group of jostling teenagers.

She fell in line with them, laughing and texting, while watching as Hughes threw himself down the stairs. He shoved by her, and she just shot him a disgusted look. Nothing too conspicuous.

Once he had descended the escalators, she tucked her phone into her pocket and began to walk quickly down the street.

Her luck had saved her, as had her short-con lessons. Now it was time to get her long-con game in order.

"Is Ash in yet?"

"Nah, think she went for a walk... so we said St Martin's, right?" Eleanor said, ever the consummate professional.

Esther nodded curtly.

"She'll be fine."

Esther gave a terse nod as she looked around the warehouse, continuing to survey the situation with barely raised concern. It was perfect. Perfect for the job; she'd have to thank Nunn later. The work was still being completed, but it looked good. Junk hidden as solid gold, she considered. She knew how meticulous the plan was, and how it hinged on so many factors: on the hidden Spanish Prisoner, on the wire... on lives. She winced at that.

"Nancy's dad is good for this stuff?" she asked, raising her eyebrows.

"Yeah, double- and triple-checked. Terry said we can have it. He'll only charge a bit extra for the sapphires... seems there's a booming trade in them," Eleanor said, walking over to show Esther the stall. "There's an extra stall for some snuff films."

"I hope you're not invested in that stuff?" Esther snapped, eyes boring holes into Eleanor, although the latter just raised her eyebrows. "Or..."

"Or it could be dodgy DVDs I got from Jock Simmons down Portobello Road." Eleanor grinned. "A girl sitting in a room for all of an hour, crying and pleading... last bit, she stands up and walks out."

"Who's the gal?" Esther snorted, imagining those perverts gazing at the screen. It quickly turned to concern. "Her face can be seen?"

"Felicity Lester-Millpond; she's this con artist from Brixton. Absolute artist with plastics," Eleanor said, gesturing at her own face. She paused and looked at Esther. "Could even hide that scar of yours, if you so chose?"

"Now, why would I do that?" Esther asked, examining the thin scar that ran around her wrist and ran up her arm to her elbow. "It's the only thing anyone can identify me by." She rubbed it fondly, then looked out.

"You know your problem, Es?" enquired the blonde, tucking a pink streak of hair behind her ear. "My grandmother would say that you have one hundred problems, but none at all."

Esther snorted rudely through her nose, trying to ignore the prickling of her thumbs. *Good old Shakespeare; always a quote for every occasion*, she thought. However, her inner Shakespearean quotation didn't hide the unease in her bones as she sensed that something was indeed very wrong.

Something was up… and she had a funny feeling it had to do with Ash.

"Also got some of the crew from Detroit in," Eleanor said, as Esther nodded. "Holmes strikes me as someone who'll like an international flavour… by the way, why is Ness charging me more?"

"Royal gems are worth more, perhaps?" Esther suggested, running her finger under her chin. "Caelan, any ideas why?"

Caelan walked around from behind her, ruffling his newly light brown hair and taking out his contact lenses to reveal the same shade of green as her own. "It's nice to be my own hair colour again, Esther. Next time we do a con, you can dye your hair." He looked over her head at the new men. "Nah, it's because some know their stuff about current cons in the States."

"I'm too dark to go blonde. I'd need to be bleached. Nice to see you light brown again. Sun-bleached brown," Esther joked. "Could you get them cheaper and quicker?"

"I'm the best fixer this side of the Atlantic beyond Terry. Course I can," he said, striding off, muttering about "ungrateful sisters" and "best fixers".

At that moment, Ash turned the corner. Esther nodded in

relief before turning her head back to Eleanor, assessing whether she read the same thing. An imperceptible squint of the eyes told Esther that Eleanor had indeed noted it.

Something was wrong.

"You all right?" Eleanor asked, raising her eyebrows as the young girl joined them. "Look like you ran a marathon."

"I had to run. Thought I'd miss the Tube. This looks good." Ash looked around, fascinated.

Doesn't want to speak about it – probably ran into that goon who was left behind, Esther thought.

"I like the good old-fashioned big store," agreed Eleanor. "We're going to need somewhere to bring them to from here; I figure I can be a pig in the car… you know, being taken from an honest job and all that stuff."

Ash listened to the two negotiate terms, jumping when Caelan handed her a cup of tea. She thanked him and looked around. A real smugglers' den of treasures and knick-knacks. Fool's gold. Then she spotted a figure crossing the large industrial estate car park, and watched them as they disappeared.

Esther breathed in the London air and promptly coughed. "I hate the Big Smoke. Funny, though, I think you always see celebrities in Kings Cross."

"Does that include me?" said an American accent to her left.

Ash spun to see a curly-haired man with wide green eyes looking at her. She gasped and pointed.

"We've met, Miss Azeri… or should I say Ash?"

Esther merely blushed and pushed her chin out. "Morning, Anton." She looked across to Ash. "Ash, I'd like you to meet Anton Volkov, grad student and international jewel thief." She leaned over and kissed his cheek. "You are late."

"Do you know how your grandmother is? Demanding I leave evidence to prove it's not an insurance job?!" the man said, raising his hands in exaggerated exasperation. "She had me there over five hours."

"Hellion is anything but kind-hearted," teased Esther, putting a pencil behind her ear. "And synagogue before you started?"

"Had to see Rabbi Wolff before we began the con," he said, reaching into his pocket, withdrawing the blood red stone and holding it up to the sunlight. "This will be my crowning achievement. I'm surprised you didn't recognise the slip with the name?"

Ash flushed as she thought back.

"Ah, you thought we were intimate and there had been an accidental revealing of my name? No need to worry. Although my Esther is hot-blooded when it comes to a con, she is as cold as an ice cube." He smirked at Esther, who just rolled her eyes. "No threat of a beating? You know, it would make a wonderful wedding ring."

"There are enough reprobates around here to beat the hell into you. Put it away; get me a Monet for our wedding day," Esther scolded teasingly.

He smirked and tossed the jewel to her.

"Now, if you're not going to be of any use to me, then go find something useful to do."

"Fine," he grumbled, kissing her cheek again before heading toward the stairs. "This is the same place as we used for the safety deposit job back in November, right?" His Russian accent had slipped faster than a piano down a flight of stairs into a Midwestern American.

Eleanor nodded.

"Good; I'll look over the books."

"Anton is our banker when he's not a thief; make sure this goes someplace safe," Esther said, handing the gem to Eleanor. "Oh, and before you slope off to bed, Anton!"

Anton leaned on the railings, looking over.

"There's some food in the fridge. It seems Ash has been missing her fry-ups."

Ash stopped dead, waiting to see the knowing look, but Esther only stooped over some paperwork with Eleanor.

"Bought some from Smithfield Market for you on my early morning run. The amount Benny James charged for it, he should be the crook, not me."

"I'll make enough for the crew," Anton said, jogging up the stairs.

There was plenty of talk from then on, Ash watching the stage performers get into their roles. There were loud discussions, and she jumped when she heard a whistle.

"Ash, get your butt up here and get a seat," Anton called. "I'll set a bed up for you too… got a big day ahead."

Ash jogged lightly up the stairs and smiled as she stepped into the office, looking at the kitchenette. "Doesn't look like much of an office."

"Oh, this door will be closed, don't you worry. Esther's got an easy ride from now on; she just has to be whispered about, not seen," Anton said lightly as he put some bacon under the grill. "Only the eggs to go and you got a breakfast."

"Are you heist-drunk?" Ash asked. She'd heard of such things among thieves.

The man gave a laugh.

"I'm being serious."

"I have no doubt you are. And, in answer to your question, I am not. I am merely exhausted from hauling stuff through the world," he sighed dramatically. "Interpol is always breathing down my neck. Seems they think I am the holder of some Van Gogh stolen in the '40s."

Ash snorted.

"Damn family."

"You?"

"Most thieves go down the family line; that was the first job I scoped for my Uncle Fyodor in Russia." He tilted his head thoughtfully. "That was after my parents emigrated from Russia, shall we say?" He grinned to himself.

"Esther kept you to herself," Ash said, sitting down opposite him as he began to pull out plates. "Was it your family on board?"

"You need have no concern," the Russian said. "I do not leave a trail of breadcrumbs. I am genuinely finishing my doctorate in geology."

"Still say that it's sneaky of Esther not to tell me about you."

"Esther will consider your grumpiness a tragedy, I am sure. I knew Luke." He looked hard at her. "He helped Esther learn the short cons… and he also taught me that love isn't a con. It's how I met Est." He glanced at the window and shook his head. "You'll have no idea how well liked that Englishman was. Oh, I have no doubt you loved him as a dad," he added. "No, to lose him was a tragedy."

"You ever lost anyone?" she asked quietly.

He nodded again, and it wasn't beyond her notice that he reached to a chain hanging around his neck, brought it up to his lips and kissed the Star of David pendant.

"How'd you get on?"

"I survived it. You learn to." He looked at her. "Why do I feel as though I should be passing on con advice to you?"

"Perhaps because you're training me?"

"Me? Oh no, I'm a thief and the banker; I deal with the necessary side of things. Plus, I am leaving. I have a job that Esther wants us to go over tonight. It'll start just as you begin your side of things with Eleanor." He saw her confused look. "Me and Est have a good relationship on both sides of it."

Ash sighed. She felt safe with Anton, just as she had done when he'd been playing a graduate student on board the ship. He had had the easiest job in con terms. "I can't imagine moving on," she said softly. "Luke was such a big part of my life."

"There are three ways people go with tragedy. At least in my experience," Anton said, breaking an egg into the hot frying pan "Over easy or sunny side up?"

"The difference being?"

"Keep forgetting none of you are cultured – means that it gets fried on both sides, but it's not cooked for very long on the second side, so the yolk doesn't cook through and stays runny. That's over easy." He saw the look. "Yeah, that's better for you?"

"You were saying about tragedy?" she asked, as he plated up.

He shot her a confused look.

"Before you were explaining eggs?"

Anton nodded, a look of comprehension coming over his face. "They either commit suicide at a later date, or they are forced to survive. Then there is a lesser-known third option." He walked to the window that overlooked the warehouse. "Breakfast is on the table!"

There were varied shouts in response, though no-one seemed to move. Anton shook his head, and began making up a bed in the corner of the room.

"That being?" Ash asked, sitting down to her own breakfast and beginning to eat.

"They become addicts." Anton continued to fluff the pillows.

"Addicted to what? Alcohol? Drugs?" Ash asked, grabbing her cup of tea and drinking it quickly.

"Whatever tickles their fancy," he said, standing up and stretching his back with a slight wiggle of the bum before walking to the centre of the room and picking up a glass of water from the table. "For example, I know of one girl – very good writer – her father committed suicide when she was sixteen, on the cusp of seventeen. Very nice, dependable girl; could already write, but after that she could only write down what she felt, not say it, for fear that she broke her father." He leaned on the doorway. "I've only ever seen it again once."

Ash nodded and looked down at the ground floor of the warehouse, watching Esther shouting out orders like a general to her men. But there she was; she could strategise like a general at least. "Don't tell me – one of the twins?"

"Not the one you're thinking of, either. See him?" Anton joined her at the window and pointed down to where Caelan was sitting cross-legged with one of the surveillance cameras. "He became addicted to the con life. Kept him alive; it's how I met him. We were scoping the same museum for a con… keeping the family whisper alive for him."

"And Esther is being forced to survive?" Ash asked, smiling blithely.

Anton turned haunted, if sparkling, green eyes to her. "What else would you call organising the biggest con this side of the twenty-first century against a man who has a vendetta against your family, but a slow suicide?"

THIRTEEN

"The kid is concerning herself." Anton ran his hands through Esther's hair as he kissed her shoulder. "She's thinking about revenge, worrying about Luke; about what-ifs."

"Don't remind me. I suppose you told her the bull about tragedies... slow suicide?" Esther said.

He nodded and hugged her a little tighter.

"Thanks for reassuring her, Anton."

"I know you're useless with it."

Esther sighed and looked sad for a moment, but only for a moment. She took the opportunity to kick off her shoes and squeeze up to him on the sofa, looking out at the city of London. The rest of the apartment was asleep; at least, the last time she'd checked they had all been sleeping. Healthy breakfasts for the lot of them, and working out the line once more.

"It's the way of the long con. It's been a long time coming to Holmes." Esther took a deep, shuddering breath. "I didn't *want* a sixteen-year-old kid to be my rainmaker."

Anton hugged her close, and she sighed softly. Anton came from a long line of thieves; Esther from a long line of con artists. Concerns came with both their heritage and their chosen job.

Anton normally had his concerns about new alarms that he hadn't had a chance to investigate. Esther would always worry about the day when her mark would be cleverer than her. For now, her most recent concern was the least experienced of their crew.

"I'd like to do some relaxing. Aren't you ready for something more relaxing? Fewer risks with more thinking and planning?"

Esther knew exactly what he meant, and didn't skip a beat. She tipped her head back to narrow her eyes at him. "You mean the risks you took with the Fabergé job?"

"That was one *fantastic* risk."

Esther rolled her eyes. He'd escaped by the skin of his teeth; how he'd smuggled himself over the border into Norway, she didn't know and didn't want to ask. She'd tended him for the best part of a week, nursing his fever. Upon hearing his explanation that he'd broken into the Kremlin, no less, to try to steal the 'Clover Leaf' Fabergé egg, she'd consulted the local hospital and made sure that he was healthy before promptly sending him back to America.

He brushed her hair off her face, kissing her cheek. "I've never seen so many police trip over themselves so fast. Now, come. What can we do for fun?"

"Is there anything you find fun that doesn't involve you almost getting caught?" Esther asked, sitting up. "No, don't answer that. This is exactly the reason you're not a con man, but a damned thief."

He only shrugged, a coy smile on his face, pulling her to her feet and swaying gently. "How about Shanghai? I could rob a safety deposit box. Nobody wants to report what's in a safety deposit box. That's international. I happen to know that an emerald from the Hatton Garden job is being kept in one of the Shanghai safety deposit boxes. It'll make a fine engagement ring. It'll bring out the green in your eyes."

Esther tilted her head to look at him. "Well, if we get married we're going to need some things…"

"What?! Just like that?! All those stupid jokes… I—"

Esther silenced him with a quick kiss. He chuckled against her lips, and she giggled. So different from the serious con artist she presented to the rest of the world.

"For an engagement present?" she said, taking a step back to look at him.

"You've already thought about this," Anton realised, shaking his head. "You… you… con artist."

"You say the nicest things," she said, smiling fondly at him before walking to her backpack and pulling out photos. "This is the place I want you to try next. I've put notes on the back of the photographs to show what you need."

"Insurance policy?" he asked, looking at the photographs.

"Insurance policy," Esther agreed. "We need this. I need it to fit into the background. This entire con is built upon the honour or dishonour amongst thieves."

"Miss Crook," Anton asked after a moment, "do you think we will ever have a normal relationship?"

"What do you consider 'normal'? We live in the shadows of 'hello' and 'goodbye'," she said, looking at him out of the corner of her eye. "Just be grateful that this time as I say goodbye, I'm not throwing you out into the Norway snow!"

"You know, you turn a lovely phrase," teased Anton, looking at the paperwork. "Even if now you are putting me on a job that could get me arrested in the United States."

"Fine," she said, catching hold of his chin. "I love you. Is that better?"

"Much better," he said, walking over to his backpack. "I will call when I get the item. Send Caelan over soon. I'll need his help."

"I'll need him as long as possible," Esther said quietly. "He has a host of duties. If you could send over the plans, I'll get things out to you."

"You're a fallen angel in disguise," he said, grabbing his coat and putting it on. "I've got stuff waiting for me Stateside."

"You calling me Lucifer?" Esther asked.

"*Zmeya*," he corrected, taking the plans and shoving them in his backpack before heading for the door, Esther following. "A snake… and I love you too."

He smiled and, before she had time to protest, leaned over to kiss her, once again thinking to himself that there were indeed worse things in life than catching a tiger by the tail.

You could also catch a Crook.

Holmes was late.

Ash stood looking at the Liberty Clock, allowing the shoppers to bump by her as she gazed above the arch that spanned Kingly Street on the south-west side of Great Marlborough Street. With growing concern, she looked at the ornate clock face that had always fascinated and comforted her. Three times St George had chased the dragon, and now his great hand was raised to strike and slay the beast to the peal of the noon bell.

Esther had been wrong. Holmes didn't want to partake in the revenge game. The con had ended before it had started.

"I'm sorry, Miss Azeri, the wife had me call in at Liberty while we were here."

Ash spun around to see Holmes standing there with an amused Innocent, who looked around to check if anyone was following them, apart from his overlarge bodyguards.

"That's all right. Please. I know a good cafe."

The two men looked unimpressed.

"It's better than what you think I'm thinking of. I promise." She looked at them pleadingly, but neither shifted. Good. It meant easier work. "Fine. I'll take you right there." She almost huffed at the indignity. She saw the two share a wry smile… they thought they were conning her. Let them believe it.

She just hoped that the rest of the team was ready.

All the way to the warehouse, she hoped everything was ready. She knew that things were moving at a convenient pace for everyone else. Too slow for her, but that was her inexperience she knew.

"Have you lived in London long, Miss Azeri?" asked Innocent conversationally as he directed her to a black car.

"Forever," Ash said, rubbing the back of her neck with unease. "Although my grandmother was born in Tiger Bay, Cardiff. Do you know where that is?"

Innocent shook his head as Holmes coughed, clearing his throat with a superior expression.

"It's where Dame Shirley Bassey is from, Ezra."

Innocent cocked an eyebrow.

"You know, the singer of those Bond themes?"

All the way there, Holmes tried to list famous people from the Cardiff area; then when Innocent showed no recognition, he moved on to Welsh personalities in general. He did this the entire journey to the Docklands.

"Honestly, Ezra, you'd think you'd be a bit of an anglophile, the time you've spent with me," Holmes said, as the car drew to a halt at the dockside factory.

"Jim Driscoll, the first recipient of the featherweight Lonsdale Belt, was from Cardiff, I believe?" Innocent asked, raising his eyebrows.

The two men accompanying him shared a look and a small chuckle as the driver clambered out of the car, frantically checking his mobile phone to confirm the idle bit of trivia.

"Pugilism and its history is a hobby of mine."

Ash didn't want to ask what other kinds of hobbies Innocent had. But when she caught his hand to help her out of the car, he winked. He had been warding off questions, it would seem, with the art of distraction – a fellow con man in every sense of the word.

"Move yourself behind there! Yes, Terry, I'm being polite," Eleanor's voice roared. She was standing with arms folded across her chest. She looked like a tyrannical leader, despite looking calm and efficient. She raised her hand in acknowledgement to Ash before barking out an order to a worker.

"That's Katherine Clarke," Ash said quietly.

"Can't even begin to start with how crap the day has been," Eleanor said, walking over to Ash. "How are you doing, Azeri?"

"Fine. These are the people I was telling you about," she said, gesturing. "After Crook."

"Then we can walk and talk. I take it you gentlemen aren't above seeing the less-than-savoury side of London? I have at least six shipments in that need dealing with," she said, shaking their hands quickly. Two curt nods and open mouths before she ploughed on. "Snuff films, art forgeries... we got it all here."

"Kat is the best fixer this side of the Thames. Outside of Terry Nunn, of course," Ash said, trying to show her knowledge through casual conversation. "She's the best screw to hold together a plan, while Terry is the best screwdriver."

"Everybody is trying to screw everybody," Eleanor said calmly. "Follow me, and close ya mouth, Ash." She stopped next to an artwork that was going by. "That sixty-five by fifty-four centimetres? I want it right, Jo."

"Sure thing, Kat. Got a few papers to sign it off to keep it safe and legal – you know, so nothing comes back on you."

"Measurements?" Holmes asked curiously.

"If you think the Cairo authorities won't measure it to make damned sure my client hasn't sold them a dud, you have another thing coming." Eleanor smirked as she continued to sign the papers. "My mother – who got me into this business – always said, 'Make them think they have what they came for and leave them with nothing.' That's my good old mama." She shrugged. "I don't ask questions... it could be for some biddy who wants art treasures."

"Even stolen ones?" Innocent asked politely as he admired one piece. "These are excellent. A hidden Van Gogh?"

"Yes. Jo?"

The young woman looked up sharply.

"Be a doll and get me those stones that Ash is after. If I'm right, that is?"

Ash nodded.

"Good. And interested?"

"Always, in good art – even if they are forgeries."

"What a nasty word! I'd say more along the line of honouring the dead. Don't you know that in his lifetime, Van Gogh only sold one painting? While my artist colleague, in loving memory of his all-too-tragic genius, has already sold two through myself to some other sap." Eleanor flashed an insincere smile at the men. "No offence."

"None taken," Holmes assured her as a young girl scampered off to collect the items. "What a wonderful piece," he added, walking up to a painting. "This is?"

"Ironically enough, Van Gogh again. It's *Oleanders in a Vase* or something like that. I don't have an appreciation for the art, Mr Holmes; just the con and the money it brings." She scowled. "Nazis stole it during World War II. Nobody has seen it since then – working from damned photographs."

"I can assure you some people have seen the original… what an amazing likeness." He scratched his chin.

"Very difficult to get, that one. Think I might keep it – I like irritating those snobs who think they know all about art."

Ash smirked at them, seeing Holmes puff up at Eleanor's blasé tone.

"You know, I heard about this art gallery gig somebody did recently – good job, too. Except for the fact that Luke Gaines was killed, poor bugger. Good man. That was for his gig. Thing was, my artist couldn't get it to him in time."

Ash raised her eyebrows.

"Esther's set to buy it for her personal collection. Thank you, Jo." Eleanor took a small box from Jo, who had returned. "I expect it back, Miss Azeri. I mean it. I have several of Crook's other buyers wanting to see it." She glanced at some people entering. "Ah, customers. Excuse me, everyone."

"Sure thing, gentlemen?" Ash said, gesturing for the others to join her.

The trio sat down with the bodyguards milling around as Holmes opened the box, to reveal the jewel inside. Innocent whipped it out and held it to the skylight. He whipped out a magnifier for jewels.

"Please don't be so surprised, Miss Azeri," he said, not looking at her. "My late wife and my sainted, albeit alive, mother had a fascination with this little gemstone. Ah, there it is!" He held it up to the light and grinned. "The fault in the centre of the gem. It makes it look as though a star burst inside it. The only fault, in fact, which is impossible to replicate." He handed it back to Holmes as Eleanor rejoined them. "It's the real thing."

"Sure?" Holmes asked, tossing the jewel lightly in his hand, only to have Innocent snatch it out of mid-air.

"As sure as I can be," Innocent said, handing it back to Eleanor with a charming smile. "Kat – if I may be permitted to call you that? Yes? Oh, how lovely – might I bring my own jeweller in to examine this piece?"

A nod.

"Thank you."

"And what would a gentleman such as myself be interested in that ruby for?" enquired Holmes. "I'm much more a... human resources man now. Reformed, don't you know?"

"Really? Human resources?" Ash said, raising her eyebrows. "Knew you were going straight. Book deals and that?"

"Yes, that's my special area of interest. Human resources and how we can resource them; I'm not in the gangster business any longer." The man opened his hands in an innocent fashion. If Ash had not known what an evil man was sitting opposite her, she could almost have bought his 'innocent gangster' look. Almost. "And you want me to invest in a scheme that could endanger my livelihood? After all, I'm compounding a felony."

"No. It's foolproof," Ash insisted, leaning forward and speaking in a considerate tone. "You just seen for yourself; Kat is willing to sell anything to anyone." She took a deep breath. "She's planning on doing the scam that Potvin did."

"And how does that intrigue Mr Holmes?" Innocent said, examining the painting again. "A failed scheme from… what? The 1980s?"

"Listen, all you have to do is go along with it. You go along with the buy. I know she'll have a few others purchasing, too… it's easy enough. I'll persuade her that I have managed to get into your good graces." She put her hands on the table and outstretched them pleadingly. "I'll bring you their receipts. I'll bring you both everything."

"What's the con?"

"You buy the stuff from me. She brings in a sting on you with the police to switch the fake for the real ruby. You're discredited, the full works," Ash said, flashing an insincere smile. "The coup de grâce is when you're arrested by Interpol for said buying and receiving of stolen goods."

"Ingenious," Innocent said, returning to admire the art on the wall. "She captures you for a crime she has committed. I can appreciate the irony."

"All we need to let her into the con to get the convincer."

"If we're so far…"

"Because I need bait. The documents won't be legal. I was rather hoping that you could speak to the police officer and bring her in on the gig?" Ash smirked. "I am in rather a lot of hot water with the Old Bill in my neck of the woods."

"What kind of trouble?" Holmes asked.

"I got caught doing the flop down in Soho; unfortunately it was a copper's son that I was trying it out on. I'd rather not give them reason to put me in the cop shop."

"I'm surprised that Crook is letting you pull this off," Holmes said.

"So am I, if I'm honest," Ash said, allowing her genuine incredulity at the faith Esther displayed in her real self to show through. "Seems she only wants to be there on the pay-off… didn't even know about that painting."

That much was honest. She'd wondered if Esther Crook had had anything to do with the art gallery scam. It seemed like something she would've thought up, advised Luke Gaines on, joked with him over the phone about what would be needed. A friendly contest, as it were. But there was nothing friendly about Holmes as he stood up.

"Boy?"

A young man with fair hair looked up.

"Bring it over here."

Ash watched as the lad walked around the painting, examining it. Like father, like son, with a panther-like grace and scowl. Where the con had amused her to no end with the son, it concerned her with the father. With the son it had been a light-hearted game, the first of its kind in the UK. A successful short con turned long. A game that had been won.

But the victory had had a bitter aftertaste.

"She like this, does she? Esther Crook?" Holmes asked, breaking her out of her reverie.

"Pardon?" she asked.

Eleanor stepped in. "Yeah. Asked for it to be packaged last night and sent to the De Braun Casino in Monte Carlo; seems she's recouping costs or something as payment to De Braun. Leaving in the next few days."

"Payment, eh? Say, how much you want for it?" he asked, looking at Eleanor, who raised her hands. "What? Won't sell?"

"Not mine to sell." Eleanor flashed a grin. She pointed at Ash. "Sell it to her; she's the one who's got to tell Es what she's done."

Ash looked at Eleanor. She'd not been told this part of the plan. In fact, from the look on Eleanor's face, she'd have to wing it. "I'm willing to take £250,000. That way I can at least pretend to Crook that I tried to make a profit on it." She smirked. "People pay for the story, after all."

"And you think you're going to sell one to the great Esther Crook?" mocked Holmes.

"Yeah, who says I can't?" Ash smirked. "I managed to get you here on a promise. Crook will more than likely be impressed with my skills. Might be able to convince her to stay… you know she has only three weaknesses?"

"As many as three? Why, Miss Azeri, do astound me with your intellect," Holmes mocked, folding his arms across his chest.

"Her weaknesses are her ego, her brother and loyalty. The woman has successfully avoided the law for the last few years, so she has a right to have a bit of an ego. She has her damned loyalty, which I don't understand, as you can see. Then there's her brother. He's on the run now, but as you hurt her ego and her wallet, I can near damned well guarantee that she will be so mad she'll fall into any good-looking trap you lay for her. She's done all the hard work by making this plan."

Holmes nodded. Ash sighed inwardly with relief. She had allowed the man to think she had thought it through to the ultimate bow and exit. That she wanted to con Esther Crook… that she wanted to break her. That she – no, her *character*, Azeri – wanted to break her in order to become independently famous in the close-knit community of con artists. Holmes and Innocent just wanted to break her. She looked at Innocent, who was wearing a frustrating little frown.

"Fine," Holmes said, with a firm nod. "I'll pay you for both items when the item is proved to be real with an independent jeweller… I'll take the painting now."

"Only if payment is on the table, Mr Holmes… after all, neither of us wants to be doing something that is totally dishonest, do we?"

Innocent let out a sharp laugh, watching Holmes withdraw a cheque book. "I admire your guts, Miss Azeri."

"Just want to make the rules of engagement as clear as you did, Mr Innocent," she stated politely.

Holmes had worn a grin after that shoot-down.

There had been a shared laugh between the three scheming conspirators before an appointment had been made to meet back there at nine o'clock sharp tomorrow morning. Ash had watched the men go to their cars after making excuses about wanting to inform Crook of the developments.

Holmes sighed to himself.

"Problem, Harry?" Ezra asked casually from the front seat.

Holmes shook his head, considering. "No."

It was a pity the kid was so determined to become like Crook. A waste of God-given talents... perhaps he and Innocent could persuade her, when all this was said and done, to join them. But for now, he scolded himself, he had to be content with what was to come.

The downfall of Esther Crook.

FOURTEEN

"I knew he was a thief but this a new low for him."

Esther was standing, hands on hips, as she looked out at the city. Ash winced as the light summer heat fell cool over London, the streets buzzing with the first hints of the British summertime. It was a Friday morning in June. Lights pulsed along the skyline and traffic clogged the streets. The air was thick with the anticipation of all that can happen in the city on the last day before the weekend.

"Sorry, Est… didn't know the painting meant much to you," Ash offered. "I can always ask for it to go missing in transit?"

"You won't!" scoffed Eleanor. "That painting was spirited away the moment it got away from those offices."

"Could steal it back?" Caelan said, looking at his sister.

"I have no need; not at this juncture, at any rate," Esther replied. "It's a victory to find a likeness."

"I'm still sorry."

Esther sighed. "Look, my part here is over. It's best that he thinks I'm only back in London when the con is coming to a close. I'll even put money on him rushing to the Met to get *them* ready."

"He'll still want to test the ruby, though."

"But of course. It'd be an insult if he didn't." Esther snorted through her nose. "As good as my brother is, I think he'd take it as a personal affront."

"I would," Caelan said, rubbing his chin thoughtfully. "Means he's slipping up."

"Nah, all it means is that Innocent is cautious. He knows we're not chasing him down. His partner is collateral," Esther said, walking to the window. She looked out. "Every one of us needs rest. Now."

"You really think any of us is going to sleep?" Ash asked incredulously. "It's only five o'clock."

"No. I just hope you will." Esther looked at her. "Being on the lam is no fun. You take sleep where it's required and move on from there."

"What about you?"

"I'm going to need a word with our Russian exile, and then I'll follow you."

Esther watched all of them reluctantly leave before she pulled a card out of her house of cards that she had been playing with when they got in. Old friends, as they were. Club. Heart. Joker. Spade. Diamond. They fluttered to the floor and Esther looked out across the city.

"God help the saints, and may the Devil keep us wrongdoers in his sights," she whispered to herself. "And if this ends, let it end in a blaze of glory." She looked upward towards the glistening heavens in contemplation. "After all, you made me in your image, you old sinner."

In the distance, thunder crackled and a lightning bolt lit up the London skies.

DCI Rebecca Banks sat gazing over the London streets from her office. Even now, people were going about their business; the black cabs served as the life blood to the London traffic. In front of her lay the heavy file containing the details of the theft of the Burmese ruby. Interpol had been wandering the corridors since it was stolen, and it would be considered a feather in the hat for anyone involved in the capture of the criminals who had committed the act, and in the safe return of the priceless jewel. Whoever it was had a fantastic criminal mind.

"Boss?"

Banks looked up into the eyes of her young sergeant.

"There's a man here to see you. Holmes."

She raised her eyebrows in exasperation. "Okay, send him in."

She openly despised the man. He had beaten the rap so many times on small technicalities. The Crook case; every agency had thought they'd had him. When the long-time Interpol agent had been murdered, all agencies had considered Holmes a wanted man. It had been a tragedy, but no evidence had been officially tied to him, and the whisper of a forced confession had done the case in despite the best efforts of all involved.

Banks closed her eyes as she remembered the two Crook kids who had been standing safely out of Holmes's view, although their sobs had carried around the courtroom. Then the defence had stood up with a single technicality. It had demolished the case.

"Ah, DCI Banks." Holmes came into the room and threw down his jacket in a blasé manner, with the triumphant smirk of a cat who'd both caught the canary and drunk the milk. "I hope you are well."

"You're lucky that I had no plans, Holmes. What do you want?" the DCI forced out.

"Ah-ah, manners, please." He sat down opposite her, still wearing that stupid grin. "I believe you, DCI Banks, have been looking for resources on a mutual acquaintance?"

"Never thought I'd see the day Harry Holmes would cry cop." Banks smirked.

"Not crying cop, just have a mutual interest," he said indignantly. "I suppose you know about Esther Crook?"

The detective chief inspector winced internally. She'd heard whispers on the wind about the Crook daughter. That she had, despite studying to become a lawyer, turned into a criminal and had masterminded several cons that led no route back to her. Banks hoped not… whispers were usually just whispers.

"I've heard rumours. And those are inadmissible. She has never been arrested in Europe or Asia, let alone on either side of the Atlantic."

"She is considered one of the finest con artists of her generation… among the criminally minded," Holmes interrupted. "I chanced upon her on my book tour. It would seem that she had something to do with the theft of that ruby. The Star of Burma?"

Banks narrowed her eyes.

"Yes, and she is on London turf… and set to make a fortune on people's backs."

Banks sighed. "Fine. Give me the low-down."

"I'm warning you, being a con artist isn't like it is in the movies," Esther had said to Ash, with a measured patience that Ash sensed was being sorely tested. "There's a lot of boring waiting around… and you have to have the patience of a saint with the long con."

As she huddled underneath a bridge, trying in vain to dodge the sudden torrential downpour that London was famous for, Ash was willing to admit, if only to herself, that Esther had been right and it *was* less fun than Ash had thought it would be.

She had meant to fall asleep. Honestly, she had. But peace was hard to come by when she thought of what was on the line for her and everyone else. Their lives balanced on a tightrope. Eventually she had fallen into a light, fitful sleep, filled with dreams of being chased by Holmes and Hughes.

After one too many gasps awake, she had found herself wandering down the side of the Thames. As suddenly as the rain cloud burst, it stopped, and Ash let out a soft sigh of relief. She walked to the wall that overlooked the river, and blew out some air. She stared out over the water, looking into the distance. The movement of the water always reminded her of 'the dip', a fluid motion of fingers and bodies as she sidestepped her mark and made off with their readies.

The dip was almost poetic when you really looked at it. What better way to get even with the flagrant cheats and reprobates of this world than to dip your finger in their pockets? Ash wiggled her fingers experimentally and smiled to herself, only stopping when she heard a gentle cough behind her. She spun around and let out a surprised huff when she saw who it was.

Esther was standing in the darkness of one of the broken street lights. Ash had been too lost in her thoughts to notice her follower until she had stepped out of the shadows and joined her in watching the fighting light and shadow at the crest of the river.

"Can't you sleep?" Esther asked politely.

"No. How long you been following me?"

"The art of the con man is to be everywhere and nowhere. I saw you leave; wondered where you were off to. I was looking for some more blankets." She ruffled her own dark hair, then pulled out a baker boy cap from her pocket, putting it on her head. "I was supposed to be meeting Mattie LeRoy. Colorado is fine, by the by, although I'd rather you didn't tell him that you're still with us."

"Yeah."

There was a pause. In Ash's mind, Esther was probably considering what to say next. She wasn't chatty at the best of times, except regarding the execution of a plan. Ash, however, was trying to think of a way to explain everything. Things that she couldn't explain. She also guessed that Esther didn't want to imply any jealousy from Colorado.

"Dee's settled in," Esther continued quietly. "Chris Adams has taken possession of her in Denver. She's a bit worse for wear but there's no lasting physical damage. Mentally… well… that'll take a while. It seems she is quite contented for the moment. And more importantly, she is safe."

"Thanks for getting Christopher Adams involved, Est. I don't like to think what it cost."

Ash was grateful for the intervention of the ATF leader. In truth, she had almost forgotten both him and Dee. Her big sister, once so confident, was so vulnerable right now. And equally she had not been forgotten, just pushed to the back of the mind with the con.

"You don't need to thank me, Ash," Esther said, looking out onto the river. "I needed him for one purpose, but he served two. You're worried about the con." It was a question wrapped as a statement.

"Think it'll go to plan?" Ash asked.

"That a question or a concern?" Esther shot back.

"I don't know. And you didn't answer my question."

"Lord willing and the creek don't rise," Esther said thoughtfully. "That's what my dad would say." She glanced at the taller young woman. "What about you?"

"I'm okay... just, I can't get rid of a million thoughts and I don't know what it's making me feel like."

Esther nodded. "I get that feeling... can't close down. It's just static. It's too hard to focus and much too hard to sleep. Just like a kind of ambient background noise that gets in the way of everything. Static is what I call it."

"What do you do about it?" Ash asked.

"Normally plan cons. Play cards or watch a movie." Esther chuckled. "Used to walk... just like you."

"Just like me?" Ash asked curiously.

"Yeah, until I almost got pneumonia... and Norway still has wolves, kid," Esther said with a soft laugh. "Every person in this world experiences it, from stockbrokers to con artists. But it becomes so excruciatingly pronounced in those of us that are deep thinkers and worriers." She breathed out hard. "Do you like the cold?"

"Yeah, that's about right." Esther didn't speak, so Ash offered her own opinion of the matter. "It's a good distraction."

"Yeah. It's easier to think when your hands and fingers are numb," Esther agreed, blowing on her own fingers as an example. She suddenly looked at Ash seriously. "You do trust me, don't you?"

"Course I do," Ash said indignantly. She knew this was true. She knew that much of Esther wasn't a con. She just couldn't figure out all the separate pieces. Yet. "Thanks again, Est." *Not just for Dee, but for everything. You said you needed a rainmaker but you didn't really… you took me on without a concern. Thank you for giving me the opportunity.* But all this went unsaid. "I appreciate it all."

"I know." Esther jerked her head. "Now, come on. I happen to know a nice late-night walk. If you don't mind my company, that is?"

"I can think of no better." Ash walked with a spring in her step behind the woman she now considered a friend. "Where are we going?"

"The Easy," Esther said, sharing a sly smile. "I need a good whisky which burns my soul… and I'll just get you a mocktail."

The expletive that Ash used to describe her was lost in the wind, but not to the second figure who stepped out of the shadows just beyond where the two young women had been standing.

"Hello, Hughes," the figure said. "Yeah… I got them, and I know where they're heading."

Company was no good when a con artist began to feel that strange melancholy, Esther thought as she sipped at her champagne, pretending it was hot chocolate and that she was sitting in her Lyon home watching an old movie instead of listening to Ash prattle on.

"Ash, I need a bit of quiet," she said finally.

Ash suddenly fell silent and looked at her with concern. Damn, the kid was beginning to read her poker face.

"Go dance. Speak with friends. You won't be here long after this is over."

"Only if you're sure?" Ash asked nervously.

Esther nodded.

"You need to switch off more."

Esther chuckled, watching the teenager swagger off. She knew she had a junior partner, as it were, if she asked.

In the euphoria that followed a successful implementing of a con, Esther had been more than willing to follow Ash, expecting the silence that she usually immersed herself in. Instead she'd found herself tagging along with Ash, the young woman chattering like a nightingale. The confusion of the static had dissipated into nothing at all for the young Ash.

Esther envied her for it. For her, it was a constant. A reminder of the pain that her decision to lead a less-than-honest con life had bought her. She had wealth tucked into her pockets, but had lost several fortunes running from cons when the whispers became too loud. She could make a living on the poker tables if she so chose. Her recent wins on that front had been proof that she could make a living. She'd considered it optimistically, but had since resigned herself to the fact that she was a con artist through and through. She'd finish her degree – ironically, in law – and then leaf her way through, trying to find loopholes before they turned into nooses.

Mattie LeRoy called her the most honest dishonest person he knew. It was the highest compliment she had received, and she had said so when she'd cancelled her meeting with him in Covent Garden. He'd been in a forgiving mood, willing to allow her an exit whilst she dealt with her own demons.

They'd laughed over always seeming to miss each other, especially in the Big Smoke. He was the only one who knew where exactly she hid out when she was in London. Not even Nancy was privy to that, unless Esther was sleeping on her sofa. The two had cut many deals together and she trusted Mattie with her life. He was the greatest con man she knew, and he returned the compliment, saying it was nice to know a fellow Dutch master who masqueraded as a con woman. She was lucky like that. She had a good deal of cut-throats on the lookout for her. Only a few disreputable souls were not on her side.

Now, sitting in a booth at The Speakeasy, Esther considered things more soberly. Her time in London was coming to a close. She was ready to become little more than a whisper in the wind again. Her work as a prisoner was up. It was a new type of prison, but she found it satisfying. Now she had to slink back into the shadows, while Ash did the legwork for the next few weeks with Eleanor. Or would it be wiser to keep it short? She'd judge that later, she thought.

She had a good crew already. God, she needed a good bath. After a con, as her beloved grandmother would say, she just wanted to soak in a bath. To purify herself of all the evil deeds she had planned and manufactured, as if laundering her very soul.

There is one reassurance without getting wet, Esther thought as she absently pulled out her cards and laid them out, remembering each as easily as an old friend. Club; Caelan. Diamond; herself, but of course. The Joker… who to… ah – Eleanor! For who else would be able to perform the trick of a lifetime? Spade; Anton, the outsider but the banker. Heart… She paused. Was Ash her heart? Her conscience? Esther wasn't even sure if she had one of those any more. Her whispering angel that should've been on her shoulder had long gone quiet.

She took a deep breath and tucked the five cards back safely in her pocket. Now was not the time to wax lyrical. It was time to move. She had stayed too long and she needed to get back before fate began making holes in her carefully constructed plans. Before she grew attached and the barbed-wire fence that encircled her heart was cut loose.

Ash seemed to have taken this as a signal to join her again. She was wearing a silly grin and holding two bottles.

Esther shot the sixteen-year-old a look. "We have got to be going."

"We need a toast before we leave," the kid was saying in a deceptively light tone. "To Luke and absent friends?"

"To Luke and absent friends," Esther said, pointing at the bottle of lemonade on the table. "That and then we leave." She had drunk herself into a stupor and lost five rounds of cards while grieving for her short-con friend. She was now inclined to move forward.

The kid, though, was wearing a sad smile, and Esther realised that she was still suffering from the static and the concerns of it all.

"How was your first inside job, kid?"

"It was great – you could've told me about the painting."

"I did like it... bloody Holmes," Esther said, smirking. Ash would make a fine trainee, and if she kept up, Esther might let her in on a few other con...

Hell.

Esther's bright green eyes connected with knowing blue ones. Hughes. Typical. The one night – the *very* night – she let her guard down just to let the kid be a kid again, she saw Hughes.

She didn't stand too quickly, trying to appear unaffected and cool before standing Ash up. "Come on, time to go." She looked at Hughes. "I'll be right back, Mr Hughes. You have my word."

Ash threw a panicked look at the gangster's lackey and began spluttering apologies to Esther as she led her through The Speakeasy's door-slash-bookcase and outside to the taxi rank. "Est, I'm—"

"Don't apologise. Just means we got to move quicker; here's £20." She put the money firmly in Ash's hand, letting the young woman feel the slip of card between the note and her hand. "You get out of here. Go on, now. Take care of her, mate."

Esther slammed the door shut and began to walk back towards the club, hands casually in her pockets. She spun on her heel and threw a blasé look, hiding a relieved sigh behind a sharp cough as she watched the iconic black cab melt into the streets amongst its brothers. Ash was safe.

"Miss Crook?"

Esther turned and smirked at the grim Hughes. "It seems I have an overdue appointment with your boss?" She offered a flash of a grin. "Lead on."

Ash watched Esther disappear into the streams of people pouring out of the clubs. She was looking amiable enough as she walked towards the men who wanted to kill her.

"Hey, miss, anywhere in particular you'd like to go?" said the voice from the front, the man that both women had barely glanced at.

"I need to be taken to Covent Garden." Ash glanced at the card again. The Jester. "Mad cow," she muttered softly.

"Sacred in India, and you'll be taken where I instruct you to be taken," came a Southern drawl over the open radio. "Vin."

Ash shrank back in her seat as she saw the familiar smile of the bounty hunter as he turned in his seat.

"Bring her in. But bring her the long way around."

FIFTEEN

Ash stood in the centre of the room, glaring balefully at the door. Vin had driven for a solid hour, and for all Ash's intimate knowledge of London, she had no idea where she was, beyond the fact that she was in a room in a building. The room was only on the first floor. She stared out into the street. There wasn't even a black cab in sight, and the street seemed empty. It was the perfect way to make an escape.

Luke always said it was a miracle how she always landed on her feet, in both her escapes and in her luck in life. A small miracle she hadn't been arrested by the police, but somehow she always managed it. That said, she might need to stop taking stupid risks. Sooner or later the miracles tended to run out, Luke had said.

What would Esther say? *You're an idiot.* That's what she would say. No, Ash corrected herself, making the quick decision that that wording would be much too simple for Esther. *You're an ineffectual idiot, taking too many small risks for a slice of puny loot at the end.* Yes, that definitely sounded more like Esther.

But Esther Crook only played big risks for big rewards. She didn't much like getting her hands dirty, preferring to keep her fingers on the marionette strings, manipulating the outcomes. She was the stage manager, the tactician and the leader.

The roping was done by Eleanor, and quite successfully too. No wonder Esther had been so proud of her team. Ash was still fascinated by how Eleanor had wound in the story of Esther's painting by a second-rate artist to earn some extra money, and how she had guided the mark into this position. She could really understand the artwork of the con there.

The fixing was done by Caelan, organising behind the scenes, much like his sister, although in amiable silence. He was a chameleon, hiding in plain sight. Nobody had cast him a second look today when he'd been handling paperwork with the American grifters, though he was set to leave to meet up with Anton for America today. When Ash had asked Esther, Esther had not uncharitably pointed out that she had other cons on the line too. It was always better to have at least three big rewards in the wings, according to Esther.

Anton was the banker and thief, something that Esther prided herself on not being. Yet, she equally took pride in managing to help him capitulate to some con-artist traits. That in itself was a reward to Esther.

Getting away from Innocent would be a big reward for *her* at this moment, was all Ash could think when Esther had told her that. And she needed to do it soon.

"Good evening, Miss Cox," Innocent greeted her as he walked into the room, not flanked by his bodyguards. He was dressed in a smart suit, and a wry smile was on his face.

"Good evening, Mr Innocent," she said quietly.

"You were on the lam, I believe?" he said, smirking. His green eyes flickered with the humour of the situation. "Seems Miss Crook was too busy saving your skin to see you step into another snake trap."

"You're breaking my heart," Ash snapped.

"You signed a contract, Miss Cox. You made a promise on paper that you near enough signed away when you escaped."

"I would've met with you eventually."

"You knew—"

"Yes, I knew you were coming. My mother knew you were coming and she's been dead for ten years. Oh, sit down," said Ash. "Stop making a spectacle of yourself."

Innocent sat on the edge of the bed.

"Now let's get to it, so we don't have to spend any more time together than absolutely necessary."

"That we can agree on. Well, what's the con?"

"The Spanish Prisoner con?"

That earned a loud, if disbelieving, laugh. "Everybody and their mother knows the Spanish Prisoner. What's it got to do with Holmes?"

"It's so obvious that he'll not be looking for it. Esther's not given me the full details, except that I get out with the bribe money paid to some dealer by the name of Desjardin."

Another guffaw.

"What?"

"A private joke, nothing more; take no offence," he sighed. "You see, the plan you spun to Holmes, I could swallow. If that's the tale that she's told me to spin to you, then I'm less inclined."

"Well, it's what she asked Nancy Nunn to arrange," Ash hissed. "It's the one she's gone through with a fine toothcomb."

He nodded thoughtfully.

"I'm telling you what I know."

"And a damn good job you are doing, too. Very good. *Plus vous en saurez, plus il vous sera difficile de vous mentir*," he muttered to himself.

"Excuse me, I don't speak French," Ash said.

"Just an observation. I'll make sure she has a burner phone and you keep an eye on her, and the girl, for that matter. A very daring escape." Innocent clicked his tongue

"I'm glad to know I'm not trusted by you," Ash said defiantly.

"Do you blame me? The only reason you came was you were

forced, as I well expected. In fact, if you'd skipped in here I'd rather think you were trying to con me."

"What're you going to do to Esther?"

"Tan her to within an inch of her life," he spat, handing Ash a phone. "You'd best call when the plan goes down. I expect daily updates."

Ash was about to spit out a retort when Vin grabbed her arm and dragged her away. Apparently, he had decided that her silence was the better part of valour, and Ash could only wonder what kind of woman had inspired such love in this heartless gunrunner, for him to hunt Esther so remorselessly.

It was a thought that haunted her all the way to the rooms where they were staying. Caelan had been leaving when she'd arrived after being shoved out of the car by Vin. When she'd told him the edited, but nonetheless sordid, tale, he'd just rolled his eyes and woken Eleanor, snapping at her to cancel his flight for the time being. He'd then flung himself in front of the door, boring holes into it with the intensity of his gaze.

Big Ben was chiming three when Esther got in, but Ash watched as she collapsed into a seat. She had a nasty cut to the forehead, which Eleanor began tending to immediately. Esther allowed her, sharing a few hushed words, and Eleanor shooting glares at Ash. Caelan had joined her a moment later, pouring a whisky for the two of them. Green eyes narrowed in Ash's direction, but he gave an almost imperceptible nod which she returned before he retreated silently to his bed.

"It's not the kid's fault... now go to bed." Esther put her fingers to her bleeding head. "I am fine."

"Only if you're sure?" Eleanor began.

"Go on now; if Caelan can go to bed, so can you."

Ash stood looking at her friend nervously, waiting for an explosion from Esther. Instead, Esther merely withdrew the familiar playing deck and threw it down, organising it with nimble fingers before reaching into her pocket and tearing open a new pack.

Silence overwhelmed the room as Esther fiddled with the cards, straightening them out and making a pattern as she sat at the table. She suddenly began humming the old nursery rhyme 'Oranges and Lemons'. It gave an ominous feel to the already tense room, which threatened to drown Ash. She was forced into speaking again to try and escape that feeling of total guilt.

"I don't ever remember seeing that kind of game before," Ash said, attempting to make conversation as she looked at the card layout, which featured two vertical rows of four cards each, separated by space enough for two more. Apparently the centre spaces were supposed to be occupied by foundations building up in suit.

Esther didn't look up. "It's called Four Corners. Features two decks, tricky as hell. But it can be played in a small space."

"You'll have to teach me."

"Why didn't you tell me about Hughes?" Esther asked blankly. The time for subterfuge was over.

"Thought you'd pull the con?"

"As if I don't have any demons following me," she said, not uncharitably.

"Well, I thought I lost him."

"You have for the time being," she sighed. "How long have you known that you were made by Hughes?"

"Never knew." Ash sounded unconvincing even to herself.

Esther fixed her with a penetrating gaze that seemed to go right through her. She was too smart to be tricked by the measly shrug of the shoulders that Ash had offered. She started firing questions at her. "Have you seen anything suspicious? Do you feel like you're being followed?"

"For God's sake, Esther, shut up!" Ash snapped. "Since when did you become a prosecutor, judge and jury, and I become a suspect standing in the dock?"

With visible effort, Esther let out a breath and unclenched her hands. She didn't say anything, just looked into Ash's eyes until she began to feel the guilt seep into her bones.

"Do you know how easy it would be for one of Holmes's men to get to you? We had a near-run thing with Hughes. He knows I'm here now, where I was hoping not to be." Esther took a deep breath. "God knows this is a crooked enough business – hell, if I wanted honest I'd be speaking to gardeners; they're about the only honest thing in this city. Except us! We have to trust each other, Ash."

She looked at Ash with concern and worry. Ash found she couldn't say anything intelligent or sarcastic in response. She was too busy staring into the depths of Esther's eyes and wondering why she suddenly felt she was on a kind of trial already. She looked away.

"I trust you so much, in fact, I *did* get caught saving your hide!"

Ash continued to look away, dreading the guilt that the master poker player would see there.

"Look at me."

"If you're looking for an argument then you've broken your arm overstretching. I did wrong, I know." Ash looked up at her and brusquely said, "All I'm asking for is a couple of days. That's all. Please."

Esther clenched her hands once more and turned her back. It was a decidedly cold gesture, and completely unexpected. "Go to bed."

"Esther?"

"Go to bed. Sleep."

Ash nodded and walked through to her bedroom. It overlooked the living room and she could clearly see Esther stacking the cards, with a glass of whisky next to her and her gaze subtly checking her charge.

Ash fell onto the bed, still fully clothed. The static sounded like cards beginning to be stacked and balanced on a coffee table. Maybe the static would not let Esther sleep, Ash thought as she drifted off into an exhausted slumber of her own, driven by the lullaby of the cards.

GIVING THE CONVINCER

SIXTEEN

"Coffee, anyone?"

"I'm not keen on strong coffee, but if you have a cup of tea?" Ash said politely.

She returned her gaze to overlook Kensington High Street, smiling as the jeweller's assistant asked everyone the same question and received similar answers in reply. It was a bustling Saturday; the tourists and the weekend Londoners had come in. It was only ten o'clock and the city was at its best.

It was a far cry from only an hour and a half before, when she had arisen to receive dirty looks from Caelan and Eleanor, and a dark look from Esther. They'd shared an almost silent breakfast before Esther had announced her intention to go into town and see the Natural History Museum with Caelan. When Ash had voiced her concern, Esther had just shrugged and told her it was up to them to persuade Holmes and Innocent that she was beyond his reach.

"Well, Durant?"

"As ever, Mr Innocent, you were astute to bring it here." The jeweller took off his glasses. "Yes, sir, this is the ruby."

He sat back and nodded in abject fascination as Holmes's

wife gasped softly at it. Ash rolled her eyes. Holmes had brought the woman here to make sure that Esther's painting was a fake – something even Innocent had shaken his head over.

"You'd swear I was lying to you; Crook said it was impossible to replicate," Ash said, smirking at the men.

"Never harms to check, nonetheless." Innocent carefully placed the ruby back in the box and then gestured at the photograph of the painting. "What do you think about that?"

"Obviously a fake – see the yellow mark here?" Elizabeth Holmes, wife of Harry Holmes, said.

"We use that to tell us a painting is false," Eleanor said, sipping her tea with a measured calmness. "Then we hide it behind the framing."

"Ingenious. What did the artist use for reference?" Elizabeth asked curiously.

"Wikipedia, of course; the original artwork was destroyed, apparently."

"A rumour, nothing more," Elizabeth said. "If you have enough money, it'll be available." She put her hands on her hips, eyes as predatory as her husband's. "Well? What happens?"

"I'm supposed to have persuaded you to buy the fake ruby – it'll be put in a fake setting. Then you show it off and she'll arrange for the flying squad to be there."

"I've already invited DCI Banks to a little soirée." Holmes grimaced theatrically. He did hate dealing with the police – even if it was in an 'honest' capacity.

"As I tried explaining to Azeri, you won't get Crook there," Eleanor said softly. "She won't step into the lion's den for any money."

"Who says she's going to be stepping in?" Holmes said, as Ash watched the jeweller sign some papers. "What are those?"

"Verification papers. Mr Innocent asked for them."

"I thought it might help other clients of your own," Innocent said thoughtfully. "So, Miss Clarke?"

"Thank you." Eleanor took these from him and tucked it into her pocket. "I will be certain to give this to Esther Crook also." She smirked. "Might help her with her other cons."

"You'll be making your leave?" asked Innocent as Ash made her way across the room.

"I need to tell Esther Crook."

"You've not told me the full con."

"You put the money into one account," explained Ash. "Then she walks away and you will be arrested, because she'll no longer have the verification documents on her."

Holmes nodded and raised his finger to interrupt, before his wife's phone began to ring.

"Would you like to take that?"

"No." The woman straightened her back. "I want to make sure that none of this attaches itself to us. My dear father is in line for a knighthood."

"Yes, it's important to us that our reputation stays intact, naturally," said Holmes. "Even if Esther is being arrested I want it made clear that I'm buying duds."

"I will make sure, when everything is discussed with Crook that the legal document will stand up in a court of law," Ash said. "I'll emphasise that you want it legal and binding with the wording." She began pulling on her coat. "I'll make sure you agree to it all legal and nice first. I'll also fill you in on what the idea is and who it is she's baiting."

"You think you can get me in contact?"

"I'll do my best," Ash said, holding out her hand to shake. Holmes ignored it. Ash knew why, too. She was now his underling and didn't deserve a handshake. She just shook her head. "I'll do my best."

"It's the best you can do," Innocent said, shaking her hand. "Anyhow, Lord willing and the creek don't rise, then we'll be on our way with the con."

Ash started at the turn of phrase.

"What's wrong? Never heard it?"

"I heard a friend use it recently."

"Esther Crook's father is fond of the expression, I believe," he said, smirking. "Never met the man, but heard Crook say it on a few occasions, normally with a deal of affection." He looked at the paperwork. "Several different buyers. Miss Crook sure is ambitious."

"Ambition is the mother of necessity."

Esther was sitting watching some old TV show, hands behind her head, as Ash came in. She threw a calm look at the door, before nodding on seeing her. Ash smirked. Esther hadn't even dressed in decent clothes. She'd had a pyjama day, and it made her laugh that even the ambitious Esther Crook had such things.

"How'd it go?" Esther asked, coughing.

"You don't know?" Ash said, walking through and hopping briefly as she pulled off her boots. "I would've thought Eleanor would've told you."

"She told me that she had some verification documents for the ruby," Esther said, looking idly at the television, and Ash chuckled when she saw the cards in front of her. "President's Cabinet, it's called, Ash; then the Leicester Square train was calling out her name… she had an appointment with Nancy to go over a few last details and get them out of the way. Then I suppose she'll be meeting her marks."

"Her marks?"

"Didn't think that I was only conning Hughes, did you?" Esther raised her eyebrows. "Hell, girl, we need money out of here if this goes belly up."

"So you've been conning other people?"

Esther nodded.

"Who?"

"First one is Eleanor's choice, by the name of Gideon Royale. He's an American loudmouth who likes nothing more than betting on the British horse-racing calendar and thrashing horses. Got away with beating up his wife last year; poor woman walked into a door so badly that she was in hospital for three weeks. But he likes prizes that he can't win, and that is one." Esther snorted. "He's in for £250,000."

"And there are others?"

"One is Terrell Custer-Parry. A self-made Welshman who loves the stories behind the stones… the mysticism and all that bull. He's not above trading in blood diamonds, however. The last one I'm very fond of: James Conklin-Pope. He's a specialist in rare gems who accused my grandmother of stealing the ruby. I made him pay an extra £100,000." She gestured for Ash to join her. "Memorise those faces and names. They'll be handy in the future if anyone asks you any questions. Use them as your layer of security."

"Something's got under your skin, though?" Ash asked, sitting next to her and looking at the printed photographs of the men.

"Aye, they're old bastards, and they want to see it in the bank. They insist on paying by cheque into a bank account. I'm setting it up in your proper name," Esther said casually. "Holmes will go ballistic when he sees that."

"So you're pulling a tiger by the tail?" Ash asked, smiling at Esther's eager nod. "That's one hell of a chance, though."

"It gets the ball in my court. He'll be that irritated, he's bound to want me all the more, and if you don't take chances," said the woman in the striped pyjamas, "you might as well not be alive."

This is one hell of a chance.

Anton stepped out of the shadows and took in the view of everything within the seemingly empty and silent house. There was constant surveillance here from one of those 'three-letter agencies', as Esther had less than kindly referred to them.

But they weren't interested in him, and, who knew, it might play to Esther's advantage at some point in the future, he mused. In any case, there was no question that the job had to be done tonight. Tomorrow would definitely be too late, and that would require the redrafting of an entirely new plan and wasted outlay in preparation for this one.

Reservations aside, and he always had them, he knew that even in the worst-case scenario, he could escape without any difficulty.

The risks were worth the challenge and the challenge was even more priceless. Esther, in her infinite wisdom, had always remarked that that was why they got along so well. They had the same daredevil nature when it came to their working alliances.

God, how he loved that woman.

Shaking his head before he began to wax nostalgic, the Russian stepped onto the ledge of the building. He was dressed head to toe in black, and his head and hair were covered in some mixture that Caelan had cooked up to hide his body temperature... damn modern technology. He glanced at the watch on his wrist, reassuringly analogue, and pressed the timer on the side. He had exactly twenty-five minutes to get in and out of the building. Anything more would be just plain sloppy. Making sure he was adjusted, he slid his full body length down the window and dropped the five feet onto the thin ledge, landing like a cat. He glanced down at the extra sixty foot. *Weirdly built property*, he thought to himself.

He quietly shuffled to the window and broke into a grim grin. The windows were locked by a fancy mechanism, and, as expected, the night provided the anonymity he required to break into it. This client – no, *victim*, he corrected himself – was not averse to spending good money on security. He chuckled. The best art galleries used these mechanisms. In fact, he'd first come across one at the Louvre three months ago when he'd been doing his 'honest' job as a penetration tester. He'd not revealed all the faults for fear that the lock might become too specialised against the criminally minded and reveal some family secrets.

Reaching into his pocket, he withdrew his small computer and decoder, hand-built for such an occasion, and a screwdriver to unscrew several screws to the right of the machine. Soon enough, the system yielded and the windows clicked. Anton grinned quick and feral, rapidly putting away his items and clambering indoors. He hovered precariously on the windowsill, checking for any observer, though he had no doubt that there was no one available. This building was on the same security detail as the rest of the street, meaning that a private security patrolman searched the house, or rather the downstairs, in thirty minutes… hence Anton's plan to be finished in twenty-five. It kept things interesting.

"Now, where are we?" He pulled out a copy of the blueprints that he had collected from the county clerk's office in LA the previous day, marvelling at how easy it had been with a small amount of flirting, and how he had devised a way around all the gallery's security measures.

Anton studied the plans, tapping the floor with his foot briefly before nodding with satisfaction at what was to come next. Kneeling to put the map back, he withdrew a set of night-vision goggles which would be useful both for any nasty little added features the place had acquired in the two years since the blueprints had been drawn, and so that he didn't need to fumble around in the darkness. Immediately, the lenses turned everything before him a shade of green and allowed him full perception of every obstacle. He chuckled as he jogged lightly down the stairs, scolding himself when he added a cocky little bounce to his step. It didn't pay to be cocky. He would have to teach Ash that at a later date, he decided.

He was barely breaking a sweat by the time he reached the room in question. Now it got interesting. This room, despite being open and easy to enter, was complete with motion-tracking devices, infrared and sonic detectors. People relied on technology far too often these days, Anton thought to himself as he paused in the corridor. It made them cocky. It made them vulnerable.

His surname, Volkov, meant 'wolf', and Anton wondered if it was something to do with his kin being like wolves in sheep's clothing. All brain, using brawn only when needed and resourceful as hell. He grinned wolfishly as he pulled out the sonic emitter from his other pocket. He had brought it here in his official capacity as a penetration tester, but nobody had paid much mind to him keeping it with him.

Flicking a switch on the device, the emission was silent. At least to his human ears. Anything canine would be going crazy, and in the distance he could hear one dog yapping. He'd sling a few dollars to a pet charity later. However, despite its cruelty to mutts, the emitter would disable the sonic detectors surrounding the room and allow him to pass through that particular safeguard without setting off its alarms.

He stepped confidently into the room, grinning wolfishly once more. The work hung there, illuminated by an expensive light that showed up each and every natural flaw. It sat almost arrogantly against the wall, convinced that nothing could be stolen. He grinned and checked the three tubes in his backpack. Perfect for carrying items he needed, and then he glanced at his watch.

Fifteen minutes.

Yes, plenty of time.

SEVENTEEN

"Listen, I can only speak to you for a brief time," whispered Ash into the phone as she looked in at where the three others were sleeping.

There had been an unspoken air of tension today. Once they'd all returned from their respective jaunts, nobody had spoken much, other than to put in requests for coffee and tea.

Innocent was equally quiet as he spoke back. "Yes?"

"You wanted to know their routines?"

"Damn it, girl, just tell me."

"Esther has chronic insomnia; she either plays cards or watches old films to try and get herself to sleep so she doesn't fall asleep while talking to Anton, her partner. She takes a walk in Hyde Park every Monday. But she doesn't keep to a set path," Ash said, feeling bile rise within her as she made her observations known. "She likes to eat in Covent Garden."

"Good a place as any for a public ambush. What about the boy?"

"Caelan works a proper job at night but hasn't said what; just that it's short term and he's glad of it. In the day he goes to Nunn's and offers himself as a stunt double."

"And this Eleanor character?"

"No idea. She doesn't trust me enough."

That was true now. Time wouldn't heal everything, especially not broken trust, and Eleanor looked at Ash with suspicion. While Esther and Caelan had seemingly accepted her escape, Eleanor didn't share their optimism.

"Fine, what about the Spanish Prisoner?"

"From the sounds of it, Esther's going to pretend that the person inlaying the jewel is going to be either raided or accused, and the cop on duty recognises it and wants a lump sum, especially given that Esther's in the wrong circles with the gambling community to be stealing from them." Ash took a deep breath. "She's really annoyed about the three other marks."

"Why?"

Ash smirked as she remembered Esther's rant when Eleanor had come back. "They've all asked to put cheques into a bank account; Esther expected as much because they're all older people. One infuriated her grandmother or something." She took a deep breath. "Do you think you'd let me get the money?"

"How much are you going to take from Holmes?" Innocent asked tiredly.

"Esther seems to reckon that we tell him £1 million for the con that he thinks we're setting up. After all, the jewel is insured for fifteen times that. It seems reasonable that a jewel setter would want it for only slightly less, so approximately £750,000."

"A fair price... do you have a timescale for this?"

Ash shook her head, but then realised that the motion couldn't be seen. "Esther has another insurance policy she's been waiting on, and she's waiting for Caelan to get out of the spotlight."

"She's a good sister," Innocent said, fleeting admiration clear in his voice. "Let us hope she provides us both with the gift of time to ourselves."

"Mr Innocent... promise me you'll not kill her," Ash pleaded. "She lost her mother too in that stunt."

"She lost more than that. Fine. I promise that, if Holmes breaks any deal we have made together, I'll release both you and her from her bonds."

"You swear? On all that you hold dear?"

"I swear on the grave of my wife and the life of my daughter… I will have no part in her killing," Innocent said.

And Ash knew, there and then, that, as Esther had promised, Ezra Innocent was a man of his word.

Done, and with time to spare.

Anton stepped back to look at his work, nodding with satisfaction. He worked his way over to the object of his desire, taking photographs with the infrared camera and smiling to himself before he walked off and picked up the sonic emitter. He sighed as he walked to the top of the stairs and glanced at his watch, heading into another room.

No security. There was no need for a dingy office with a safe blatantly on the wall, looking old-fashioned. Practically invited hijacks… but then, the fact that it was in plain sight probably meant there were more valuable things inside. Oh, how Anton loved the human condition. So vulnerable to being read – hide the valuables in plain sight.

Pulling out a stethoscope – what could he say; he was a technophobe – he began the easy process of breaking the safe. Nine… back four… six… forward… two… one…

There was a satisfying click, at which point Anton tore open the safe door and grinned as he saw the boring brown pieces of paper. Quickly, he withdrew them and placed them on the table, studying them as reverently as a vicar studies his Bible. Nevertheless, he'd met a few churchgoers in his time and none had been particularly holier-than-thou.

"Aha!" he said aloud, smiling happily as he jabbed one piece of paper, taking off his backpack and pulling out the matching papers. "Just as I thought; exactly the same. Let's see what we have here… aha! We have the proof that aliens exist! Ah, for you American fans out there, we have where Hoffa's head is buried… who shot JFK… who *really* shot JR? Where the rest of Hoffa's buried…"

The silence answered him as he began to study the items intently, nodding as he photographed each item with the infrared and then tucked the one set of papers back into his bag and the others into the safe. He reached into his backpack, added one last item and withdrew another, tucking this into his trouser pocket. He quickly shut the safe and locked it again, leaving behind a practically useless little gadget he'd picked up in Russia when he'd been visiting Uncle Fyodor.

He glanced at his watch and smirked as he looked outside, seeing a Keystone Cop. Correction – these were bargain basement cops who relied mostly on technology to do their work rather than actual mental and physical competence. He could make out the shape. Poorly trained. Probably spotty as anything. Really, for their security, the people in this neck of the woods were rather lacking.

"Must add a bit of spice to his day," he said to himself resolutely.

Anton walked to the door and turned on the light, grinning as he saw the car that had just started down the driveway in the distance stall. Poor boy. Poor girl. He chuckled and broke into a run, heading towards his entrance point. Poor kid wouldn't find—

"Freeze!"

Instantly, he skidded to a halt and then laughed as he realised the kid had entered the entrance hall. Good diversion tactic to get a bit of a lead on where the intruder was. His expectation of poorly paid security guards went up. Damn, their response time was fast!

Running by a vase that looked decidedly Ming Dynasty (but his years of training with his family told him was categorically fake), Anton grinned as he grabbed the item and flung it behind him.

The noise brought footsteps up the stairs and Anton beamed in delight as he stepped into his forgotten escape route, hidden behind a doorway. Feet soon thundered by him and he ran in the same direction they'd come from, straight outside to the still-running car with the keys in.

Arrogance didn't pay, but seizing golden opportunities did. He laughed as he heard frantic yelling from well behind him as he sped down the drive and through the still-open gates.

Once safely three miles away, he pulled into an alley in a less-than-savoury neighbourhood. He dug into his pocket and withdrew both the book and his burner phone. He held up the book, admiring it as he made a call. "Got it, for the right price, of course. You have it? Good. I can't wait to tell Esther about this. And don't you worry... no evidence of it being me or her. Does this mean I can start calling you Dad now?" He smirked with satisfaction as he terminated the call to a verse of expletives worthy of a sailor.

Such a family business, he thought as he got out of the car, tucking his leather gloves in the pocket before walking away. He'd wiped down the car thoroughly, and quietly withdrew Caelan's bottle of 'magic goop' from his backpack.

"Stinking habit," he muttered, lighting a cigarette that somebody had lit for him when he'd faked struggling to light up outside the City Office today. They'd soon receive a knock at the door from the LAPD. He threw the goop in with particular viciousness and tossed the lighter and cigarette in together, before stepping back as he put the phone once more to his ear. He watched for a brief moment as the magic goop took light, consuming the car in flames. As the handler buzzed a greeting in his ear, he answered in his best Bostonian accent. "Yes, 911? Oh, fire and police, please. I just saw somebody set fire to a car. Yes, I'm on 91st Johnston Street... oh yes, as soon as possible. I think it's been stolen... yes, I can wait. Oh, wait, you want a witness? I think you misunderstand... I'm the person that stole it and burned it up."

Anton broke into a grin before throwing the phone into the

flaming car. All evidence destroyed bar his backpack and himself. He smiled as he strode away, the flames highlighting his shape as he walked into the shiftless morning sun.

And Esther thought that con artists had all the fun.

EIGHTEEN

"Nancy, I've said it before and I'll say it again: you're a goddamned gem."

Nancy laughed as Esther held up the jewel to the light, studying it intently with a grin on her face that could've swallowed a watermelon "You should've seen their faces when they seen it, Est. It's gorgeous."

"It's a beautiful setting."

"I had LeRoy ask his brother to design it. It's an eighteen-carat rose gold with that bloody ruby centre."

"Didn't know Greg LeRoy had such a talent," Esther said, fishing in her pocket for the payment. "How much do I owe?"

"Oh, you didn't know? Greg's working for Asprey of London now. Honest boy, unlike us," Nancy said, shaking her head in amusement. "And on the tick, says the father, if you can get Caelan to consider that stunt."

"Caelan would sooner chop his left hand off than do that stunt; he told me that last night," Esther laughed. "Seriously, how much?"

"Just do it on tick, for me this time," Nancy said, smiling. Sadness overwhelmed her eyes for a few seconds. "Luke Gaines was good to us when times were hard." She saw Ash and patted her shoulder, then held out her hand to Esther. "It's been an honour working with you officially for the first time."

"Well, we'll meet again soon enough." Esther shook hands with the young woman. "I'll make sure to invite you to the wedding."

"The first wedding in the cells of Monte Carlo," joked Nancy, before looking at Ash. "Good luck, kid. You've been trained by the best short-con man and long-con woman… you shouldn't need it."

Eleanor jogged in lightly and smiled.

"Eleanor, Dad got you tickets. You'll get into Denver nice and early. You need to get out of here."

Eleanor nodded and handed over an iPad to Esther, before sharing a hug with her. "As Ash can see, the payment is all in the account, and as far as they are all concerned, we have walked away into the sunset like Butch Cassidy and the Sundance Kid."

"You do realise they get shot at the end of that movie?" Esther teased.

"But live on in the matters of eternity," Eleanor shot back, looking hard at her friend.

Esther gave her a dirty look from where she was beginning to make her way out of the building. There was a taxi waiting outside, which made all three of them stop dead. It felt like a final hurrah and a farewell mixed together.

"Hopefully when this con is over," Eleanor said, before sharing a hug with the two of them.

Ash asked quietly, "Est, are you sure about this?"

The two looked at her.

"You're sure you don't—"

Eleanor smiled and gave Ash a tight hug. "Don't worry. Es is usually right… and I'm sorry for treating you so rotten lately."

"Understandably; you thought I'd betrayed you all."

Eleanor patted her cheek a few times before looking at Esther. "Ciao."

"See you in a few days," Esther said, kissing both of Eleanor's cheeks in the French style and offering a small smile in fond farewell.

The two watched her clamber into the taxi and drive off into the distance. Ash felt her heart sink lower than her knees. All Esther's colleagues and friends were out of the picture. There was just her and Esther. The woman she was set to betray, but equally aimed not to. She'd just have to work like a devil, get the money and get set to run for their lives; make them believe it was a day or two. She'd never given dates. They'd believe that.

"Where's your head at, kid?" Esther's voice broke through and Ash spun on her heel to see her standing over by the wall, leaning on it. "Certainly not on the con."

"Yes, it is," Ash said, a bit too quickly. "Just…"

"I told you once that you should take any deal that Innocent offered to you," Esther said quietly. "I advise you again: take him into your confidence."

Ash coughed nervously. "Est…"

"Make the call; I have to go to the Natural History Museum," Esther said, beginning to walk off. "When the con is off, just text me. We'll be on the run from now on; I'll meet you at Leicester Square Tube Station."

Ash watched the shadow disappear into the distance, before looking heavenward. Redemption did not offer itself. Instead she texted Innocent of the plan with silent tears dribbling down her cheeks as she realised she had signed her friend's death warrant, and had now waved a merry goodbye to any chance of redemption as hastily as she wiped the tears away.

After all, she had an appointment to keep.

"What do you mean, the artist won't hand it over? Let alone that Esther Crook has already conned the others?!"

Holmes had never heard of anything so ridiculous. A con woman being conned by an understudy whom she'd hired to do a job. It amused him to no end.

Azeri stood in front of him nervously. "I can't help it! I know that Innocent's told you part of the line, but Crook moved so quickly I couldn't do a goddamned thing to stop it."

Holmes looked across at Innocent, who was leaning on his desk, a silent predator as always.

"How much is he asking for?"

"£750,000," she said demurely.

Innocent scoffed.

"Well, the other marks have paid!" She thrust out the iPad after unlocking it and the payment screen. "All via cheque, which has really wound Crook up."

"They take days to clear," Innocent said, realising exactly what Crook was supposedly angry over. "Payment's there, but hasn't cleared yet."

"So Crook doesn't have the funds to pay him off." Holmes let out an evil little chuckle. "So I'm saving the little con that Crook has in line for me? Oh, the joy!"

"The irony is not lost on anyone," Innocent said drily. "And when is Crook planning her con?"

"This weekend," Ash said quietly. "She's gone to the Natural History today to do some last-minute research into the jewel."

Holmes looked at the bank account with a smug grin. £750,000 wasn't a great amount to someone like him, and it meant direct funds. He would have Crook in his grasp. He watched Ash's face. It must've been hard to admit that her great mentor had failures, but there was no time for sentiment. He smirked and watched her retreat, satisfied.

"Happy with yourself?" Innocent asked suddenly.

"Of course I am. From both your information and Azeri's, we will have Crook in our grasp by this weekend."

"Strange about the jeweller. You've not met him until now... and yet he needs money," Innocent said, as Holmes watched Ash disappear into the mist of Hyde Park.

"So? He got nervous, or saw how Crook was raking it in;

decided to get in on it himself," Holmes snapped, then froze. "Wait. A friend in trouble who can't be seen… Crook's played the girl! It's the Spanish Prisoner."

He began to pace in horror. The Spanish Prisoner was one of the oldest cons (that still worked) in the book. It was based upon a confidence trickster using somebody or an imaginary friend needing finance, under some sort of pressure. Many years before, the tale had been built around a person of high estate who had been imprisoned in Spain under a false identity and needed funds. Supposedly, the prisoner could not reveal his identity without serious repercussions.

"I swallowed it! I actually swallowed it, and from the look on that kid's face, she swallowed it too!" Holmes looked out of his window, praying to see Azeri but seeing nothing but the mist. "And she walked out of here! She modernised it, made it seem like she was the hostage."

"Crook likes the classics, and it's just as well, as I got the address and have already sent Vin." Innocent flashed a nasty little smile. "He's been following Crook since she left the Natural History Museum. The tiger is within my trap. Let's go collect the hide."

"This is Leicester Square."

The sterile tunnels of the London Underground were familiar territory for Esther Crook, just as she knew nearly every public transport system in most major cities. They were her escape routes and her salvation. She knew every crack in every tile, every dot of gum on the floor, the optimum places for the musicians who performed in the winding passageways to stand to achieve the best acoustics. She leaned on the wall briefly, as she listened to a rather impassioned violin playing 'Clair de Lune'.

"I thought we were meant to be running?" Ash asked, playing with her bag as she joined her.

Esther chuckled darkly. She had sent the young woman to buy an Oyster card, not allowing her the old trick of dodging the train fare. It was dishonest to say the least. Something no honest crooked individual would involve themselves with. "I am. You are sulking in the moment, but I'm just enjoying the atmosphere," she replied.

"You can be sneakier than a polygamist at a family get-together when you get an idea stuck in your pretty head." Ash squinted thoughtfully in the direction of Esther's gaze. "What're you thinking?"

"I'm thinking we've just been made by Vin." Esther's voice was calm and collected. "Hand me the bag, please?"

Ash felt all the blood drain from her as she handed Esther the bag. She suddenly felt an iron grip on her elbow. She turned to be met with bright green eyes aflame with concern.

"Don't you dare run!" snapped Esther out of the corner of her mouth. "You run and we are stuck. I warned you about that before."

"Why are you so calm?" Ash snapped, directing her rage at Esther, the two surveying the room as calmly as possible.

"Patience is a virtue for both cards and cons." Esther looked around casually. "You got it?"

Ash turned her gaze and saw the Tube coming into the station. Their exit. "I got it," she replied. She held out her hand to Esther, regardless. "Nice doing dealings with you, Miss Crook."

"Likewise." Esther shook the hand with the firm brusqueness attached to business dealings, before waiting to be jogged along by the commuters.

The two allowed themselves to be pushed along, Ash watching as both Esther and Vin occupied the same carriage as herself, but Esther remained at the end, within Ash's view. Ash watched as Hughes boarded her carriage. She pretended not to notice as they juddered through the various stations.

Esther tapped the window and spoke loud enough for Ash to hear as they came into a new station. "Our change. Next platform."

The two exited, walking towards the platform, buffered by the midday commuters. When the next Tube came in, Esther grabbed Ash by the elbow to stop her getting on. She waited until most had boarded before they stepped on, Hughes and Vin joining them.

"Nice to see you both again," said the oily Welshman.

"Nice to see you too, Lenny," Esther said politely with a firm smile.

Ash tensed as she felt Esther's hand once more on her elbow. As the train doors began to close, she realised what Esther was about to do and prepared herself just as Esther threw her through the doors and followed in one swift movement. Behind her, Ash heard the slams of two bodies against the door. She spun on her heel and let out a small laugh as she saw Hughes and Vin rammed up against the glass. Vin was looking wryly at Esther departing up the stairs, while Hughes was obviously cursing at her. She merely smiled and followed Esther up the stairs; they kept a respectful distance.

Ash dodged through the crowd, blending and blurring with the people. She waited for that iron grip before Esther dragged her to one side outside the station.

"Where are we going?!" Ash snapped. "That's not going to slow down a bounty hunter on our heels."

"Easy – back to the apartment where we spent our last evening!" Esther looked around. "I'll take the long route; you get in and wait for me!"

Ash darted into the dark, busy street, quickly making her way to the next street where the building was. The tingling sensation of being followed was more intense than before, but adrenaline helped her navigate the streets as quickly as she ever had. Vin had the advantage of being a bounty hunter, but she knew this area and he did not. *Home advantage and all that stuff*, Ash thought to herself. Her heart was thumping from both excitement and more than a tinge of fear.

A young man was exiting her building and let her in, recognising her from that brief interaction the previous week. She knew the door would lock behind her, and ran up the stairs to the flat. She didn't see anyone, but knew in her gut that Esther had led them away to give her time. She threw open the door to her floor and scrambled down the corridor, then rounded the hallway corner to open her door, her key falling to the ground in her haste.

Finally, she let out a long breath as she stepped inside, followed by Esther a few minutes later. Esther panted and went to lock the door, when it burst open and sent her sprawling to the ground with the force of it.

"Did you really think you'd outrun me?"

Instantly, Esther let out a loud yelp as she began to thump at Vin, who deftly grabbed her and heaved her up.

"Stop it! Christ!" The two ended up on the floor, Vin straddling Esther over her middle and holding his hand over her mouth. "Will you shut your mouth and just listen to me, you little shit? And don't even think of hitting me, Ash, or I'll have you upside down from an outside window."

"Hi, Vin," Esther greeted him as she lay on her back, him still straddling her. "Rather glad you bumped into me in the Natural History, right now."

"This way, brat!" he said, dragging her up. "You know how worried your father has been? You know how much effort it took to arrange everything for you?!"

"Well, it's not my fault," she said, as he touched her forehead where the cut was healing still. "Needed to get him good and distracted. I take it, it worked?"

"It worked all right."

Esther brushed herself down as Vin cursed. "What happened to Hughes? I thought I saw him with you?"

"Seems he was that busy watching your skinny ass, he forgot to look where he was going and fell into the gap between the Tube and the platform edge."

"The man had enemies of his own," Esther replied ambivalently. "As I am sure you are well aware."

"He'll be out of commission from that fall." Vin looked hard at her. "Might not walk again. Might not even survive."

"What a shame," Esther said, smirking. She jerked her arm free of his hold, ignoring his glare. "What?!"

"Holmes is after you. There is no honour in that man."

"Then you shouldn't be helping Innocent, should you?" she snapped. "The poor kid is beating herself up thinking that I was annoyed thinking she'd done the betraying here."

"Well, she can stop that for a start," he muttered. "I promised your old man that you'd see each other shortly. Your con is over."

"Fine. Can I pack—" She broke off as she heard the front door being opened. "No one's due home. I have them timed." She ran over to the still-open door, to the stairs that Ash had fled up only a few moments before. She returned a few seconds later. "They're earlier than I thought, even for Innocent."

"Somebody's ratted you out that isn't this little fool," Vin said, throwing her a look. "Somebody has you made."

"Quick, Ash, get your boots off – I'm not kidding," Esther said as Vin took off his belt. "Do you trust me?"

"You've never given me reason not to trust you with my life; just not to when you're playing cards," said Ash, as Vin pulled Esther to him.

Vin looked hard at her, already using his belt to fashion a lasso around Esther's wrists. "How're you with knots, Est?"

"Crap. Can't you just handcuff me and I can make a daring escape like the last time?" Esther asked, wincing at the tightening. "You're doing that on purpose."

"Should've just told me that you were planning this scheme," he said. "Spanish Prisoner, Est? Even I know that one."

"Innocent told you?" Ash asked, smirking at him – of course he would've.

"Damn it, Ash, keep your mouth shut!" snapped Vin, tying her hands behind her back. "Est, do you mind taking a hit?"

"Slug in the face, if you please," Esther said. "I don't fancy any more hits to the st—"

She fell silent as Vin smashed his open palm across her face, knocking her out. Ash looked at him, surprised.

"What? Did you think she'd go with hair all combed? Now, give me your hands… need it to look good at least."

Vin had only just finished tying Ash's hands together when, as one, Holmes and Innocent strode decidedly into the apartment. Holmes wore a triumphant look on his face, but it faltered when he saw Vin standing there, putting Esther in some sort of trunk that barely fit her body.

"I figured the girl was willing to come," he said politely. He glanced at Holmes and Innocent. "Since you've all been working together."

"Good. As soon as you get her to the townhouse, tie her up and fix her cheek. After all, I have a party I wish her to attend." Holmes smirked.

THE STING

NINETEEN

The apartment overlooked Hyde Park, which looked strange from this high vantage point. It was a pretty green pasture in an urban jungle. Harry Holmes looked at the view with jaundiced eyes.

The girl Azeri stood in front of him. She had tried to run with his money, taken her chances with a woman he'd looked to break.

"The Spanish Prisoner? Did she really think I wouldn't see it?" scoffed Holmes, as Innocent stood with arms folded across his chest. Innocent looked displeased at the suggestion that Holmes had thought of it himself, but then again he was annoyed that Vin had only *just* managed to capture them.

"I think she was working on the idea," Ash said patiently, "that it would be so obvious that she'd not be spotted."

She was bold, Holmes had to give her credit for that, but he was done being played; he wouldn't let himself slip in front of this comedian. "Do you know what you cost me? The honour?"

"What honour?"

Holmes snorted. "You know everything in this world; our – and yes, I mean our – world, is about reputation. I couldn't let it get around that I let a grifter make a fool of me, could I? You understand that, Azeri?"

Holmes worried that Azeri could tell that he half-wanted to see that she did indeed understand. It was pure business. Even Innocent understood that. She was an added bonus.

"Yeah, I get that you're nothing but business—"

Before she could get any further, Innocent moved and punched her in the stomach. She doubled over, coughing and spluttering.

"Silence, my girl, would be wiser."

The girl threw her head up, still struggling to catch her breath. Openly hurt, but defiant and angry. Holmes was almost admiring of her insolence in the face of the cold, harsh reality that awaited her. A quick death was too easy, much too easy.

"Yeah, I was never exactly good at that."

Holmes walked around the desk and got in Azeri's face. Brown eyes glared balefully at him. He opened his mouth to speak, only for the girl to spit at his cheek. He growled and wrenched her in so that they were nose to nose.

"I can't let it get around that you were in my city and escaped punishment. When I'm done with Crook, she'll be begging to be sitting pretty in one of my brothels."

"Just get on with getting your pound of flesh." The girl flashed a nasty little smile. "You follow?"

"Want me to give her to the boys?"

The girl's head jerked to the left at this implied threat from Paulsen.

"No. Just… make her less pretty tomorrow night. It's too bad she has a dinner party to attend." Holmes tossed a look at them. "And you didn't know?"

"Not really, no; Crook told me that the job had altered slightly and it was time to bow out once your funds were in. I could see the funds had gone in and I phoned Innocent to warn him of exactly that."

Ash winced at a particularly loud bang from inside his office. "What's going on?"

"Making sure everything is safe and secure, including that

beguiling jewel Esther Crook had secreted on her person," Holmes said.

There was a string of loudly spoken Eastern European, though whether curse words or not, Ash was unsure.

"New safe. Keeps things safe... unlike your little deal with Innocent... now I know who you are underneath it all."

"Christ, Harry, I gave the kid my word!" Innocent snapped, trying to step forward to stop them, only to be shoved back.

"I didn't give mine." Holmes looked at Paulsen. "Take her away." He smirked. He could see the anguish on the girl's face, but he had plans for her. Not nefarious ones... or not, at least, in the way she was thinking at the moment.

She'd be a good lieutenant, with the head she had on her shoulders. If this plan of hers worked out, he could mould her into his shape; beat the ridiculous idea that she was a con artist out of her head with kindness. She couldn't be much older than Henry. Perhaps he'd suggest a merger. He'd had to kill fathers of useful sons, sons of useful fathers. Other times he'd offered them power; other times offered them mercy. It occasionally worked, and often didn't.

He wondered if, when she heard Esther Crook scream for mercy, she'd break too.

"Do you know what time it is?"

"Well, the sun's down, so it must be after six," Ash said, frowning.

"That makes sense. Was just wondering."

For someone who had been betrayed by her protégée, Esther was dealing with it remarkably well, Ash thought. Or...

"You knew I'd do it, didn't you?"

"Take Ezra Innocent's deal? I was rather banking on it," Esther said, smirking at her as she wiggled her fingers.

"Think they're going to cut you down from there?"

"I doubt it. It reminds me of that poem by Noyes. Or is it

Robert Louis Stevenson? Something about a landlord's daughter... I remember that much."

Ash looked up at where Esther had been tied up. She had several ropes tied around her wrists and arms. One wrong move and her wrist would break; Vin had emphasised that point. As Esther's 'honest' work was playing poker, she'd quickly acquiesced. Ash was lying spread-eagled on the bed, each of her limbs tied to a bedpost.

"Noyes... it's *The Highwayman*." Ash looked up miserably. "I did it for my exams this year. Luke drummed it into me."

"Really?" A nod in her direction. "I had to do three Shakespeare plays between fourteen and sixteen. I did them for fun then until I remembered the quotes."

"Any in particular that you like?" Ash said, tugging uselessly at the rope that bound her.

"Have a preference?" Esther said, throwing a hooded glance up the bed.

"How about one about death? Seems like we're walking to our own."

"Nah, we're just acting in a play called life," Esther said, before smirking to herself. "And actors are better con artists than us. They get paid for being liars in honest capacities."

Ash snorted through her nose. "Shakespeare?"

"Nah, some American actor. True enough, though, con artists are actors," Esther hummed, as the doorknob was jostled. "Ah – our hostess."

Elizabeth Holmes entered, sharing a scowl with Esther, before pulling out some dresses. "I've estimated your sizes."

"You know, I never had you down for a trafficker," Esther said, smirking at the woman as she shot her a glare. "Oh yeah, plausible deniability."

"You'd know all about that, Crook. By the time we're done with you, you will be known all through London." Elizabeth glared as she cut Esther down before holding the knife to Ash's throat. "And any more smart-mouthing will lead to a few new cuts."

"I'd sooner die than become your pawn, and if you lay that knife on the kid's throat, I'll make sure you never recover from the storm I will arrange to hit you," Esther said, sticking her chin out defiantly.

"You haven't got enough power?"

"I'm on first-name terms with most of the social elite in Monte Carlo, who, I hasten to remind you, you are desperate to fit in with. Not to mention that I was the ward – as dated as the term may be – for Chris Adams, an ATF agent whose team has a 100% success rate. Think it over."

Elizabeth Holmes scowled. "Fit the damn dress and get out of here, or I get one of the boys to bring you out in whatever state of dress or undress you are in." She smirked. "And don't bother with the windows. We've upped security here since our apartment in LA was broken into."

"Anything stolen?" Esther said politely as she rubbed her wrist. Elizabeth Holmes shot her a look.

"Now, now. I'm not a thief, as you well know."

"No. Now get your backside down the stairs."

"Now, who am I to turn down such an invitation?" Esther flashed an unerringly false smile at her hostess, who stormed out at this slight. "Come on, we'd best bow out in style."

If Ash hadn't known any better, she would've sworn that Esther was deriving pleasure from being caught.

The party was the pinnacle of false high culture in Ash's opinion. She was being escorted around by Innocent and his bodyguard Jesse, who was talking extensively to her. Once Ash had been dressed in a red ballgown she had been dragged away from Esther and kept within her gaze.

Esther wore a black georgette satin one-sleeved gown with a black-and-gold metallic floral brooch. The long sleeve practically hid her arm to the fingertips. But then she opted to pretend to be networking, talking animatedly about the artwork on the walls, looking every inch an aficionado of the arts. Ash just felt, and knew she looked, like a fish out of water.

"You don't seem to be having a nice time."

Ash turned to see a dark-haired older woman standing next to her. "I'm… a bit indisposed," she said politely, deciding against irritating the gargantuan figure guarding her. "Mentally occupied, shall we say?"

"If you don't mind, could you read this?" the woman asked, gesturing to the card below the painting.

"Sure… it says it's a replica of Van Gogh's *Still life: Vase with Oleander*s. It was purchased very recently." Ash gestured at another painting on the wall. "*The Painter on His Way to Work*, also by Van Gogh… they all seem to be replicas of artworks that were stolen by the Nazis."

The woman nodded courteously.

"I think that is her work… looking at old paintings."

"So I have heard, and my particular interest lies with these pieces especially given their history," the woman said, smiling.

Ash was about to question this statement when there was a sudden clink of a spoon against a crystal glass that had everyone spinning around. Holmes was standing on a small platform wearing an ingratiating smile.

"It is with great honour that I welcome you here today, especially given the circumstances. As many of you will know, our very home was broken into a few weeks ago, but the perpetrators got away with nothing but indignity."

There were a few hollow laughs around the room.

"But we are here tonight because of one young lady. Esther Crook. Esther, if you could come over?"

Instantly, there were whispers. A lot of the bankers in London had heard the name spoken in corridors, almost as reverently as a prayer said in church. The underworld had naturally heard of her, but there was respect, too. Innocent raised his eyebrows as he saw several men tense, as did Ash, but unlike Ash, who remained in place, Innocent walked over.

"Miss Voleur?" he called as she made her way over.

"Yes, Mr Innocent?" she said, pausing to look at him as he stopped briefly next to Ash and the large bodyguard.

"Have you got your way out?"

Esther raised her eyebrows, and walked over at his motion for her to join them. "Holmes intends on breaking our deal?"

"Miss Crook?" called the man in question.

Esther raised her hand. "Voleur and I have some financial dealings."

There was a titter around the room.

"Of course, but if you could keep an eye on my friend? Once my business with Holmes is concluded, then we can discuss my options to escape."

"Why, yes, my fair lady."

Esther gave a tilt of her head in acknowledgement and winked at Ash as she passed by. She quickly stepped up to where Holmes was waiting.

"Now, as many of you here will know, me and Mr Holmes have a long, chequered history. He insists on calling me Esther Crook when I much prefer the name of Darnell Voleur," she said, taking on the speech and the box before he had a chance to move.

Holmes glared at her, the spotlight having been stolen.

"He once turned to me and said that the greatest gift for a woman is a blood red ruby." She smiled ingratiatingly at Elizabeth Holmes. "That is why I take delight in handing this beautiful ruby necklace to your lovely lady wife."

There was muted applause around the room as Esther stepped back, smiling at Holmes and gesturing for Elizabeth to take her place.

"Of course, there are necessary documents to sign?" Holmes said, baring his teeth in a very flimsy semblance of a smile.

"Of course," Esther said, smiling as Holmes handed the documents to her to read through.

Ash winced. The piece of paper set to hang her, and Esther had handed over the death warrant.

"Here's my John Hancock." Esther signed the document with a flourish. "Enjoy your moment in the sun."

"Now, DCI Banks."

There was a murmur through the crowd. Many in the room began looking at the walls anxiously.

"Please don't worry, ladies and gentlemen; the DCI is here to arrest the notorious criminal, Esther Crook."

Esther, however, walked by DCI Banks without an air of concern on her face, pausing to kiss the older woman who had shared the conversation with Ash about the Van Gogh. There was a quick nod, and Esther grinned before joining Ash.

"You took your time," Ash groused. "We need to get out of here."

"Just waiting for the fireworks," Esther said.

The police officer looked down at the ruby that had been set into the necklace. It looked so innocent, almost false. But the pigeon blood red colour and the star-like fault in the centre revealed what it was. If they hadn't already seen the news, she and her compatriots would be holding Esther Crook and reading her her rights. If they hadn't already walked through it with the Natural History Museum and Interpol, let alone that Isadora Cross-De Braun woman, then she would've been grinning delightedly. If she hadn't known any better, she would say she was going to derive some glee from being wrong.

"You know, Holmes, you're lucky I'm not charging you with wasting police time," DCI Banks said, smirking at the man's sudden change of expression. "You've bought exactly what you paid for. A good one, I grant you, but an imitation. Let alone, I have been on to Border Control, who assure me that Esther Crook has not entered the UK, and when I enquired with the Norwegian authorities they told me that she hadn't left the country since the last time she visited her grandmother, Isadora Cross-De Braun, in Monte Carlo last year."

"That's impossible. I heard it verified by a jeweller of good repute," snapped Holmes. "See…" He looked frantically in his pockets, patting them and finding nothing. "There… she's taken them."

Ash looked at Esther. "How—"

Esther just rolled her eyes and put one finger to her lips to indicate silence.

"Not quite. You see, it got caught up in the geologist Dr Victoria Jones's exhibition. It seems that they mixed it up somehow with the exhibition items that were going on to the Natural History Museum. Her poor graduate student sat through hours of interrogation with us, but it looks to be an innocent mistake." She handed the ruby back to Innocent. "It was verified this morning in the early hours. Seems your appraisal may have been done for *a* jewel… but not that one."

Holmes felt himself flounder, and all hope sink below his knees. The kid. The kid had sold him out… or Crook had allowed her to. Regardless, she was dead. Forget the bordellos or the backstreets. Dead.

Then he saw her face; pure shock and horror. Crook had conned her too. For all Azeri's planning, Crook had got around it. Half of him felt a strange delight; the other half still felt rage.

His feelings were interrupted by the police officer. "But this… this interests my learned colleague here," she said, pointing at the artwork on the wall. "This is *Vase with Oleanders* by Vincent van Gogh – am I correct, Mrs Du Barry?"

The older woman with greying hair stepped forward and appraised it in silence before nodding in satisfaction. "Do you have a receipt for this?"

"But of course." Elizabeth smirked, as her assistant went into the office for her.

They waited in silence, everyone captivated by the front-seat drama that was taking place. The assistant soon returned and handed her a billfold of the documents.

"I didn't realise that police salaries stretched to this. A very good reproduction."

Du Barry ignored Elizabeth as she studied the invoices that had been given to her. She, herself, brokered a small smile. "The very best kind, Mrs Holmes. Go ahead, Banks."

"Mrs Elizabeth Holmes, I am arresting you for the purchase of stolen goods."

"I've not… they are verified receipts!" snapped Holmes, gesturing at the paperwork.

The older woman merely put these into an evidence bag.

"What're you doing?"

"This, at first glance, looks to be the verified original which has been missing since 1940. These documents seem to suggest they fell into the Göring collection, that you purchased them from a well known dealer in Nazi artworks so these documents prove ownership to yourself." Du Barry smirked. "It's rare that someone hands something to us so willingly."

Innocent froze and spun towards where Esther Crook had been standing, to see only an empty space with no sign of Crook or Azeri, whose Christian name he hadn't even bothered to get.

"I hate you."

"No you don't. You love me with a passion. You just hate my methods because you don't see the madness. That's your trouble, you know; you don't see the creativity behind the methods. That's a new hint for you."

Esther ran down the stairs, practically skipping for joy. They'd slipped out of the room after she had quietly asked for the ladies for them both. Innocent's bodyguard had been willing to allow for bodily functions but then Esther had produced a derringer pistol – God knows where from – and cold-cocked him. Once in the toilet, Esther had reached beneath a sink and pulled out a bag, sticking her hand in withdrawing a set of uniform waitress clothes that had been walking around the party all evening. They'd changed into the clothes and then joined the mass of waitresses already leaving as the police made their way up the stairs.

"You could've told me."

"I told you the basics. I used your con; just improved it. You told him the truth; he just chose to believe that I would be stupid enough to fall into that trap. I'm surprised you didn't recognise Anton's voice when he was swearing in Russian... from my brief understanding, the safe was being awkward."

"How'd they do the painting?"

"Oh, that switch? Happened under Hughes's nose. All that security and it's all focused on you and me, who made *no* attempt to escape. Pity about the professional thief that's fixing your safe on the wall with his retired Uncle Fyodor."

Ash glared, feeling angry that it wasn't so much that she had been blind to the truth; it was just that she had seen the truth differently.

Esther looked at her as she walked down the stairs with measured calmness, Ash allowing herself to radiate the disapproval that she felt.

Esther evidently felt it burning into her back, as she turned her head slightly. "What?! You can't con an honest man," she recited. "Or woman."

"That you can't."

Esther stopped on the stairs, spinning around to glare at Ash.

"I have just opened the Pandora's box for Interpol's art fraud department?!"

Ash froze, realising her intention. "You got his reputation."

"The one damned thing he cares about beyond riches and the bitch who will sell him down the marketplace. The very reason he knocked her up was so he could leap on her family's respectability. And that high-born lady is nothing more than a Nazi-hoarding bitch. The rumours that have been whispered but were dismissed? They are true." Esther threw a defiant look up at the gallery. "That bitch has stolen artworks that were plundered by the Nazis and hidden behind doors. They've suspected her for years, but had no proof. The pieces belong to the families who were butchered. If she was a good, honest person she would've handed it over – this… this is a revenge for them. Plus, we've hit him where it hurts."

"But his family?"

"I never said I was below working at his level." Esther glanced at the man's Rolex Submariner watch on her wrist. "Now, we need to go; we don't have time for this debate." She slipped out of her heels and into a pair of flats in one fluid motion and began to run. "Come on, Ash! We have to beat the hangman!"

TWENTY

Holmes's goons slid into the parking area of the apparently newly named Henson's. Holmes got out of the car, closely followed by Innocent, who was wearing an equally grim look.

Holmes knew that Liz knew everything about his business; a silent partner, as it were. He loved the woman desperately, and that much was clear. She, he knew, loved their son and the notoriety, but had little affection for her fling that had resulted in a shotgun marriage thanks to her strictly Catholic father. She knew where the bodies were and where to bury him while playing the grieving widow. His only chance was Kat, who would have the invoices to show that they were being set up.

"Can I help, mate?" asked a foreman as Holmes approached.

"Where the hell is Kat?" Holmes snapped, seeing Innocent glaring balefully at him.

"Kat? Don't have no Kat here, mate," said the foreman, folding his arms across his chest. He'd seen how carefully she'd put away those verification papers.

"There was art stuff here," Holmes said, looking at him angrily. "People milling about. Kat was an overseer."

"There would be... it never closes, except Christmas Day

or for official business. And all the overseers are the grandsons and granddaughters of my father. This has been in the family for more than two hundred years, mate. The only time we vacate is when something big is going on – take last week, for example," the foreman said. "A couple of people came in from the London Commission. They were checking the building for asbestos. They closed the place down. They were verified, before you ask." He whipped out some papers. "Some worked for Terence Nunn; really nice job they did, too."

"May I see?" Holmes asked, as he looked at the paperwork. "Verified… and you said Terence Nunn?"

"Yeah, he's the best fixer-upper in all London."

Terence Nunn. Holmes's hands trembled lightly over the sheet of paper as he remembered what Hughes had told him. The blonde girl who had so kindly promised to help, no doubt closely resembled the girl he knew as Kat.

"The little bitch!" Holmes didn't wait for a reaction from the man as he stormed back to the car, where Ezra Innocent was glaring at him, looking as though he'd heard every word.

"She conned you again, didn't she?! One hell of a big con!" snapped the American, green eyes flickering with pure rage. "This has been one set up job from start to finish! And she got away!"

"I have Hughes after her right now!"

"I had her half an hour ago with Vin! But no. You had to go and make it into a con. Even I admit the pure balls of that girl make me wonder if they mixed up her gender at birth, and you walked right into it. You wanted her, you got her!" He slammed his hand on the car door. "Now I've got to go hunting again for her. Believe me, I have some serious thinking to do with my associates about my business dealings with you."

Holmes froze. The press. His press deals would disappear; he knew that. He'd be hung out to dry, and Innocent had always been prideful of the distance that he maintained between himself and the press. Would that be maintained? He'd almost certainly lost his business partner, and his dealings would never be the same. All the respectability he'd worked for, lost.

And Esther Crook was set to lose her life when he caught up with her.

"I don't see how you knew I was working for him."

Ash looked over at Esther as she put together the last of the boxes to empty the room. Esther glanced at her, before returning to writing on the boxes. They'd arrived back safely.

"I told you to, didn't I?" Esther said.

"There was no guarantee that I would listen to you," Ash said, sighing heavily. "You have an awful lot of faith in your team... Vin included."

"Vin's not a member of my team. My father? Yes, he runs with him. Me? Definitely not. As I said, he thinks I'm a brat," Esther said, with a small, dry chuckle. "But he did teach me a valuable lesson: that it's just a matter of looking and listening. You are terrible at cold reading, but I'm not."

"Am I really that bad?"

"In the words of Buck, you're a whole mess of tells to those of us that know you." Esther smiled.

Ash nodded, breaking into a grin as she looked into Esther's eyes. They were comforting... but also hid a thousand things. "So how did you get the other three's money?" she asked.

Esther laughed. "You have got to pay better attention. I got them to pay via cheque... which will bounce all the way to the bank."

"Wait..." Ash paused on the stairs, staring at Esther's retreating back. "They're con artists?"

"Yep, which is why I wanted the big reward." Esther laughed happily. "Do you know how much reputation he's lost being conned by me? Let alone that he spoke to the police... there's nobody in Europe who will deal with him right now."

"Est... Ash..."

Ash looked up straight into the eyes of Vin, and then Caelan. The latter was wearing an expression of grief.

Esther stood carefully. "How bad?"

"He's got us, sis." Caelan ruffled his hair. "I was sliding in Covent Garden when I saw some of his goons coming here. Lucky Vin was there. We got the bastard, but the text had been seen and sent."

"Est, there's no exit. He's watching the ports, including air…"

Esther ran her hands through her hair. There was a slight tremble to her countenance now.

"Listen, Est… I can get the kid out. Caelan told me some of the plan."

"Yeah, I know he did," Esther sighed as Caelan looked at her from behind Vin. "Cael, you have got to get out of here. He doesn't know you too well."

"Sis, I'm not leaving you."

"You damned well are! This is the only route that gets you out of here safe." Esther bit her lip. "In the safe, Vin, you'll find some needles. They've been pre-measured. It's quick, painless and easy."

"I won't leave you."

"Shut up, Caelan. I'm not telling you again. He's not looking for you. Organise the flights. Go on!"

"There's method in this madness," Caelan muttered, hugging his sister and then holding her out at arm's length to look at her. "When will we meet?"

"Soon, little brother, soon," Esther hissed, walking into the bedroom with Ash following. "Ash, I ask you to put your full faith in me from here on in." She held out her arm. "I'm ready, Vin."

"It's the best option, Est," he whispered. "And everything will be arranged. Sure you're okay with this?"

Esther merely maintained her gaze, even when she winced as the tracker tightened the belt on her arm. "You swear to me that you'll take care of her, Vin?"

"Never broken my word to you yet," he said.

"Don't BS me right now," Esther said, flexing her arm one last time. "Go on, Vin."

He looked at her sadly, and she caught his cheek with her other hand.

"Hey. It's for the best... do me a favour, though?"

"Anything."

"Don't let the kid see me die like this."

Vin tenderly touched her cheek and lay her back down on the bed.

"Shut the door, please, Vin."

"I'll stay until it's over, okay?" He looked through at Caelan. "Keep her in there; we'll arrange the rest."

"Arrange the rest of what?!" Ash demanded.

"My sister's last wish was that you have faith in her," snapped Caelan, as the door was kicked open by Vin.

For a brief moment, Ash saw that Esther was lying still on the bed, and she looked at the man with panicked eyes but saw only comfort and gentleness. The last image that Ash had was of Vin offering a wink to her, along with a sharp pain in her neck.

Then the world slid into nothingness.

TWENTY-ONE

Paulsen interrupted Holmes in the middle of a card game. Subtly, of course; a mere murmur in the ear. Paulsen knew better than to be rude in front of important friends, especially these days, with Holmes running so low on friendships. Nobody in his fraternity would touch him with a bargepole since the suicide of Gaines – there had been steady whispers, growing louder, of the man being pushed. With Crook in London, he knew where the rumours were coming from, let alone his wife's arrest. He was the laughing stock of the criminal fraternity – not helped by the fact that there was no trace of any of the marks.

The very victims he'd wined and dined in top hotels, upon Azeri's words and the fingers that she'd pointed. The victims who had been vetted by his personnel, and whom he had gone to great lengths to convince that they were being conned. These people Azeri had shown to him, as well as the private account that their cheques had been paid into successfully.

These interested parties had attended the same party where Esther Crook had performed her greatest conjurer's trick and, amidst the excitement, vanished with Azeri, the money and another notch added to her legend. Holmes's compatriots in the con had equally vanished into the night, along with their donations to Esther Crook. The bank transfers had gone through legally and the contract that he had signed with Crook showed the money going into a perfectly legitimate business named Desjardin Ltd. The accounts were feasible and, with the wording on the contract that Esther Crook had signed in the name of Darnell Voleur, were shown to be for a business transaction regarding a fake ruby necklace in the style of the Burmese ruby's original setting.

It was a miracle, at the very least, that Innocent hadn't flown home. The charming American from the Deep South had persuaded several prominent members of London's criminal society to join them, and there had even been a few laughs shared as the police wandered in and out, looking at his books.

And now his business was needed desperately.

"I need to talk with you a minute."

"Not now." Worse than being interrupted when he was about to win, Holmes was sure he was about to lose again. Nevertheless, this particular friend had to be placated. Innocent had been annoyed with Holmes lately, and Holmes was trying to be diplomatic, give him a small win. Innocent had been decidedly angrier and won several hands with vicious satisfaction.

"It's important."

"Can it wait?"

"Not even ten minutes," Paulsen said, and he hovered in the background, buzzing with so much energy that Holmes could barely focus on his game.

"Christ, Holmes, just fold and speak to your damned friend," said Innocent as he lost a hand. "He's putting the spectre of misfortune on me."

Holmes trembled with rage as he joined Paulsen again, well aware of the glares at his back from the other players. "What is it?"

"Azeri," Paulsen said. "And her partner… Esther Crook."

It was enough to take the breath away. Esther Crook was still on his stomping ground. The notorious con artist had really stayed here, alive and breathing.

Holmes hoped it didn't show; of course, he could trust Paulsen, but he knew he shouldn't be quite as shocked as he was. The woman was as ruthless as him, and had a reputation to uphold. She'd already be angry with him for the factor of his 'theft' of 'her' painting. She'd escaped once, but had lain so low that he'd not been able to touch her since that night.

"What the hell?"

"I'll tell you in a moment, but it begins with two pretty young girls together."

"A pretty girl with a huge tangle of secrets remains dead no matter what those secrets were, and I want them dead. Anyway, Crook and Azeri together?"

"Our source saw… he phoned it in to me, said they were looking pretty calm and collected for two people trying to con each other."

"Where did he see her? When?"

"About two hours ago." Paulsen scratched his chin. "I was due to meet him, but joined you on this little venture when Innocent phoned with that fancy solicitor of his."

"And the boys with him?"

"No."

"And he didn't attempt to bring her back?"

That was the next step, of course. Holmes had thought about what he would do if Esther and her band of merry men were in London and still breathing. He could confront her, take her apart piece by piece for what she had done to him, for the shame of her escaping him on the boat. The humiliation he now endured because of that. Not to mention her latest getaway.

Paulsen put his hands in his pockets. "No – the kid followed her and it looks like she was heading towards where Vin caught her."

"Damn it…"

"Lost all contact."

Holmes cursed under his breath; another friend lost.

"It'd seem, also, that Crook forgot herself too… she's heading to Denver. She left her travel plans with the most disreputable source. She told our source's unwitting partner that she is heading back to Lyon to pay some respects and then going on to Denver. The flight plan has been booked to the final detail."

"Good. I need to show my business plans… and show Innocent I am a man of mettle and my word."

There was a sudden flurry of curses and Innocent stormed through, his green eyes glaring balefully into Holmes's. He was holding his phone in his hand, shaking in rage. "Two young women have been found dead in a suspected murder," he announced, his fingers shaking lightly in what Holmes took to be barely contained rage.

"Why should that affect us?" Holmes smirked, continuing to play dumb until he suddenly felt his tie tighten as Innocent tugged him in.

"Darnell Voleur was last seen playing poker on the charity cruise where, guests have reported, she became downhearted after being accused of being a crook. She was last seen exiting a party that *you* were throwing and, during which, *your* wife was arrested." He held the news report in Holmes's face. "The damned girl has got one over on you one last time. The man found at the scene of the crime is none other than your damned watchdog, Hughes."

Holmes stuttered for a reply. He was saved by a cough from behind him, followed by a flurry of curses from Innocent. He spun on his heel and felt his stomach drop from under him.

Chris Adams.

The ATF team leader was something of an unlucky legend to those in his path. His team was known within the gun trade as the 'unlucky-for-us thirteen'. The man had a fantastic conviction rate. He'd been chasing Innocent for years, although had so far been unsuccessful in capturing him.

"You know, Innocent, I've been running after for you for over four years and you've never been so helpful."

Christopher Adams's smile was a strange one. It was a smile filled with lethal longing as he looked at Innocent, who had suddenly gone stiff as he sat down at the end of the table.

"Mr Adams." It was impossible to miss the slight quiver in Innocent's voice as he faced down the agent whom Esther Crook had tauntingly used as a threat.

"Fascinating array of details you have here," Adams said, holding up the innocuous-looking billfold.

"I have no business dealings in the United Kingdom, as you are, no doubt, well aware from your sojourn to Companies House," Innocent said, looking paler by the second.

"None legal, but that's just semantics… imagine my delight when I got phone calls from both Interpol and the CIA to tell me that they'd found this billfold in your UK apartment. The search warrant covered the place, just to keep things nice and legal, and the search turned up this lovely little book."

Holmes felt his heart sink. The black book. The one that held all his illicit business dealings and his whispers on the winds. It was supposed to be in LA, where his wife's ownership papers had been. So far away from the eyes of Esther Crook; from her knowledge and her wicked ways.

According to his security form, he'd written off the attempted break-in as the work of an opportunistic thief who had stolen nothing of that level of importance. He'd even assumed that his wife had made one of her habitual mistakes, with months being switched.

But then Crook left nothing to chance. Not even death, apparently.

"We have enough information here to put you away for several lifetimes. I must confess that Mr Holmes is nothing if not thorough."

Holmes looked at the leather-backed book, feeling his stomach swirl inside him.

"What the hell is that?" Innocent had lost all traces of his typical congeniality, and the tremor in his hand was now evidently from rage, not a healthy dose of fear and respect for the ATF agent.

"This is what got us your extradition paper, Innocent. Over a hundred pages with dates, places and names from past transactions, future transactions, warehouses, safe houses," Adams said, grinning as he handed him the paperwork.

Innocent read it in silent contemplation, the tremble in his fingers becoming more apparent.

"Every team with three letters in, as my beloved god-daughter is fond of telling me, is going to root through this. It'll take days. Months, even. Especially with the two bodies in the morgue that your friend Hughes mixed up... with any luck, we might get you soon enough, Holmes." Adams flashed a grin as Innocent stood up. "No screaming?"

"Any point – except one courtesy?" Innocent asked, as he turned and allowed Chris to put on the handcuffs. "Keep my name out of the papers until it's proven... after all, it could be just a minor infraction of an understudy grabbing for a lead role."

"Don't worry yourself; I'm sure you will be a leading man for the rest of your days," Adams said. "Gentlemen; Holmes..." He looked over Holmes's hand. "My, my... black Aces and Eights. A dead man's hand?"

"The last hand Wild Bill Hickok got before he was shot in the back of the head by a man he had helped." Innocent coughed, sounding miserable. "A more appropriate term I'm yet to hear."

Holmes looked around. The eyes around him held nothing but contempt. For his betrayal, for everything. Esther Crook had signed his death warrant without even saying a word. But he couldn't resist one dig at the leader of the ATF. "Well, it's a pity Esther Crook didn't get to see this day."

"Fait accompli," Chris Adams said, pausing in his walk. "It's a great turn of phrase; it means a thing that has already happened or been decided before those affected hear about it, leaving them with no option but to accept it. Esther Crook is well enough in Norway; there is no trace of her arriving in the UK and joining the cruise ship as you claim." He looked at Innocent. "Makes you wonder, doesn't it? Kid hides in Norway from you and America because of all those tales that he spun to you about her mother being the reason for your wife's death. Tells you on multiple occasions that she's as much a victim as you. He pays off the kid to buy a painting that is a forgery, kid turns up dead and you're caught… great tale."

"You've got to admire the criminal act. Makes you wonder who the real con artist is!" Holmes tried to step back as Innocent lunged for him. "And you got that kid killed! A poor sixteen-year-old! Spinning…"

"Now, now, Mr Innocent, it won't do." Christopher Adams grabbed his hands and offered a smirk. "I want you in the USA, not the UK… I might be back for you, Holmes."

Holmes looked around at his former friends and quietly prayed that Adams would be true to his word, and wished he could join those he had thought to be Esther Crook and Azeri in the mortuary. He was just resigning himself to this thought when his phone received a text. He looked down at it and broke into a feral grin at the one word. *Laudanum.*

"Paulsen!" he snapped, the man coming quickly to his side. "Get hold of the morgue. Tell them I want a blood check on those two."

"Boss, that's the coppers' job," said Paulsen.

"Well, get them to go with you; we're on a timescale," Holmes said. "I got a feeling, in the words of Ezra, that Esther Crook has been watching too much of *The Sting.*"

"I can't believe it's your last night, Bart."

The younger porter flushed. Nicholas Russell looked at him. The pay was terrible but the young man had proved to be a good gurney-pusher for the mortuary.

Apart from one clerical error on the part of Brixton Mortuary, where two Jane Does' bodies had ended up going missing on their watch this morning, Bartholomew 'Bart' Proulx had done a wonderful job in Russell's opinion. Might've been able to work his way up to transporting living people, the way he was going.

"Better hours, better company… not that yours is bad," Proulx hastened to add.

"I don't take offence," Russell chuckled. "Any plans?"

"Apart from to lock up tonight, not really." Proulx grinned. "Say, why don't you go on ahead of me? Get a few pints in?"

Russell nodded. It was against protocol for one person to leave, but the kid was trustworthy. "Sure. Got two kids in there need to be put away."

"Don't worry. Are they young?"

"Yeah. Shame. Looks like murder, more than likely, or pushed into suicide… heard some cops talking upstairs. They're taking a pool on the boss that they reckon sold them out. They think he'll be dead within two months definitely."

"Ah, it's a tragedy for the poor kids."

"True… any pint in particular?"

"Nah, any will do."

Russell watched Proulx walk into the mortuary and sigh heavily. Perhaps it was better that the boy was out of this job. It'd seem that it had affected him more than Russell had thought.

If Esther Crook had been living, she would've told Ash how, at the beginning of the classic movie *Sunset Boulevard*, the scene where William Holden is lying face down in the pool had had to be shot at the last minute due to poor test audience reactions. Holden's narration suited the scene better.

She would've gone on to explain how the scene was supposed to open in Los Angeles Morgue, where three dozen corpses were having a discussion about how they died, which both opened the film and closed it. Not the famous maddened gaze, but the very narrator being wheeled away as a nobody after telling his story.

Ash, if living, would've remarked on the situation with a laugh, as in the London Morgue there were only four bodies; two carefully stored and dressed in clothes that didn't belong to them. If they could've spoken, they would've thanked their new friends for the duds, then queried the reasons behind them and listened in fascination to Esther's explanation.

But this was not a movie. And the sleeping remained deathly asleep.

THE BLOW-OFF

TWENTY-TWO

Esther gasped for breath, jerked and cursed as she fell halfway off the table. She rubbed her eyes and looked around, half relieved and half disappointed to be alone.

She'd always wondered what it would be like to come back from the dead, as it were, just as she was wheeled in for an autopsy. She had read somewhere that curare numbed you so efficiently that, in the olden days, a few unlucky victims had woken up mid operation. She had to read better books, Esther thought to herself as she surveyed her surroundings.

Ash was on the next table, still unconscious. Esther took a deep breath and slid off the slab, walking towards her clothing that was in a bag at the foot of said slab. Once she had dressed, she walked to the telephone, stretching her still-stiff limbs. She glanced casually around as she dialled the numbers, humming to herself as she waited for her designated contact to pick up.

Caelan's voice soon rang out. "Yeah?"

"Ready for our pickup. Tell everyone to wait for me."

"For two?" Caelan asked drily. "Or has she clocked you and stormed off yet?"

"Not even up." Esther heard a quick intake of air and a choking cough behind her. "Never mind; antidote has finally kicked in. Make it fast."

"See you soon."

"No need… I figure the kid wants to say goodbye," Esther said, rubbing the mark of her scar. "You get out. Leave the appointments in with one of the guys. I'll track it down."

"Sure thing. See you soon, sis."

Esther offered a similar greeting before watching as Ash began to truly rouse. She smirked as she watched Ash's panic turn to confusion, then alarm, then calculation.

"Welcome back."

"Est. What…?" Ash looked around the room, then down at her own naked body. She shook her head. "Never mind, I get the 'what'. How?"

"Nice little drug I know. Curare. Once used for anaesthesia but produces enough of an effect to knock us out… good old plastics." Esther tugged at a fleshy piece of neck and pulled it off, smiling at Ash's yelp of distress. "Don't worry, it's a trick. Hides the slightest of pulses that curare still lets you have; if you give a tug to the right of your neck you'll get it off you. Right, now, let's just say we're good and dead. There are two unfortunate souls that went missing from Brixton Mortuary that suit our needs." She threw the bag at Ash. "Now, if you can learn a thing or two more, we might just have a bright future ahead of us. A really long one. You interested?"

Ash's wicked grin was enough of an answer.

There weren't many people in the airplane hangar when they arrived in Denver via a small light aircraft. Of course, they had been the only passengers. But there'd been little conversation, despite the close quarters, due to Esther's focus on finishing up several loose ends of the plan when they'd stopped off in Oslo for exactly three days. She'd been very busy.

Esther had needed to make sure all bases were covered, visiting the French Embassy to confirm her identity and that she was safe. Some ridiculous notion that she was Darnell Voleur when her passport quite clearly showed that she had been in Norway since the tail end of the previous year, and now was heading to America for her wedding and to see her family before finishing her degree.

Ash was travelling with her, under her own name once more. Safe and sound, with little need for anything else. Esther had taken the opportunity to teach her Four Corners, and later on President's Cabinet, which Ash had witnessed her playing. Once she had shown her the basics, she'd left the precious cards in her friend's hands, then began to read over some documents that she had brought with her.

The two ran through the hangar, Ash glancing at Esther. How they had gotten here, she was convinced, was with steam under her. Eleanor was up ahead, waving, with what looked to be Caelan and Anton.

"You managed to get him here?" she asked.

Esther flashed a grin. "Isn't that the way all good films end?" She spun on her heel. "With the lovable rogue walking off into the distance?"

"Ash!"

Esther looked behind her at the same time as Ash. Dee. She looked healthy. Happy *and* healthy.

"Dee!"

Dee laughed as Ash ran forward to catch her foster sister in a tight hug, the two sharing tears and kisses on the cheek. Eleanor joined Esther for a handshake, before giving her a bear hug.

"How was the flight?" Eleanor laughed. "Less than your usual five-star service?"

"Private and surprisingly quiet. Everyone get off okay?" Esther asked.

"Yeah, love the ranch... pity about the agents wafting about. They banned Anton from leaving when they saw he was reading a book on Monet."

"I hope he didn't take my wedding joke seriously," Esther said, grinning roguishly.

Ash looked up from her hug. Esther looked at ease, like a great weight had been lifted from her shoulders, though this was soon ruined by Anton charging over and heaving her up off the floor.

"Anton!"

He laughed and planted a kiss on her lips. "You are the triumph of the world, my love!"

"Get your thieving Russian hands off of my girl!" Chris Adams had approached, as silent and deadly as a panther. Esther merely threw an amused look in his direction, though Anton dropped her. "That was a damn dangerous trick, Est."

"It was. How was your flight?" she asked politely.

"You know the damned man complained the entire time."

"Pernickety," Esther said, with almost hearty affection.

"Probably wanted to smoke, too," Caelan agreed, the two siblings sharing a hug. "Nice death?"

"Pity about waking up; you must show me how you do your version. It's utterly fascinating," Esther said, as Chris growled a warning. "Mind, I give Holmes all of a month before he either sells out or gets killed. I have no care which."

"How'd you mean?"

"Death is easy. It'll be a madman who'll get off on lighter charges… has he?"

"His wife has already agreed to show the brothels in the UK for a lighter charge." Chris flashed an insincere grin. "Seems she didn't realise she was exchanging one sentence for a worse one."

"Any news on Holmes?" Esther asked, although there was renewed tension around her eyes at the sombre look on Chris's face. "It wasn't enough, was it?"

"No. The man is more slippery than an eel. He broke it down to his wife buying goods, and until she can prove that then it's not of much use. He managed to correctly guess that the bodies in the morgue weren't yours as they hadn't been filled with the drugs that would've still been there if they were you two. Even thought, wrongly, that it was laudanum. I had to release Innocent."

Esther shot him a betrayed look.

"Est. You've done more than your fair share." Chris placed his hands on her shoulders. "You can let it go."

"Not until the fat lady sings." Esther's voice was a guttural growl of warning as she looked at Ash. "I promised Ash I wasn't above working at his level... but I most certainly won't work below."

"You didn't trust me?"

"I don't trust my own shadow, and besides, I told you. I knew what was going on."

Ash frowned and continued to look into the distance over the rugged landscape of the Colorado ranch. The Adams Ranch was 525 acres of spectacularly remote landscape surrounded by farmland. In the distance, horses grazed, and from the bunkhouse she could hear the whoops of Vin and the others. Esther was quiet, reading through an overlarge book, while Anton lay half in her lap and half out. Caelan and Eleanor were bickering about their movie selections.

It turned out that Chris Adams lived a two-hour commute from Denver, in his 'proper' home with his wife Keri, two sons and one adoptive daughter, with horses on the pastures. It made an ideal hiding spot for Dee, who'd given evidence. It was also a second home for the twins and where they had spent their last years of childhood, and where Esther had touched base with her adoptive family to keep track of her mischief.

So far, though, Esther was polite, quiet and busy playing cards. She occasionally helped with the horses, or fiddled with a jeep. An ongoing job, according to the ecstatic Vin, who enjoyed listening to her curse in French. Sometimes she went on long, solitary walks, returning at dusk, looking exhausted but with a calmer air around her. When Chris drove in, she generally went into Denver with him and looked irritated when Ash asked to join them.

It was about the only time since the argument in the airport that Esther had seemed annoyed. That could've been because Chris had basically manhandled her back into the car with a torrent of warnings about what he would do if he caught her going on the con-artist game again. Esther had remained quiet and promised not to try anything until Chris and his team – which, she discovered now, included Vin, Buck and Wyatt, as well as three other individuals, one of whom was her own father – had done what they needed to do first.

"Dee said you did well in your GCSEs?" Eleanor said to Ash, looking up from waving *The Brides of Dracula* in Caelan's face.

"Any plans to go back to college?" Esther asked, evidently changing the subject.

Ash scowled at her, and Esther shook her head in amusement.

"I take it that's a no?"

"Not sure."

"Good... I have an opening?"

"New crew?" Ash asked politely.

"Semi-crew. The three letters that I so adore," Eleanor said, as Caelan coughed. "Oh, hush... they want an interdepartmental group."

"Basically, a con-artist group who work *with* those agencies but not *for* them officially. An independent espionage agency, as it were." Esther smirked. "You know, we get to select our own missions, get paid handsomely and, if we can, make a side profit."

"So, kind of like Robin Hood?"

"We just get to err on the wrong side of caution," Eleanor finished. "Now, we seem to have done pretty good on a small scale, but we figure a small-time operator like yourself still needs guiding hands."

"And we're willing to teach," Caelan agreed, leaning on the wall nearest to them. Anton joined him, and they shared a grin. "It's got to be kind of boring to be totally on the straight and narrow."

"It is. Fingers have been itching," chuckled Eleanor.

"Feels all kinds of wrong," Anton said, rubbing the back of his neck. "But this job does offer a kind of freedom... Est, El, what do you think?"

"I don't know – this whole business of being crooks but on the straight and narrow..." Eleanor said, scratching her chin. "It raises a whole bundle of questions about what kind of jobs we can get... let alone what fun we can have any more?"

"Less fun than committing them?" Esther asked, half-agreeing with her best friend.

"But we didn't commit any crimes," Caelan joked, giving Anton a nudge with the edge of his knee. "And I know it seems overly complicated... in fact, downright wrong."

"Even if you know someone's guilty, it hardly gets you anywhere," Esther said, deciding to argue the case that an ATF agent had put to her when her father had pulled her to one side. "You know the old adage?"

"'There's no honour among thieves'?" Eleanor said, smirking at the young woman.

"No, not that one. Although I suppose it applies well enough," Esther said thoughtfully. "'Set thieves to catch thieves.' We get the profit. We get the fun. After all, not every criminal is merely an amateur with good taste and modest desires."

"Well, right now I want to make sure that Vin doesn't get my burger from the grill," Caelan said, standing.

Ash considered. It promised everything. A legitimacy that would satisfy Dee, and she had no doubt that, if it involved Esther, she'd make sure there'd be some sort of education involved. The woman who, before she'd left the US, had been studying for a degree in law, ironically enough.

She glanced at Esther, her eyes narrowing as she saw her setting up the cards again. Solitaire. Esther threw her a quick smile before returning to her game.

"I don't see why we're even bothering with movie night, Est," said Anton, eyes still closed as she swatted him away with a book lying to one side of her. "You've got those damned cards out again."

"If it helps me sleep, I'll take anything."

"Even if the night air gives you pneumonia?" mocked Ash. Then a sudden realisation washed over her as she looked at the two, a memory slipping through her mind.

It's just static. Normally plan cons. Play cards or watch a movie.

Esther *wasn't* done.

The distant crowing of cockerels ran through Esther Crook's mind, replacing the diminishing static. While it had once been an irritant, it now proved to be disconcerting in its absence. Yet, as if to prove that the universe can occasionally be kind, the rest of the house remained innocuously asleep, allowing the con artist to sit back and consider her actions.

The dawn was just beginning to break, and Esther looked yearningly over the mountains. She longed for the day when her name would no longer be the stuff of legend… but while Holmes remained, those days would never be.

"Penny for your thoughts?"

She looked up sharply to see Chris standing there, arms folded across his chest.

"Or is there a French version?"

"There is," Esther said, smirking. "But I fear it'd be butchered by you."

Chris chuckled darkly and joined her, as she poured him a good, strong coffee. She'd loved living here since she was sixteen, and had attended university here. It was good to have a second father in the wings, although he was even more distrusting of her God-given con-artist abilities than her own father.

"You're going to have to hang off getting him, aren't you?" Esther asked quietly. "You've not been saying anything but you're a terrible poker player."

Chris sighed and nodded. "Hoping that we'll get him in a

little bit, but we'll be back with his head on a silver platter for you, Salome."

"Just bring him back," Esther said tensely. "I promised Ash, and I'm not one for breaking my word."

Chris nodded, stepping over to plant a kiss on her head before pacing off to the waiting Dodge Charger. Esther stood in the doorway and waited for him to go down the drive, before pulling on her shoes and running out to the barn, yanking back the canvas on the jeep that she'd been playing about with. She'd kept the job ongoing, tossing oil on various tool parts and making sure she looked good and dirty when she returned. She'd spent too many hours tracking the ATF team, remaining in plain sight. Ash had nearly ruined one day's surveillance when she'd asked to join her, but the day hadn't been a total waste; she'd got to hear Ash be a kid. For her, the static had stopped.

She was just smiling at this thought when she saw Ash seated on the wall outside. She considered, biting her lip as she turned the engine on. The look on Ash's face was feral. It was a promise to scream her head off and interrupt whatever plan Esther had in mind. Esther jerked her head in defeat, smirking as Ash clambered in, putting the seat belt around herself.

"I knew I shouldn't have taught you to cold read," she muttered, putting the car into drive and speeding off with Ash clinging on for grim death.

TWENTY-THREE

"I figured you out."

"Well, it took you long enough, and you'll be the latest in a long line of people who think they have," Esther said as they drove down the highway, not taking her eyes off the road. "I've been hunting down the operation while Team 13 has been waiting and Judge Waters has been twiddling his thumbs."

Ash threw a look at her. "You signed the paperwork, didn't you?"

"We already did; I'm dropping it off with Chris."

"Don't bull me – there's more to it!" Ash snapped, Esther raising her eyebrows. "You're going after him again."

"I always have a backup plan."

"Are you going to tell me it?"

"You know, I never counted on rainmakers being so intrusive, so no." Ash glared and Esther sighed. "Listen, I have a feeling that I'm being ratted on and I know the source. I need to check if my father's side is done up tight."

"I thought Chris and your dad told you nothing?"

"They didn't. But their body language did. They're going in for a raid. It's a surprise one. Looks like Holmes is a desperate man."

If Ash expected further conversation, she was sorely disappointed. Esther was silent and foreboding all the way into Denver, manoeuvring through the traffic like a pro and looking calm and efficient.

Eventually, she drew the jeep to a sharp halt. "Listen. You wait at least two hours... do the normal stuff that people of your age do. Then you go to this address." She fished in her pocket, flipping out a card, which Ash took. "You go there. Chris will be there."

"*950 17th Street, Denver*?" Ash read. "I don't bring backup? I can call Caelan?"

"You bring no one." Esther's glare was hard. "I don't want any slip-ups, as I have no doubt in this world that you'll do as I say."

"It wasn't our—"

"No. He's got a mole that's warning him for some parts," Esther said, closing her eyes as she clambered out of the jeep, waiting for Ash to do the same. "When you get to Chris, you tell him this: I'm intending on seeing him soon. Tell him I know what Dad's thinking of and I'm going to see the lay of the land. Tell him everything about my little scheme... and tell him he'd better move his backside. It's not often a killer sees their victim walking by when they're long dead."

Ash had gone through the story a third time by the time Chris came down to the ground floor. She immediately jumped to her feet on seeing him, and saw the green eyes flash with amusement.

"I had a bit of a surprise when front desk told me they had a young Brit waiting," he said, handing her a visitor pass. "What's brought on this visit? Did Esther lose badly at poker?"

"No. I don't think I've seen her lose, except to Innocent," Ash said, pinning on the visitor pass and sharing a bright smile with him.

Chris chuckled.

"And even then I think it was a fluke."

"Could very well have been... now, what exactly is the reason for your visit?" he asked.

"Est told me to tell you everything," she said, fishing in her pocket for the envelope.

"What the hell is that kid up to now?"

Chris narrowed his eyes as he stepped into the lift, opening the envelope that had remained closed all that time. Ash witnessed his hands beginning to shake and a glaze coming over his eyes as rage rattled through him.

"I just gave the son of a bitch coffee," he snarled. He cursed as he looked at the watch on his wrist. There was no time; even Ash could see that.

A young man was sitting in the centre of the room, his head turned away from Ash as she pondered over the note and its contents. She poked her head over Chris's shoulder to read it for herself.

> *It'd seem my little trap worked too well, Christopher. We've been betrayed by a source that I set up for you. Just think of the old John Denver song 'Rocky Mountain High' and you'll work it out. He's probably holding court right now.*
> *Love, Est.*
> *PS: Don't shout at Mattie!*

Ash threw her head up as the realisation hit her that she knew both the laugh and the expression. "Colorado?"

Max 'Colorado' Ying turned on his heel to look at her and flashed a grin. "You rang, milady?" he teased, looking behind him to where another young man was sitting. "Hey, Mattie, I'd like you to meet an old friend, Ash. Ash... you still mistaking me for a mark?"

"Mattie LeRoy?" Ash asked, offering her hand to the long-con man. He looked much the same age as Esther, and from the handshake, Ash realised he had accepted her into Esther's con-artist family. "Esther told me about you."

"And she told me about you, too." Mattie gave her hand a

tight hold and an even tighter shake. "Fantastic approach to the job… pity about Holmes getting away with some of it. Esther had that fantastic idea, told me all about it. That drug, wow, one hell of an idea."

"Yeah, that's great… it was laudanum," said Colorado confidently.

"How'd you know that?" asked Chris immediately.

For a moment, Colorado looked as though he had been struck. "Ash told me."

"I've not spoken to you since the con began," Ash said quietly. "Especially since I've not had Facebook. But you've been in contact with Esther, Mr LeRoy—"

"Mattie, and yeah, she is one of my closest associates – no, no. Friends." The young man scratched at his beard. "She was planning for us to meet, the night you went wandering, so cancelled it. Imagine our surprise when Holmes knew where the usual haunts were." He coughed.

"So?"

"Well, when she gave herself up, she managed to lose Hughes in the Tube stations. She phoned me from an antiquated phone box… harder to track down," he said, frowning. "We agreed to meet at one of my secret hiding spots. Apparently, I was listened in to once again. By the time I got to the spot, Holmes's goons were swarming."

"But… Esther got away?" Ash said.

"Yeah, with a cut to the head and a nice slice added to her hip. If it hadn't been for a mutual friend," Mattie glanced in Vin's direction, "she'd be dead. That friend managed to warn me of a future change of scenery, even managed to find somewhere else for us to go to tend to her, but there was only one person who knew of my secret cove."

Colorado raised his eyebrows disbelievingly. "Seriously? You're accusing me?"

"Esther was." Mattie flashed a grin. "You see, it's so easy to delete social media that that was part one of our little test. He knew the haunts that you were going to. I got that you'd been chased… from him." He offered a dark smile. "Esther thought something was up. Bad feelings and all that. Then when I mentioned it, innocently enough you knew that she'd been chased. You were the only one apart from Esther to know that *particular* hiding spot. That clinched it a few days ago when I met Est. And then what really clinched it? Was you just spilling it wasn't curare poison… I was the only one outside of Caelan and Est to know of that tiny lie. In fact, Est told me when I brought it up in conversation to tell *you* nothing… except to mention it in messages to her… the exact same thing that Holmes assumed."

"Why?" Ash asked, staring at the man she'd called a friend as he sat his eyes narrowing with rage.

Colorado, who had fled London the same time as her due to the equal weight of Holmes on his shoulders, had betrayed her, Dee and Luke. He'd probably guided Holmes right to the house to arrange Dee's kidnapping. He'd portrayed himself as a victim, and Ash had believed it because she had no reason not to. She'd believed every word and Colorado had laughingly led her along the merry path.

"Why?" snapped the slightly older man. "You dare ask me why?"

Things began to click into place. "Because I got sent to Crook and you didn't, God. You didn't even keep the small con you had going in Trafalgar Square," Ash replied, staring hard. "How much silver did he line your pockets with?"

"He made me a partner in his business, junior, better than being abandoned by Esther Crook midway through."

"She held on to her," said Mattie, stepping forward. He offered a slight, if predatory, grin. "I'm not the second-best con artist and best con *man* for nothing you know."

Ash lunged at the older man who barely held off the attack as she scored punch after punch. "You rat bastard! You murdered my Dad! You set him up. You tried to kill Dee and me! You broke the con!"

Chris who'd held back a few moments paced over and pulled her back. "Ash! Ash?!"

"He murdered my Dad!" she bawled.

The others of the team put their heads down. The calmness of the girl's calculations had fled, to be replaced by the true girl that Chris had spotted before them. He merely went to the floor with her as she collapsed in his arms, sobbing harshly. He cradled her as he would have any of his own children.

"She was—"

Instantly, the angry, bespectacled eyes flew up at him. "Get him out of here before I do something I won't regret!"

Colorado smirked for a brief second before the girl turned her gaze on him. There was something in her eyes.

"Remember me, Max, because every con artist will know that you betrayed her, and I will make sure, if anyone asks, that I end you. You sanctimonious… pray nobody asks."

Colorado was led off by Wyatt, thrashing and trying to look pleadingly at Ash through a rapidly darkening eye. Ash, however, was sobbing into Chris's chest.

After a few moments she collected herself and wiped her eyes. "She said she's gone to check on her dad's side of things… is this why?"

Realisation flickered into Chris's expression and Ash recognised the look of fear in the eyes, the one she had seen hidden behind Esther's emerald green.

Esther had committed the suicide that Anton had spoken of.

TWENTY-FOUR

"You have always said that you have an impressive inventory. I have no doubt this will interest our... clientele."

Innocent said this confidently and Holmes shot him an amused look. It had been no small act of mercy that his lawyers had managed to get him off on a technicality. Liz was pleading with him for help, and, while he had once been cautious, he was now eager to get his hands on money that nobody but himself would see. Liz could wait for a time.

It had all led to this moment. Innocent had arranged for the goods to be brought into a complex that Holmes had rented out to him as part of his 'legitimate earnings', and that Innocent normally used strictly for his vehicles.

It was a vast complex, isolated on the edge of the city. It was made up mostly of offloaded truck trailers stacked side by side and several levels deep, with one large warehouse. With Denver's status as a distribution hub, no one gave a second glance to trucks coming in and out of the area, and there were far too many vehicles for a decent monitoring system to be in place.

The door opened as the gate was unlocked. Three armed men appeared, lowering their weapons when they saw their boss. "We have some samples for you, Mr Holmes, as ordered. The other weaponry is with Mr Innocent's men. Also, your present is all wrapped up."

"Excellent. These gentlemen are likely to become regulars here, so expect to see them again in the future."

Innocent, Holmes and Innocent's bodyguard Jesse stepped inside, while the others remained on guard. Innocent led them towards a side entrance, stopping just a few steps away and reaching to unlock what looked to be a service door.

"As you can see, Ezra, a fine array of weaponry for your needs." Holmes gestured at the ground. "Automatic rifles, machine guns... all for your basic needs."

Innocent nodded, rubbing his chin. "Very interesting. I admire your foresight."

Holmes smirked, delighting in the reactions. "I also have a gift for you."

"Another gift?" Innocent asked, surprise evident in his voice. "How pleasant."

"It'd seem that we have a mole in our operations," Holmes said. "An undercover man... Esther Crooks' father."

"Never had the displeasure," Innocent said shortly. "Do you have a description?"

"None clear. My source, a rather cocky young grifter, assures me that he's on the case... apparently his 'tutor' went out for dinner with Crook, and she used a particular phrase when she told him that the con had failed. *Qui court deux lievres a la fois, n'en prend aucun.* It turns out I rather like that expression."

"'Who runs after two hares at the same time, catches none'?" Innocent shook his head. "I don't see the reasoning."

"I caught myself a hare while Crook and her father were busy chasing me. Your gift, my friend."

Innocent stopped dead with a look of surprise and incredulity written across his face. Holmes grinned proudly at the sight before them.

Esther Crook had walked by his warehouse, thinking she had not been seen. Scoping the lay of the land, as it were, before heading to the jeep that she had been driving. Paulsen had followed her. She'd been so wrapped up in her thoughts of possible cons – at least, that was what Holmes supposed she was thinking about – that, by the time she'd realised she was being followed, there was something in her neck and she had slumped into Paulsen's arms. Holmes had made sure that she made a pretty picture on entry; he'd swapped her shirt for a halter-neck vest that left her bare back exposed, and her lower half was clad only in underwear. Her arms were lashed together and hung expertly from a hook, her bare feet dangling a foot or so off the floor.

"Seems we found a dead woman walking," said Holmes spitefully. "Most unscrupulous law-abider I've met." He stepped forward and stroked the underside of Esther's chin, the young woman maintaining her rage-filled emerald gaze. "Now, I have some questions for you."

"None that I will answer," Esther replied shortly.

"Ah, bravery – misplaced, however," Holmes said, picking up a cattle prod and holding it out. "It is your choice... now, where is your father?"

"I still don't know the answer to that in *any* language," hissed the Frenchwoman.

"Ah, so you will answer?" Holmes mocked, smirking. "You know, you remind me of a young man. A rather good young man from a Southern French family." He leaned forward, holding the cattle prod over the exposed flesh of her armpit. "Now, first question... where is your father?"

"Christ, she's a kid," snapped one of Innocent's bodyguards.

"She's not a kid. You all keep thinking of her as that... and she ain't," Holmes said, smirking as Esther glared at him.

"The art of a con man is doing everything illegal, but legally. You got away with it," Esther snorted. "But yours was far worse than mine. At least I'm in the clear."

"You honestly thought I'd just let you walk away? Be like Butch Cassidy and the Sundance Kid?"

Esther pretended to consider. "Well, it did cross my mind. And I love a good Western... rather like *The Magnificent Seven*. The original, of course."

Holmes brandished the cattle prod like a gun. "You know what you cost me, Crook?"

"Just the same as you cost me," Esther snapped, as she looked into the eyes of a rapidly unravelling man who had lost everything. "You cost me a very good mother and a very happy beginning of my adult life... do you have any idea—"

"You have cost me my friends, my family, my reputation!"

"And that's what it comes down to, isn't it? You don't know whether to check your ass or scratch your watch... make your mind up. Your family? Expendable; easy to manipulate you there," she snapped, eyes glittering without much fear. "I told you before that trial that if the law didn't get you, I would... and I went after the thing you value most."

Holmes kicked a lever that was in the centre of the room, and Esther Crook landed hard, her head hitting the stone floor with a loud crack. She was ominously quiet for several moments before groaning as she came to. As he passed, Holmes gave her a sharp kick in the ribs.

"Where is your father? My source tells me that he's finishing his reports," he said, as Esther bucked under the kick and pulled herself to a kneeling position – green eyes, no matter how dazed, tracking Holmes around the room.

"I always kind of liked the idea of going down as a dead living legend," she said, as she raised her hands, now free. "You can see I'm not armed. I'm the perfect victim."

"You're right on that one." A cruel smile creased his face as he pulled a gun from his waistband. "Sorry about this, Crook. Like I said, I think under other circumstances, things might have been different. Shame about us both—"

"Being ghosts from a distant past?" Esther chuckled grimly. She didn't look frightened, and she kept her gaze unwavering. Damn, she knew it would come down to this. Just like him. "And there's no need to raise your voice; I assume that your colleagues are all dead bar Mr Innocent, and I can assure you that he would not have taken refuge to escape his own colleagues if he were law enforcement."

"Law enforcement?"

That brief moment of distraction meant Holmes was completely caught off guard when the shriek of sirens and the squealing sound of tyres filled the air. There was an all-too-familiar pounding of feet as the raid began.

"Nobody move!" echoed from a loudspeaker.

"Son of a bitch!" Holmes grabbed Innocent, spinning him around. "How'd the cops get here?"

"You ask me such a question? This is your operation! You turned yellow and handed me over to the ATF!" snapped Innocent.

For Holmes, the implications were becoming clearer by the moment. He'd walked into friendly territory and right into a trap, and taken Innocent with him. Esther Crook had guided him through this, engineering the ultimate con. But he had to save face, if nothing else. "You can't think this was our fault?"

"Can't I? Exactly who else should I be blaming, then? I've been using this spot for months with no problems; I bring you here and suddenly half the cops in town are on my doorstep!" Innocent looked at the girl. "Best thing you can do is spin around and leave her behind."

Holmes gulped air and looked at his acquaintance – or, rather, his enemy – Crook.

Crook. He had forgotten her all over again. He kept forgetting the ruthless con artist and it kept costing him more and more. Friends in high places and the lowest of low places – even those he'd rubbed out on his way to the top – none would admit to a friendship with a man who'd apparently thrown in his chips with the ATF, and whose wife was talking with Interpol about his criminal intentions.

"You!" Holmes pointed his gun at Crook, jerking it away from Innocent in his rage. "You!"

"Put it down!" ordered Chris Adams. He was crossing the floor, arm close to his chest, but with his gun trained on Holmes. "You drop it, Holmes, or I fire!"

"Forget it."

"Damn it, Esther, we can't get a kill shot!" snapped Chris, keeping his gun trained on Holmes. "Will you just come in, Holmes; let the damn kid go?"

Holmes watched as Adams stared at Crook, his green eyes connecting with hers. He could kill her; take care of this thorn in his side. He'd be extradited; he'd take the punishment. Holmes smirked as she lifted her gaze to him just as a shot rang out from his gun and she fell to the ground.

Time stopped ever so briefly as everyone tried to process exactly what was happening. Instinct and reflex took over and time took on a slow, almost ethereal quality. The gunman who had been at the door was momentarily blinded by the flash of the canister being fired, and was taken down quickly by a charging ATF agent. The only sound Holmes was able to make was a shriek of pain as he hit the ground with his arm twisted violently behind him. Holmes found himself on the ground with Adams's gun pressed to the base of his neck.

"You lost all your deals. You might have had one with Interpol but you lost them, and we have enough evidence to take you down," Adams hissed, before speaking into his radio. "Come in, come in. Medic, damn it, I have a civilian down."

"She's dead," Holmes said triumphantly. "All that matters."

"I'm sure that'll comfort you on death row." Surprise and horror filtered through Adams's eyes. "You didn't know, did you? First-degree murder is punishable by death in Colorado if the defendant kills a person who is kidnapped or held as a hostage by him or anyone associated with him."

"I didn't hold her hostage."

"Then why has she got rope-burn marks on her arms? Plus, there was the abandoned car so her father filed a missing persons report." Adams snapped the radio onto mute. "And let us face facts here. Even if she *doesn't* die, they'll kill you inside the joint… you ratted out a lot of friends. She knew every card you were going to play in that deck."

Holmes felt everything drop below his legs. Crook had allowed herself to be tied up and captured. She'd positioned herself as the Spanish Prisoner. Unheard of. Unseen.

As he screamed his way into federal custody, a calm Ezra Innocent being taken with his bodyguard to another car, Holmes thought, as he gazed at the girl with Chris Adams kneeling over her, that he was worse than dead. One girl had brought him to his knees and was now probably going to talk the Devil out of his job so she could make his eternal damnation more of a misery.

"How's she doing, Chris?" Wyatt asked into his headset as Ash fought to be freed from the vehicle, the mountain that was Buck holding her firmly but protectively. The girl had guts, pleading with the big man to let her travel in the van with him, pleading that she'd never forgive herself if anything happened to her friend, and that she at least deserved to have someone with her if she died.

"Weak. Barely breathing. She's coughing up blood."

Through the surveillance van's CCTV system, Ash watched as the medics gently rolled Esther onto her side, confirming the bullet wound and placing pressure on it and putting an oxygen mask on her. Ash let out a gasp at Esther's first cough. The oxygen mask was spattered with blood flecks. Esther had forced her to watch horror movies in their time off, so when a second, stronger cough coated the interior of the mask, Ash realised that she was drowning in her own blood.

"Esther, can you hear me?" Chris said, clutching at a bloodied hand. "Esther!"

A rapid fluttering of eyelashes was the only response they got. It took several seconds for the movement to stop.

Chris looked into Esther's rapidly glazing eyes. "You had to go and do it your way. Couldn't see my way through."

Esther's intense green eyes connected with Chris's own as she forced out her next words. "Ash safe?"

Chris glanced over to the building where Ash was standing next to Buck, who had his big hands on her shoulders as she shook with silent sobs. "Safe."

Esther nodded once and her eyes began to flutter again.

"No, keep your eyes open and look at me." The medics pushed Chris away to have better access to their patient. Reluctantly, he allowed them to do so. "You keep fighting. You aren't allowed to give up – you understand?"

There was no answer. Esther's body tensed as pain shot through her when the medics shifted her, going slack a second later.

"She's not breathing – we need to move now, sir."

Chris stepped back to allow the experts to take over, moving in time with them as they hoisted her onto the trolley.

"I was her guardian; let me stay with her." He glanced behind at Ash, who was now struggling against the combined efforts of Buck and Wyatt to get to her friend. "Ash, we'll meet you in the hospital. Buck, team debrief."

Buck nodded, taking Ash's arms and forcing her back into the van. "You did good, kid."

"She's dead, isn't she?" Ash asked.

"She's risen from the grave once… what's once more?"

Before Ash could reply, the doors shut in her face.

Hospitals, no matter what side of the Atlantic you were on, were uniformly white and exceedingly depressing. Ash decided this as she watched Buck pace back and forth. He paced the length of the hospital waiting room again. He was wearing a path down the tiled floor. It was almost amusing as he was wearing Chris's patience down as well, regardless of the fact that the man himself was busy pacing the width, still wearing the shirt stained with Esther's blood.

"Buck, stop moving," Chris snapped. "If you have to walk, go outside. This room isn't big enough for the two of us."

"Only way I'm leaving here is if I get permission to follow through to get hold of that doctor and put…" Buck said, then suddenly noticed Ash sitting next to Wyatt, "…and put some strong words to him."

"No. I've used strong words and they don't work." Chris sat down hard on the seat behind him.

The doctor who had thrown the lead ATF agent into the waiting room, amidst curses and promises of murder unless he had an update soon, had been cold in explaining that Esther's condition was dire and would just have to wait.

Chris shot Buck a look before he returned to his pacing.

"Where the hell is he?" Buck muttered, smoothing his handlebar moustache with one hand as he ruffled his thick brown hair with the other every now and then. "He ought to be here."

"Who's he waiting for?" Ash asked Wyatt, who was sitting with feet up on the sofa.

"Her dad… he's been undercover and he's being debriefed now." He leaned back in his seat as an auburn head shot by. "Caelan!"

Caelan ran back, followed by Eleanor, both grey in colour and looking concerned. "What—"

"You didn't tell me she planned to get shot?" Buck snapped.

"Oh yeah, because I look in the know," Caelan scoffed angrily. "Last I heard from the damned fool was that she was going into Denver for the day." He looked around. "Where's Dad?"

"Still being debriefed," Chris grumbled. "It's taking longer… seems he lunged at Colorado when he was being taken into Interpol custody. It took three agents to drag him, however reluctantly, off."

"Well, I'm sick of waiting," Ash said, getting to her feet. She stepped outside and saw a familiar thin figure walking down the corridor towards her. "Anton!"

The Russian-American was looking exhausted and nearly fell over from the crushing hug that Ash had swamped him with. He chuckled softly. "Got to improve your poker face," he said, wiping her tear-tracked cheeks. "She's in an induced coma; seems the crack at the back of her head is a real cause for concern." He looked beyond Ash. "I figure the crew and Chris and Buck can go to see her… Vin's already gone up. Hoping her pop will arrive soon enough."

Ash had seen people in intensive care before, most recently Dee when she'd misjudged the flop in Camden. She'd thought she was well above anything that they could throw at her. She was mistaken, and couldn't hold back the shocked gasp that left her mouth. There lay Esther, who always took such care over her appearance, who was always in control, now almost invisible under the tubes and wires and machines, her head swathed in thick white bandages.

"Oh God, Est, what have they done to you?" whispered Chris, walking to her bedside.

The doctor stood beside him. "It looks worse than it is," he assured the team as they crowded into the room.

"It would have to; if it didn't, she'd be dead," Chris told him, because to him it couldn't look any worse.

"Thanks for your most reassuring words."

Ash jumped as Ezra Innocent took off his jacket and placed it over a chair, ignoring her shocked glance at the silent Anton, who looked as distant from the event as she felt. He shushed Esther and pressed a hand to her forehead. She remained ominously quiet, apart from the steady beeping that reassured them she was alive and the soft whoosh of her oxygen mask. Ash went to remove the offending hand, but felt her shoulder gripped by Chris.

"Hush now, *ma belle*," Ezra whispered softly to the prone figure. "We're just waiting on you to open those green eyes."

"Ashia, I think I'd best introduce you," Chris said, as Ash threw a confused look up at him. "Ash Cox, meet Ezra Gardener... Esther and Caelan's father. You didn't think they didn't have their own teacher, did you?"

THE CON MAN

EPILOGUE

"Are you coming to the party tonight, Ash?"

Ash looked up at the handsome young man. Troy – of course he'd be named Troy – Allen was standing next to her, looking both confused by her scowl, and imploring.

"No thanks, I have a prior appointment," she said apologetically. "Maybe next time."

Troy grinned and walked off, and Ash rolled her eyes at his retreating back. She felt like an illegal alien. Not a comforting feeling in the 'land of the free'.

She sighed as she looked out over the campus, feeling a weariness creep into her bones that was both unwelcome and unheeded. She'd been in D'Evelyn Junior/Senior High School for the best part of six weeks and, in all honesty, they could keep it.

She'd had her GCSE results back and discovered that she was en route to university if her A Levels met the required standards. Dee had been delighted, and a few careful words from Chris and Buck in the ears of social services had ensured that Ash stayed in the woman's care. Ezra Proulx Gardener, however, had persuaded the authorities that the two needed to be placed in witness protection as they would be giving televised statements in court, and that the safest place for them to be was the USA. So far, Ash had enrolled in a Denver college, was part of the debating society, and had despised every moment of sophomore, as the Americans termed their last year. She despised that her name was now Ashia – thank God Chris and Ezra had won that bout – Colt-Sallow.

This all paled as she compared the life of luxury she was currently living to that of poor Esther. The gunshot had, unsurprisingly, nearly killed her. It had fractured her skull and the fall to the ground had caused an epidural haematoma, but then the wound to her chest had been a through-and-through. It had taken Chris to explain that Ash's timely intervention had probably saved Esther from a bullet between the eyes if she'd kept with the "damned foolish plan" she'd had originally.

When Esther had eventually come around, she had been awake for only a few moments before she collapsed back into a heady slumber due to the drugs that the doctors were pumping into her, and promptly suffered a fit. Ash had watched in horror as the urbane woman had lurched around the bed, her sharp green eyes thrown back into her skull like a shark about to attack. Ash had often made this comparison, but the failure of Esther's body to control itself had left her as weak as a kitten.

The vomiting, shaking and high-pitched beeping of machines had lasted a total of fifteen minutes before Vin realised Ash was still in the room, and shoved her out. A priest had gone in not five minutes later, and Ash hadn't been sure what was worse, from her perspective: the priest praying over her unconscious friend and Caelan sobbing as he pleaded with his twin not to leave him, Anton's silence, or Ezra's threats about what he would do to his daughter if she didn't "stop playing about".

Ten minutes later, the steady beeping had resumed and Ezra had sat back down to read to his daughter. He had taken up his position as her protective father once his paperwork was done with, and he took that position seriously. Immediately after being reassured that she was recovering once more, he'd informed the doctors that they had facilities on Mr Adams's ranch and they would be travelling there post-haste.

Despite the doctors' protests, Esther had been hooked up and returned to the ranch, where Chris had a room ready for her. She remained in a semi-comatose state. There were days when her eyes opened and days when they remained closed. Each member of the team had taken turns in reading to her. Ezra was the exception to that rule as he had sat with his daughter, talking softly and occasionally apologising.

There had been moments of clarity when she'd asked questions about the con, but fallen asleep before the answers could be given. There had been a relapse, but that had been efficiently dealt with by Nate. She'd soon learned that Vin, Nate, Wyatt, Buck, Chris, Jesse and Ezra were from the same team that had lost the fight against Holmes in the not-too-distant past over the murder of Esther's mother.

Ash didn't need to remember Ezra's gentle persuasion to carry on without her, explaining that Esther would need physiotherapy for her injury. There was never a threat of her dying; he wouldn't let her. He'd spent far too long on opposing sides to his. He'd offered weeks away from London where Elizabeth Holmes was set to go on trial, and where the criminal fraternities had turned their backs on the Stateside Harry Holmes. She was safe; Esther had covered her.

It went unsaid that Esther's plan had gone almost *too* well, and that it had almost cost her her life.

Ezra's soft explanation that it would be best for Ash to take up residency in the States had reassured her that she was doing the right thing… even if the others seemed to have moved on. Eleanor and Caelan were working on the new agency that Esther had spoken about; while Anton still kept an emerald engagement ring in his pocket, and when he'd helped Ash and Dee move into their new apartment, he'd invited them to the wedding.

She had so many choices to make. Too many to name, in fact.

Dee wanted out of the con life, that much was certain. She wanted to keep Ash safe, and Ash appreciated the offer but it still stung to think that the others had moved on.

"Ash Cox?"

Ash turned to see a freshman – yes, freshman – standing behind her with an outstretched hand. "Yes?"

"A woman asked me to drop this off for you, but didn't stick around." He held out a large envelope.

Ash took it between her fingers. "Thank you."

She studied it for a moment as she waited for him to leave. It was made from fine, heavy paper, the handwriting on it as small and neat as a spider's. She opened it carefully and smiled as she saw the news that Harry Holmes had been killed in a prison riot… that was expected.

Ash leaned against the wall. They'd done it. They'd gotten even. It was then that she paid attention to what she had not expected; the note attached.

My dear Ashia,

I am glad to see you're enjoying the benefits of a good old-fashioned American education. I have no doubt you'd like to catch up; unfortunately, I find myself confined to this bed for meetings that forgo an immediate assembly of like-minded souls.

It is nice to meet old friends and read about new ones, don't you think? So I was rather hoping that you'd enjoy reading up on a like-minded soul by the name of Victor Lustig. Unfortunately he's long gone from this world, but I feel I have several new friends who might need an introduction to his methods.

Oh, and please remember, if you will insist on following me into the legal profession, this valuable motto:

You can do what you like with the law; bend it, twist it, hide behind it… just don't break it.

E. C.

Ash tucked the note back into its envelope and studied the extravagant invitation that had also been inserted. A small smile flitted across her face as she came to the realisation.

The con was on.

CON JARGON/
TERMINOLOGY

Con: *What is a con?*

Well, it's simple, really. A con can be played out long term, over weeks or even months, with a large payout; or it can be short, a quick scam for a smaller amount of money. Either way, for a con artist, the con is what pays the bills.

The con that Esther specialises in is called the long con, or, in US terms, the long game. This refers to a more complex, planned con whereby the mark is taken for more money than they have on their person. If a long con is done well, the con artist can walk away unscathed as otherwise the mark will have to admit duplicity in an illegal scheme of their own.

The con man can't be classed in the same group as thieves, since he doesn't actually do any stealing – the victims give him the money.

The players in the con

Extra: Unemployed con man playing a supporting role in the con. Also known as a shill. In short-term cons such as Find the Lady or Three-Card Monte, they can play enthusiastic members of the public to lure the marks in.

Grifter: An informal name for a con artist. A criminal who lives by their wits, rather than by violence. A gentleman thief, you might say.

Fixer: The person who works out the logistics of the con. They arrange for the con artist's needs, such as the big store, to be met

Insider: The key player; the member of the long-con mob who stays near the big store and receives the mark whom the roper brings.

Manager: Manages the outfit, and is often the bookmaker for the group. They often work hand in hand with the fixers.

Mark: The key to a good con is its intended victim. This person is known as the mark. The term derives from the chalk mark once surreptitiously placed on the back of someone seen as an easy target or thought to be carrying a lot of cash. Although this practice is no longer employed in the long con, the nickname remains the same.

Roper: Also known as the outside man. This is the grifter who finds a mark and gains their trust, persuading them into the con.

Victor Lustig: Bohemian-born hoaxer who posed as a government official to 'sell' the Eiffel Tower as scrap metal to the highest of twelve bidders in 1925. The 'winner', Monsieur Poisson, was so humiliated when he realised he had been conned that he told no one and Lustig escaped to Vienna with a suitcase full of cash.

The steps of a con

A tell: An unconscious signal or discrepancy (e.g. an involuntary spasm) that the educated observer can use to determine that someone is lying or trying to cheat.

The blow-off: Any technique used to get rid of the victim of a con after it's complete. Also the climax to the con itself.

Giving him the convincer: The process of allowing the victim to make a substantial profit on the first scam, thereby gaining his trust.

The mark is lured in: In the first instance, by the con man allowing him to make money on one of his scams. Having gained the mark's trust, he then stings him for a load of money.

Playing the con for him: Gaining the victim's confidence.

Putting him on the send: Another term for a long con or big con.

Roping the mark: Steering him to meet the inside man, who will eventually fleece him.

The two types of con settings

Real life: e.g. restaurants and hotel rooms.

The big store: Empty offices rigged out to look like a real-life setting.

 Matador

For exclusive discounts on Matador titles,
sign up to our occasional newsletter at
troubador.co.uk/bookshop